Wireless

Hap Hapner

The characters and events in this book are fictitious. Any similarity to real persons, living or dead, is coincidental and not intended by the author.

Ultraist Group Publishing

6193 W Mill Rd, Flourtown, PA 19031

ISBN-13: 978-0615630007

DEDICATION

In memory of Justin Barrett, it's a shame that you ever saw the Sunshine Skyway Bridge. I am better for having called you my friend. I miss you and wish you well in the universe.

ACKNOWLEDGMENTS

I want to thank my lovely wife Camilla. Sweetheart, had it not been for you, I would have never started this book let alone published it. Thanks for all of your support and for your tireless reading.

Prologue

Pelicans plummeted through the cloudless azure sky in fearless freefall toward the choppy water. Towering sails of steel rose overhead like elegant oversized kites. Twin ribbons of sun-bleached concrete trailed in the rearview mirror toward the northern shore of Tampa Bay.

The postcard image bounced off her brain. Desperation drove all beauty from her sight.

The car careened onto the shoulder near the bridge's apex. She'd hoped traffic would be lighter by nine o'clock on a Thursday morning. Just one idiot fumbling with his cell phone could kill a person.

The bridge felt alive, vibrating with the force of passing vehicles. She struggled to climb the concrete abutment. She kicked off her heels and scrambled upward. The space between the spans was solid concrete, no opening for her to plunge into the waters below.

For a second, she felt one with this new *friend*. At sixty-five miles per hour, the bridge looked pristine, even picturesque. Up close, paint peeled from every surface. Like so many things in her life, under scrutiny, the spans had lost their attraction. Corrosion and decay were everywhere.

The morning heat mingled with exhaust fumes heightening her nausea. The steady drum of tires over expansion joints drove her vertigo to a climax. Each passing vehicle created chaotic torrents of wind; hair lashed her face and shoulders.

She caught a glint of sunlight from an opening door. A brown-clad figure appeared on the periphery of her myopic journey. Someone had dispatched a Florida Highway patrol officer.

His eyes riveted on the woman, the trooper dipped his chin to the side to speak into his shoulder mike. She scrambled over the median and darted across the northbound lanes. Cars lurched and swerved to avoid her, brakes and horns protesting her presence. A big rig geared down, its engine deep and throaty.

She gripped the railing. Far below, the wind whipped the water into a frenzy of swirling whitecaps causing her stomach to lurch and her head to spin. Her body drew back but her hands wouldn't release the railing. She had to do this.

Some two hundred people had jumped from this bridge, just one had survived the fall. Odds were she wouldn't survive.

"Ma'am, please come back here where it's safe," the trooper yelled over the din.

Her petite frame floated upward as another huge truck thundered past. Fear brought her heart into her throat. She gripped the railing tighter.

"You need to get this traffic out of here!" She shouted.

The trooper hesitated and then waded into the stream of metal and stood across from her in the outside lane.

"What's your name?" he called over the roar of traffic.

She decided it wouldn't hurt to make one last friend. "Gillian Anu. You?"

"Reid, Mike Reid, pleased to meet you, Gillian."

He turned away, faced the traffic and began to direct cars past. After several minutes of hand motions, he looked over his shoulder, toward Gillian. His face contorted in confusion and terror.

It was too late. Gillian settled in to watch the end of her life. The future flashed before her eyes—her own daughter living the rest of her life as an orphan.

Chapter 1

Friday, November 15

The pilot stared into the black New Jersey morning. He sat strapped into the womb-like cockpit, peering at a formless, empty world punctuated by the amber glow of runway lights.

A cell phone startled him. Smith, the First Officer, spoke. "We'll be in Chicago around nine-thirty. Yeah, talk to you then." The cell phone snapped shut. "Mac, plan for an additional passenger coming back."

McAfee sighed as he engaged his seat belt clasp. "We're nothing more than high-priced taxi-drivers."

The controls squawked and air traffic control cut in. "Challenger Five-Eight-Quebec, this is Teterboro. Keep it on the roll; runway six cleared for takeoff."

McAfee steered the plane onto the runway with his left hand. With his right, he pressed the throttle to increase power for takeoff.

The jet rumbled down the tarmac. Smitty called off the velocities. "V one . . . rotate."

From the point where Mac should have eased back on the stick and lifted the bird off the ground, things went awry.

"My yoke. Holy shit, it's stuck." He grabbed the tiller with both hands. "She's not rotating. The yoke won't move."

Both men fought the unresponsive controls. The plane accelerated beyond normal liftoff speed. McAfee made a split-second decision. "Abort. I repeat, abort. Damn it! Implement Reject Takeoff procedures." He deployed the maximum thrust reverse and all braking systems. "She's not responding."

Seven seconds of bumping and hopping ensued as the small aircraft traversed the remaining runway and rocketed through an undulating grassy field toward Friday morning rush-hour traffic. As though drawn by gravity, it ploughed through a chain-link barrier and raced toward the newborn sun. Mountainous warehouses rose on the horizon, threatening to blot out the dawn. Steel howled against steel protesting the brutal impact.

The abrupt collision released incredible energy in the span of a single heartbeat yet the concussive blow made that second stand still. Time contracted and expanded as the escaping energy sought equilibrium. Particles of glass exploded past the pilots with abrasive force.

The aircraft had left behind a six-lane wake of damaged vehicles and stunned motorists on Route Forty-six. It came to rest in an empty warehouse. A long train of twirled chain-link fence clung to the landing gear. Galvanized posts with dirty concrete bases lay among the mass of commuters emerging from their vehicles. Acrid smoke drifted along the highway, accompanied by the stench of burned rubber, ripped steel and jet fuel. Small flickers of flame pierced the darkness of the warehouse.

The jet's nosecone had crumpled on impact, pushing the floor and rudder pedals into both pilots' legs. The punctured fuel tanks spewed their contents in an ever-widening arc around the wounded plane. Precious seconds remained before fire engulfed the craft. Muffled shouts accompanied by a rhythmic pounding filtered through the flight deck door.

"Thank God we're in one piece," Mac said. "Smitty, get these people out of here before something bad happens."

Smitty's words came in gasps. "I'm trapped. My legs are pinned." Shock kept him operating; he remained calm in spite of excruciating pain. "I think my shins are broken."

"Goddamn it, I'm pinned, too." Mac unbuckled and began to reach for the ceiling. "Stay with me, Smitty. We've got to get out of here."

The odor of fuel drifted through the collapsing windshield. Mac managed to get two of his fingers around the overhead bar, then pulled and gyrated until he freed his legs. He had to check on his first concern and responsibility, the passengers.

The main exit stood open as he emerged from the cockpit. Low-level lighting pulsed through the swirling smoke. An eerie stillness hung over the cabin; the passengers were gone. The superhuman force of panic-induced adrenaline must have led them to attack the door, pushing, kicking, and prying their way to life.

Mac turned back to the flight deck and killed the engines. Heat and smoke swirled around him. Survival instinct alone kept Smitty conscious as Mac wrenched him free. Smitty slithered through the main cabin door and slid down the escape chute. Several passengers grabbed him and dragged him from the twisted fuselage. Mac crawled through the cabin area one final time to ensure that everyone had evacuated. At the exit, he called out, "Is anyone in here?"

There was no answer.

He gazed at the tunnel of light as it gaped around the tail, beckoning him toward safety. He slid down to the concrete floor outside, almost impaling himself on the remnants of a giant warehouse rack.

Baffled he stood in the bright New Jersey morning. *What the hell had just happened?*

Chapter 2

"Skip!"

Gunfire echoed as Levi Morgan bolted up. A draft chilled his sweat-soaked body. He felt the firm mattress under his weight. Stale, dry air gusted from an overhead duct creating the breeze. No monkeys howled; no birds screamed.

He looked around the dark San Francisco apartment. He'd had the dream again, the twenty-fucking-year-old nightmare that offered no opportunity for penance.

He stretched in vain to wrest his psyche from its stupor. Anger pooled in his thoughts; dream fatigue robbed him of an otherwise good night sleep. Exhausted, he groped his way out of bed and staggered through the dark, stubbing his toe on a misaligned heating vent.

"Shit!" He cursed the strange setting of the unfamiliar safe house.

The elite top-secret crowd held Morgan in high esteem. Some of his younger 'fans' demonstrated a level of worship reserved for the mythical champions of old. To them, he didn't just epitomize a genuine American hero. He reinvented the category.

Morgan had a different perspective.

He had a job to do and did it, no different from any one else. He didn't care that some considered him a patriot and a hero. He knew otherwise; he knew the truth. Failure littered his personal life.

Reason nipped at his heels as he felt his way down the hall, toward the kitchen. "Goddamn dreams," he muttered.

He flipped on the television, started the coffee, and began his morning ritual. A hundred sit-ups and pushups as fast as he could, with just a brief rest between each, then leg lifts, three sets of two minutes each. The ritual always ended the same way; he scrubbed and flossed his teeth.

With rare exception, every day started this way. His father had always said that even the toughest solider couldn't handle an abscessed tooth in the middle of the jungle. Morgan often wondered if that was the voice of experience or just the words of a cantankerous old son of a bitch.

Back in the kitchen, he lifted a large chrome case onto a table. The *cleaning crew* had dropped it off yesterday, before he'd flown in from Chile. A dossier detailing his operation and target sat within it.

He flipped the clasps and opened the case. The upper tray contained fifteen hundred rounds of 9 mm armor-piercing ammunition. Beneath the tray lay an illegal cache of weapons: two Glock-18 automatic handguns, along with forty thirty-three-round magazines. He didn't touch those, but examined a container with several RDX wedges. RDX was stabile but one could never be too careful with something that could take out half the block. He checked the RF triggers and receivers, looking for defects. They'd be adequate to detonate the explosives from a safe distance.

Satisfied, he closed the lid and locked the case.

He poured coffee into a travel mug, grabbed the case, and headed out to face the day.

Chapter 3

Morgan approached a white Malibu no different from any other Malibu in the area, plain and unobtrusive. His needs were simple and he wanted to avoid attention. The car, like everything else, was a rental. His father had said possessions have a way of possessing us, just another one of the old man's bullshit axioms; but Morgan lived by it.

He lived like a vagabond, staying in prearranged safe houses, driving the cars provided, and expensing things necessary for work and life. He traveled light; some might even say unprepared. He preferred to think of himself as unattached and flexible.

He threw his gear into the trunk. Steam rose from the chilled streets of the Mission District. It was going to be a clear crisp San Francisco day.

Just shy of forty-four, he was a manhole-cover of a man, not in size or girth, but in toughness, durability, and spirit. An incessant flow of circumstances had proven the strength of his mind and will. That indomitable nature had served him well throughout his adventurous life.

Morgan exchanged personae like most people changed clothes. He was a man without footprints, not easily placed within any context, always passing through, rootless and unknowable. His wake was a trail of vague memories of *a* man but nothing of the milieu that had generated him.

All his adult life, he'd hidden under the leaves according to the samurai way of life.

A homeless man approached, clutching his dirty coat around his ragged clothing in vain against the fall chill. The coat fell open revealing his gaunt frame as he extended a dirty palm. "Please mister, can you help an old vet?"

Without a word, Morgan reached for his wallet and gave the man a Ben Franklin. Extravagance toward this Vet who could never repay him gave him great pleasure. He turned and got in the car wishing the man wholeness.

Parked cars were like temples to him, sanctuaries from the random disorder of life: a place for everything and everything in its place. The modern automobile screamed structure and organization. Morgan found them comforting and used the precious time of isolation in them as a green room, a place of solitude where he could unify the disparate compartments of his life.

The man knocked on the window. "Thanks mister. God bless you for being so kind!"

Morgan didn't look up, but rather sat in the car, eyes closed in meditation. The homeless man no longer existed in his mind.

He started the car and joined the stream of commuters wending their way through the Mission District, toward Highway 101. For a few minutes, he felt normal, just another member of the human herd.

A rare, mid-November sun illuminated the spectacular view of the small mountains rimming San Francisco. In spite of the heavy traffic, he dared a glance over his shoulder. Old Candlestick Park seemed to grow from the mountains and rise out of the bay at the same time.

He exited the highway at a little burg just south of the airport. It was one of those narcissistic California hamlets. The town council had decided to slow vehicles on Main Street to foster pedestrian traffic among its quaint, upscale boutiques, salons, and eateries. Morgan turned from the commuting throng and headed toward the bay.

He stopped the Chevy in an empty parking lot for a vacant office complex. The building had been closed for renovations, and he'd picked this secluded spot for its privacy and proximity to the main event. His prey wouldn't want to travel too far from the action.

He backed into a space along the bay. He had his pick of 70 spaces along the waterfront, but picked this one in advance. From there he could survey the lot and the tiny sliver of shoreline between the riprap and water. Everything looked good.

Taking a walking stick from the trunk, he hopped from the asphalt onto the rocks, and stepped down to the coarse sand. The foggy waters contrasted with the brilliant fall day. He shivered in the damp November air and dropped the stick beside a stunted bush.

For many years, he'd followed a modern adaptation of the samurai way, a life consisting of service and loyalty. The samurai had freed themselves from fear and indecision by accepting death as part of life. Those warrior-scholars had lived simple lives free of materialism and flawed logic. Death in the service of one's master demonstrated the highest integrity and love.

The samurai practiced the Mushin Way as proclaimed by the Zen Masters. *Mushin no shin*—mind of no mind—created warriors of unparalleled prowess and capability. They tuned themselves to the Tao, becoming one with their weapon and their enemy so they could anticipate and respond to a coming blow. Neither thought nor reaction was required; these Mushin Warriors moved through their work like water through a river.

His own masters had taught him well. From the beginning, Morgan had fully embraced the Mushin philosophy of life and death.

He looked back to check the distance from the water to the large riprap. With the case in place and the tide coming in, this was the perfect spot.

He returned to the car. Across the street, an unending parade of bellmen scurried from cars to the lobby at the Hyatt Regency. Friday pre-lunch traffic had exploded in anticipation of a special guest.

The Philippine president was a valued target. Her engagement that night would be the high point on the greater San Francisco-Filipino community's social calendar. They had lobbied for and obtained her unanimous election to head the Asia-Pacific Economic Cooperation's counter-terrorism task force. But her pro-American, anti-terrorism rhetoric didn't sit well among certain factions. Her alliance

13

with the previous American administration had served to align diverse terrorist cells within the twenty-one-country APEC community. Those forces intended to kill her that day. Her death on American soil would rank among the greatest anti-American statements ever made.

From his position, Morgan could see the front door of the Hyatt. In a few hours, the Filipino president would appear. The irony of the situation wasn't wasted on Morgan. If he failed his mission, his prey would use the weapons from the chrome case to kill her.

Prepared for the meet later that day, Morgan started the car and drove off.

Chapter 4

The mid-afternoon sun had started its lazy slide toward the sea when Morgan lifted the case over the riprap, onto the tiny beach. At its highest now, even the tide supported his plan. He took a long nylon cable tie from his pocket and flipped it under the bush, next to the walking stick.

He returned to the car and moved it to an adjacent parking lot across the street from the Hyatt's lobby. Ready for his sales meeting, he meandered back to the empty lot. He used to call this fun, but of late the work had lost its appeal.

Sunlight glinted off a black Ford Taurus as it backed into one of the spaces. A dark-skinned Filipino in his mid-thirties opened the driver side door. His malnourished frame and sharp features gave him a menacing look. "You Nasjolay?"

The thick glottal quality of his accent made him difficult to understand. Morgan gave a twisting nod of acknowledgement and extended his arm toward the bay.

* * *

San Francisco Bay sprawled before them, separated from the asphalt by a mere ten feet of rock and sand. The smaller man shifted position, his wary eyes darting back and forth, in search of predators.

"This is the place." With the agility of a mountain lion, Morgan leapt from the edge of the deserted parking lot, onto the rocks. The late afternoon breeze gusted warm against his face. The sun peered down from a cobalt autumn sky, and the water lay flat and vacant.

Morgan climbed out over the first of the large rocks far enough to ensure privacy. He stooped to open the bulky metal case. The buyer had requested RDX and RF triggers, as well as two automatic handguns, along with fifteen hundred rounds of ammunition. The client could trigger the explosives from a safe distance and follow through with a wall of bullets if necessary.

The swarthy Filipino stepped onto the rocks and looked around. He took several more steps toward the beach. His eyes locked on the chrome container as though it were a hypnotic talisman. He advanced to examine the goods.

His brain didn't register Morgan's trap fast enough.

Morgan thrust his foot backward and caught him around the Achilles, then pulled his leg forward, altering the Filipino's center of gravity. His prey's head whipped back and cracked against the gnarled riprap. Blood poured from the man's skull and nose.

He pulled the long nylon cable tie from its hiding place and cinched it around the unconscious man's neck. Every move appeared choreographed as he lifted the body to the edge of the water and placed the man's head in the murky bay. Spinning around, he found the rocks that had caused the skull fracture and threw them into the water. After the nightmare in the Columbian jungle, he'd vowed to eliminate all carelessness from his work.

He made every second, every move, count. He was the picture of efficiency as he shoveled bloody gravel into the water. The body would stay submerged in the cold water for three to five days. Gas from decaying organs would fill the body cavity giving it buoyancy. At that point it would resurface. By then, he would be long gone. He wanted this victim to be anonymous. The irony of a terrorist suffering an ignoble and unrecognized death brought a smile to his face.

He surveyed the scene quadrant by quadrant, searching for any bit of forensic evidence. Satisfied with his cleanup, he cut the tie from the man's neck and pushed him into the bay.

The lifeless body lay face down in the seductive current. Reeds swayed in the breeze. A Boeing 757 hung over the bay on its final approach to San Francisco International. The picture would have been surreal if it hadn't been so commonplace in his life.

The body sank into the turbid depths.

He performed one final scan for evidence. He felt the nylon cable in his pocket, then used the walking stick to obliterate all footprints, and tossed that into the bay, too. On his way back to the car, he strolled through several parking lots, looking like just another bored businessman after a sales presentation.

* * *

Morgan placed a call as he strolled in the late afternoon sun.

The brusque voice of his handler answered with a hint of a Boston accent, possessing an intimidating quality that made most men cringe. "Hello."

"The party tonight is a go. The obstacle has been removed."

"How did it go?"

"Let's just say it's quite the political statement about terrorism if anybody ever gets all the facts."

"Be at the office in the morning. I'll brief you on your next job."

"Affirmative. Talk to you in the morning." He hung up and got in the car.

Chapter 5

David Masters smiled as he gazed at the wonderful old building dwarfed but not upstaged by a forty-two-story glass structure in the background. Tampa's City Hall remained old Florida in the midst of a modern skyline. The luminous limestone followed a classic Beaux Arts style, harkening back to the time of America's Twentieth Century industrial barons.

An eight-story tower with a copper-roof cupola topped the edifice, flanked on either side by two three-story wings. It looked like a fortress; the outer corners set with vertical quoins of dressed stone, creating an appearance of impregnability. A muted coral molding ran along the face of the building emphasizing the true height of the lower wings of the building.

As the couple entered the building, a breeze bent the palms toward the granite stairs as though paying homage. The edifice itself seemed to shake out the garlands and ribbons festooning its limestone pilasters to salute this man.

David turned to his assistant Gillian Anu. "I'm a lot like this place—an oddity, out of synch with the times, a defendant awaiting the deliberation of his peers."

"Just because they don't understand doesn't make you wrong," she countered.

Without a doubt, David Masters was a lightening rod of public opinion. He created uneasiness within the established structures of contemporary society. For some, he embodied hope, for others, evil.

City Hall's interior was no less impressive than its exterior. The massive staircase leading to the second floor of the main tower wasn't opulent, but rather, solid and time-tested. The doublewide marble risers and stocky balustrades beckoned the eye toward the mezzanine level and the Mayor's offices. Those offices whispered the names of bygone eras and cigar-laden stories of power and wealth.

The pair ascended the stairs and moved away from the offices, toward the council chambers. That massive auditorium encompassed the second floor of the east wing. Its sheer size and grandeur were overwhelming. A lack of people in the seats accentuated the room's size.

Gillian fidgeted with her hair.

As people trickled into the seats, David moved to the speakers' table and signed in. He'd come to pitch the City Council on a new strategy for dealing with homelessness, drug abuse, and crime.

She watched as he sat back down, his eyes closed, his breathing calm. He looked over at her and chuckled, "I remember my first meeting here—about ten years ago. This place was deserted, but I was shaking in my boots. I almost threw up. The Council members kept asking me to repeat myself."

She admired him as he sat confident, a master of the room and himself. Public speaking wasn't her thing. In fact, she hated it. She felt at home with a gun and a target, with the chase. This place, this situation, felt like Mars.

By the time the Council members filed in, people occupied every seat and lined the walls. Christian *lobbyists* had turned out en masse to counter the Ultraist Group's proposal. They packed the room to force the *nonbelievers* into an overflow area in a nearby school gymnasium. Hand-lettered signs sprinkled the room, "Pinko", "A social gospel is no Gospel", "He preaches another gospel", "Works won't get you into "Heaven", and "Hell awaits you . . . Baby Killer".

This type of crowd could get out of hand.

Sound and energy filled the space creating a cauldron of animosity, but the din calmed as the Mayor stood. "Please remove those signs or I'll instruct the officers to do it for you."

A murmur passed through the crowd, but they put the signs away.

The Chair Pro-Tem called the special session to order with the usual preliminaries. Tampa had long ago dispensed with sectarian prayers, a fact not wasted on many in this restless crowd.

Gillian didn't understand Evangelical Christians. They made no sense. How could they condemn all other religions, even fellow Christians? They were hypocrites, plain and simple. They ran a modern day inquisition but justified it because they shed no blood. Theirs was a spiritual slaughter of those who wouldn't convert to their brand of religion.

A Council member explained the resolution before them. Tampa would divert funds supporting existing faith-based initiatives and join forces with The Ultraist Group to clean up the community. The Chair then yielded the floor to David Masters, founder of the Ultraist Group, TUG.

He approached the podium, his hands steady and his voice true. "Thank you, Madam Chair and Council."

Someone called out, "You're going to Hell."

The gavel came down. "That's enough."

The Chair peered into the auditorium looking for the heckler. Snickers ran through the crowd and heads wagged in disapproval. David acted as though nothing out of the ordinary had happened.

"All of us have done things we're not proud of. No one's perfect. Frankly, I've done things I'm ashamed of."

The crowd breathed a collective sigh; maybe Masters would stop trying to steal their funding.

"But, if I allow my imperfection to hold me back from doing the good I see needs to be done, then I'm no better than a criminal." He paused and made eye contact with individuals in the audience. "A hypocrite knows what's right but doesn't do it." Another pause. "Whether or not I can do something perfect isn't important. Do I even try? That's the issue. Trying and failing is better than not trying at all. If I don't try, then I have no faith or ideals."

He turned to his assistant, "Gillian, can you bring me those charts?"

She handed him the supporting materials they had prepared. Masters would leave them nowhere to run, nowhere to hide.

"I guarantee you; no one in this community grew up hoping to be a drug addict or prostitute." Most averted their eyes as he searched for compassion from them. "No stable person wants to be homeless." He talked the crowd through charts that portrayed the decline of inner city America over the past fifty years. "TUG doesn't care what people believe. We believe in people—that they have the right to pursue their God-given potential. You've seen the charts that outline our predicament; now, look at one solution."

He went on to elaborate how TUG could provide an important service to the community. The Ultraist Group circulated among the less fortunate, looking for those who strove to better themselves but didn't have the means to do so. He detailed how TUG provided opportunities so the less privileged could help themselves. They didn't give free handouts. They searched for people interested in escaping a hopeless life; people trapped without money or means.

The efforts had already paid off in New York City. Ultraist volunteers had helped prostitutes off the streets. Interested men and women received a business card with a number on it. If they called the number, they got free dental work. TUG also offered free medical checkups, as well as educational and career-counseling opportunities. It was a self-filtering program where the recipients decided on how much change they wanted.

This cycle of opportunity and action allowed the underprivileged to move forward with dignity and confidence. The process let them begin their journey of realizing their potential and encouraged them to give back to the less privileged.

"There are other elements to the program, like food banks, life crisis centers, and free clinics. This approach has met with surprising success in New York City. Fifty percent of those taking the first step continue on to subsequent steps. Seventy-five percent of those in the second step graduate from the program. Over the last five years, the relapse rate for those completing step three is less than five percent."

A faint hubbub ran through the crowd. Some nodded, impressed.

Masters continued. "We cannot ignore the plight of our neighbors. Jesus said, 'Whatever you did not do for one of the least of these, you did not do for me.' All TUG asks is that you allow us to do for the least of these here in Tampa."

The crowd became agitated. Several signs popped back up. Someone yelled from the back, "But you don't do it in Jesus' name!"

Confusion reigned throughout the assembly. Across the room, a man shouted, "He's a communist!"

A woman screamed, "He's an apostate turned away from Jesus!"

A well-known preacher waved a sign that read, "Poacher."

More signs appeared.

"He's a wolf in sheep's clothing, stealing our flocks!"

"He's a false prophet!"

"Anti-Christ!"

"Order!" The Chair banged her gavel. "We'll have order or I'll clear this chamber!"

Gillian wished she'd brought her gun.

The tumult died but the crowd lost none of its fervor.

Masters frowned and stepped back. He rubbed his beard, turned, and walked away from the podium and sat next to Gillian. On her way to address the crowd, the Mayor stooped down beside him.

David spoke first, "I'm not asking for special treatment here, Gail. I'm just asking the Council not to block our ability to help people."

"I know. We'll see how it goes." She walked toward the lectern and then turned back with a smile. "Hell of a way to spend a Friday night, huh?"

Chapter 6

Liz searched for any sign of imperfection as she moved through the living room toward the front door.

Unlike her two siblings, Elizabeth Rose took after her staid British mother, who had come from an aristocratic line that had all but lost the appearance of grandeur. Her life was one of duty and obligation, a perpetual audition for an unavailable role.

She took one last look in a strategically placed mirror in the foyer. After wiping her finger over the corner of her mouth to remove an imperceptible smudge of lipstick, she opened the door. "Hi, Mike."

Her guest stood on the stoop, a handsome man in his mid-forties towering over her from the bottom step. It was their fourth date, and it would be a romantic Friday night on the lanai, an intimate dinner and soft music. Her quintessential perfect evening.

She made a sweeping motion to usher him into the foyer.

He put a massive arm around her shoulder and leaned down to give her an affectionate kiss on the cheek. "God, you're beautiful. I couldn't wait to see you."

They moved through the kitchen, into the family room. Two glasses sat on the countertop next to a bottle of red wine and a corkscrew.

"Would you like a glass of wine before dinner?"

"Let me open that." His voice contained a baritone quality that made everything sound romantic and enticing. He called over his shoulder as he popped the cork, "Is your son around?"

"No, he's up in Tampa, getting ready for exams."

He approached her as she put on soft music. Handing her a glass, he raised his own. "To life's pleasant surprises." He smiled and took a short pull on the wine. "To us."

She smiled as though she'd never smiled before. "To life's very pleasant surprises." She directed him toward the sofa, where she snuggled up to him. Her body and her voice became apprehensive. "There's something I've wanted to say."

"You know you can tell me anything."

She fidgeted somewhat, until he put his arm around her shoulders. "Doctor Levine's been treating me for depression over the past few years." She shifted in his arms, searching for any hint of disapproval. None registered. "I've had trust issues with men. He says I'm struggling with the empty-nest syndrome because Thad's away at college, spending more time with his father." She pulled away and looked him square in the eyes, giving him a do-you-still-love-me face. "It's hard to believe, but for the first time in my life, I feel like I'm with a man I can trust."

"I'm flattered." He turned her face up toward his. "And honored." He gave her a lingering kiss, tender yet voracious.

She felt a newfound sense of trust. "Shall we have some dinner?"

"Sounds good." He pulled his arm back, freeing her to get up and move toward the kitchen.

"Take the wine out to the lanai. The table is all set. I'll be right out with the salad."

She disappeared into the kitchen as he went out to the candlelit patio. An immaculate table set for two stood in the middle of a spotless screened-in porch. Orchids and geraniums spilled from hanging baskets pouring down toward grass-filled pots on the floor.

Liz entered the lanai, and placed the salad plates on the table. Mike handed her a glass of wine and pulled out a chair.

He sat across the table. "It must be gratifying to have all of this. I mean you've done really well for yourself."

"It's a daily struggle. I've been a single mom for more than ten years. My ex made sure we could keep the house. He said it was for Thad."

"What's Thad like?"

"He's a good boy. I don't know what I'll do when he really leaves home."

"I'm sure you don't need to worry." He lifted his glass. "Here's to family and all the pleasure they can bring."

They drank and ate.

"I worry about him a lot, especially in that rickety old car of his—no air conditioner and so noisy. It's a mess."

Mike smiled. "Not too trustworthy huh, maybe I can help get him out of that situation."

As they finished their salads, Liz said. "Wow, I must've really overdone it today. Can we move back to the sofa? I must be coming down with something."

"Sure, let me help you."

She lay in his arms, drifting toward unconsciousness. "I've tried to be perfect for so long," she slurred. "Since I was a kid, I've shaped everyone and everything to my standards." Her eyes kept fluttering. "Now that I've met you, I realize it was all in vain. You accept me, faults and all. You've stepped out of my dreams and into my life."

She smiled and slipped into her final sleep.

A smile creased Mike's lips. He pulled a pair of surgical gloves from his pocket, took the wine glass, and washed it. He poured a small amount of wine into the glass and swished it around. Putting it to Elizabeth's lips, he pressed her chin up to create a lipstick mark on the rim. He started her computer and typed a note. On the coffee table, next to the printed note, he placed the bottle of wine and a container of pills matching the drug he'd used.

He gathered his dirty dishes from the lanai, put them into the dishwasher, and filled the appliance with clean items from the cabinets. He wiped everything—the lanai, the counter, the front door, everything. No fingerprints would point to him—not that anyone would dust for prints at a suicide.

He placed a fresh setting across from her dirty dishes. The police would assume her date had never arrived and she'd fallen into a deeper depression.

He left the candles to burn out, finishing the scene, then turned on the dishwasher and slipped undetected into the balmy Florida night.

Chapter 7

McDonnell hung up and turned toward a twerp of a man seated across the table. "Morgan eliminated the Filipino threat."

Smoke swirled from his cigarette. "The President will be pleased."

McDonnell laughed in disgust. "Don't give me that bullshit. This organization is maintained to ensure plausible deniability. The President doesn't even know SAP exists. You and your cronies keep the sensitive intelligence so hyper-compartmentalized only your masters get to see it all." Leaning across the table, she asked, "By the way, who holds your leash these days, Roberts?"

He gave a smug son of a bitch smile. "That's beyond top secret."

As a career intelligence officer, Debbie McDonnell had seen plenty of action. She had balls. She was a cold woman who would do whatever it took to get a job done. She was, in every sense of the word, a company man. She'd bullied her way to her current role as Director of Covert Operations for the top Special Access Program at the National Program Office. She was the spymaster for the most elite group ever assembled, the Mushin Warriors.

"Morgan's our choice for the Ultraist job," she said.

Roberts took a drag on his cigarette, his nicotine-stained mustache twisting with distaste. "The selection of Morgan for the Tampa operation is a mistake." His croaky voice belied both the strength of his will and the depth of his authority. "I know some of the punks in the NPO are awe-struck by him, but recent events in his personal life put him at risk."

"Who do you think you're talking to? I built this program from the remnants of your bullshit." Her growl had a wild, yet not quite rabid tone. "You may have wheedled your way higher up the food chain, but the final say is mine. Morgan is the best we have, and I'm using him." She thumped the table. "And I don't want the NPO crawling up my ass on this, either."

"You have to admit, since his injury, he's not the same. And a PhD in philosophy . . . what the fuck is that?" He shrugged, flicking ashes toward a glass tray. "He doesn't have the stomach for this anymore."

"Morgan is my number one agent in the field. He's without equal. The Mushin don't think; they act. Battle is second nature to them. You bought your own elite special forces, a cadre of assassins who'll kill or die without remorse or hesitation. They move like shadows, serving 'the greater good of mankind' as prescribed by the program." She made air quotes around her words. "Remember, these guys answer to me, not you."

"Are you threatening me, Deb?"

"No, just stating the facts."

Roberts nearly came out of his chair. "Listen to me—and this is a threat—two of your boys died recently." He took a long draw on his cigarette, sat back, and exhaled. Smoke blew across the table. "That was no mistake. They got cocky, and we eliminated the problem."

Two gnarled veins pulsed on McDonnell's reddened forehead. She stifled her fury. "Morgan's our choice."

The little man stubbed out his cigarette and rose. "The consequences fall on you then."

Chapter 8

The shower ran in the background as Morgan paced the sterile room, listening to a special Friday night edition of a cable talk show.

"We're here tonight with Robert Hardigan, Jr., son of the late billionaire philanthropist, Robert Hardigan Sr.. Welcome, Bob."

With his cigarette-strained voice and grey suspenders, Don Millar had been a late-night interview god for more years than Morgan could remember. "Tell me about your relationship with your father."

"Well, Don, my father gave me a legacy of confidence, pride, and self-worth. We spent a lot of time together while I was growing up. He always said, 'Do what you think is right and don't care about what others think.'"

Millar leaned across the desk. "That sounds pretty aggressive. Your dad never struck me that way."

"I think he meant I should ask myself what's the right thing to do in any situation and do it. If you live to please others, you'll never do anything worthwhile. When it's all said and done, all a person has is his integrity. If you lose it, you've lost everything. My dad believed in me and gave me self-confidence. He made me feel I could do anything, be anything I wanted to be. That's a powerful thing to give a person, maybe the most important gift one human can give another."

"Now, that sounds like the Robert Hardigan I knew." Millar kicked back in his seat. "Let me ask you a tough question. Suspicious circumstances surround your father's death. What do you think happened?"

"I'm sure the government was behind his death. It's clear to me they were threatened by his beliefs and power."

The camera pulled back to reveal Millar leaning forward, straining to catch every word. He'd started in radio but had perfected his persona after migrating to cable television. The picture cut to a close-up of Millar as he broke in. "Thousands turned out as the nation mourned the passing of Robert Hardigan. Don't go away. When we come back, we'll be joined by Melissa Hardigan to discuss the alleged conspiracy against her late husband."

"Goddamn it."

Morgan stripped and got in the shower. He'd conducted the Hardigan operation; it had felt ambiguous from the start. Several of his recent ops had felt that way. He'd questioned McDonnell about them but she had derided his sensitivity suggesting that he had a mutated *Oedipus* complex. *What the fuck did she mean by that? And how did it fit in with questioning those ops? Does she see herself as a father figure to me?*

He struggled on trying to understand the contradiction between Hardigan the man and the assignment to kill him. It felt strange. He stood under the torrent of water contemplating the notion that he might have killed a great guy who hadn't deserved to die.

Jack Morgan, his father, would have never faced this struggle. Jack had been eighteen years old when the Chief of Naval Operations established the SEALs. He moved through those closed ranks with honor and respect. He was senior instructor of SEAL training when his own son took the course. The younger Morgan was sure that no one had ever endured more through those twenty-five weeks than he had at the hands of his prick of a father. The other trainees and instructors must have seen their escalating competition as insane. He could still recall his words. *This is not a fight; you will never be in a fight. In a fight, you think of how you will win; remove that from your thought process. In every operation, you will kill all contacts as quickly and quietly as possible. All contacts must be eliminated. Stealth and anonymity are the rules of the day in all operations. Your teammates are your family and friends; our government is your parent. You are to live as ghosts, supernatural warriors that cannot be detected or identified.* His father was the ultimate kill 'em all and sort 'em out later guy.

Thank god the SEALs had changed. Even that was part of his father's doing in a round-about way.

To best his son, the forty-year old father had chosen to lead a night drop from a C130 just off the coast of Grenada in a raging storm—a first for SEAL ops. Meanwhile, the son airdropped onto the island to secure the safety of the Grenadian Governor General who was being held under house arrest by communist forces. His father drowned with three other team members when their Boston Whaler sank in a squall some forty miles off-target. Enemy machine gun fire pinned down the other team. As two American gunship helicopters flew over, the SEAL team realized all communications had been knocked out. They were on their own—out gunned and out manned. The younger Morgan slipped into the mansion and placed a long distance call to Fort Bragg requesting a fire mission. An hour later, a C-130 gunship responded with supporting fire.

The poorly planned invasion led to the creation of the U.S. Special Operations Command along with numerous communication improvements that enabled the near flawless invasion of Panama and perhaps the greatest military victory in American history, Operation Desert Storm.

Of course, in the end, all it meant to Morgan was that he had officially become an orphan.

Morgan turned off the water and stepped out of the shower. The mirror provided a foggy landscape, but he knew what lay reflected behind the veil—a pudgy jaw line signaling the inevitable approach of middle age—his father. He wiped the film away with a damp cloth. Picking up his glasses, he surveyed his face. Three days of growth revealed that his beard was picking up the first strands of grey. A scar near the base of his neck was a vivid reminder of his vulnerability.

He'd acquired the scar on the Hardigan mission. Hardigan had died long before he'd lost his footing and had fallen nine feet, onto his head. A stupid mistake.

His skin flushed as he recalled the pain. Over four grueling days, he'd willed his body to make it to the extraction point. Unable to hold his head up, his arms tingling every time he raised them perpendicular to the ground, he'd walked out with a broken neck.

That accident had prompted him to take stock of his life. For the first time, death—his death—had become a real possibility. He could have died. It was an odd realization for a man who'd had no fear before then.

Watching Millar's interview had raised his one regret. Unlike Hardigan, he hadn't passed on any legacy to his only child, unless absenteeism could be counted as heritage.

He turned off the TV, hoping his thoughts would power down with it. Miserable, he slumped onto the bed and tried to shrug off the feelings as mere distractions. He drifted into a restless sleep.

The room lay shrouded in darkness when he woke, no street noise or movement, just black silence. He clambered back toward waking reality from the depths of a dream he'd had off and on for months. Not like the guilt-ridden dreams of Columbia; this one felt dark and ominous. He could never remember the details but sensed that it was important, about something he needed to get right or he would screw-up his future. It wrapped him in a grimy ring of helplessness and an overwhelming compunction to change the focus and direction of his life.

Hungry as hell, he glanced at the clock, squinting to connect the blurry images swimming through his vision. Four-thirty. He'd slept all night. Exhausted, he rolled out of bed and prepared for the drive to the office.

Chapter 9

Saturday, November 16

Gillian sat halfway back in the ballroom of the Tampa Convention Center. The place was full—hard to believe for ten o'clock on a Saturday morning. David Masters stood on the dais to speak.

Gillian couldn't concentrate. Her mind drifted as she looked at the happy families and hard luck cases around the room. She knew one bad decision—one brutal twist of fate separated one from the other. Happy families and hard luck cases were two sides of the same coin. One never saw the other except in the mirror of fate, which rendered all onlookers incapable of appreciating the past.

Her parents divorced around her tenth birthday. Her dad didn't leave for another woman. He left for crack cocaine. Since then, she had struggled with relationships and chosen men badly. Or was it that she chose bad men. She could never figure that out. Because of work and lifestyle she tended to isolate herself. It can be tough explaining an out-of-wedlock child. Why do people make you choose between right and wrong when love is the true need?

Her daughter, Maddie brought life; had saved her life. She had nothing to explain; nothing to be ashamed of.

Marrying Maddie's father had never occurred to Gillian. When he'd learned of the conception, his first words ended all hope of a relationship. Those words still rang in her ears. "Get rid of it."

David broke through her thoughts.

"Jesus, Einstein, Gandhi, Dr. Martin Luther King—they all had a vision, a shared dream for humanity. Their hopes will be realized as we allow ourselves to evolve."

Magic seemed to fill the air. His words tore the veil of time and space, revealing another world where the past and the future mingled together, a world of possibilities.

"As one race, we need to denounce the ideas of social and economic inequality. We should no longer tolerate the injustice of racial, social, or economic inequality. We must stand against the political, religious, and economic oppression."

His words cast a spell; everyone became entranced, believing they could change themselves and their world.

David was a handsome man with salt-and-pepper hair. He possessed a peculiar magnetism. His charisma felt gravitational, defying description. Whether speaking in public or one-on-one, he radiated confidence and authenticity. He had no hidden agenda. Sometimes, watching from a distance, Gillian could see people listening, leaning forward, and struggling to get closer. It amazed her, but listening to him seemed to bring them closer to one another.

Gillian had come to the Tampa Bay area eighteen months ago, under the guise of a single mom on welfare. It hadn't taken long for David to recognize her potential and bring her into his protégé program. David was passionate about giving others the means and opportunity to re-establish their lives. His altruism allowed people to overcome their coping mechanisms and enter a life of meaning, fulfillment, and service.

Gillian felt somewhat guilty that her opportunity was a sham. She was there to do a job—to stop the flow of terrorists' funds. But she was happy to be living near her mother.

Her FBI handler and his superiors believed TUG was leveraging tax law to hide money for terrorists. They saw the Ultraist Group as the ultimate tool, created by David for the sole purpose of channeling money undetected into the hands of the highest bidder. Over the months, Gillian had seen plenty of documents indicating odd, but not illegal, behavior. People contributed billions to TUG's coffers every year. Since nonprofits didn't have to be audited by outside groups, there was no way to know what they were doing with all that money. How does a Fed analyze that kind of information? They come to the worst possible conclusion, racketeering. Executives at the Federal Bureau of Investigation believed Masters had pioneered a New Age international terror community. He had brokered peace and unified diverse groups around a single goal: topple the Great Satan.

David arrived at the apex of his presentation.

"Will we continue to tolerate the injustice of a have and a have-not economy? Don't all men and women have a right to food, clothing, healthcare, housing, education, and employment? We must stand for the weak, the powerless, and the defenseless, protecting them from the corporate looters at their doorstep. Natural disasters around the globe have exposed the inequality among us. The rich escape unscathed and prosper while the poor die en masse. This should not be.

"The great Irish playwright, Eugene O'Neill wrote, 'There is no present or future, only the past happening over and over again'." He paused, allowing the inexorable force of those words to collide with his listeners. "This is our moment. We need to secure a different future by refusing to let our experience be the past happening over and over again."

Risking the cliché, he called for action. "Let us stand united and be the change we want to see."

On that note, his speech ended without pleading for commitment or an extravagant outcry to evoke guilty penance. He turned and walked away, letting someone else close the session.

After the meeting, there would be no slipping away. Every person would accost him with handshakes and congratulations, declaring how he'd shared their innermost thoughts and desires. *Could you meet with me sometime? I've got a great idea for . . .*

Gillian couldn't face the hypocrisy. She slipped out the back, unwilling to break tradition by mingling with others.

Chapter 10

Morgan loaded his gear and wound his way through the Saturday morning streets of the Mission District. Fathers gathering their children for soccer punctuated his loneliness, highlighting all that he had sacrificed. For the first time in his adult life, doubt fed on him.

He made his way down to the corner of Bryant and 10th. The Office, as the NPO referred to the brick building, was an old manufacturing facility. The small company specialized in selling high-end furniture to the upper class.

He circled the block and pulled up to the gate. A tall chain-link fence topped with barbed wire surrounded the parking lot. A pleasant female voice responded to his arrival, "May I help you?"

"I have a meeting with Mr. Papadopoulos."

His response started a series of events on the other end of the intercom, including a retinal identity scan.

"Just one second, sir."

The receptionist had been doing this kind of work at various government facilities since the Cold War. She would check his retinal scan for a positive identification, then the readings on explosive detection meters, infrared scan images, and audio sensors. She would note the C4 trace signature coming from the case in the trunk. Body heat of one, one heartbeat, interior/undercarriage video scans clear, and his identity confirmed. Then she gave the prompt to seal the deal. "Do you know which department he's in?"

"I believe he's in folding chairs."

She coded the proper sequence into a computer and released the gate. "Pull into bay number three; the door will open as you approach. Place your parcel in the scanner before entering the main facility."

As the door closed behind him, he stepped to the rear of the car, pulled the weapons cache from the trunk, and walked to a door marked AUTHORIZED PERSONNEL

ONLY. He placed his palm on the biometric scanner, and the door unlatched. Inside an eight-foot-square room, he approached an elevator. The door opened and the receptionist spoke over an intercom. "Drop the parcel in the freight elevator to your left and then board the north elevator."

He obeyed. The elevator had no buttons. He engaged another biometric scanner. The high-speed unit dropped at a fantastic rate, yet the pressure-control system prevented any discomfort. In thirty seconds, the car descended to a depth of nine hundred feet. After a series of clicks, it began to move horizontally, accelerating toward its final destination, then gliding to a gentle stop.

Debbie McDonnell waited for him as he exited. If her growl could make men shudder, her five-foot, pencil-thin frame and wiry brunette mop made them laugh. Her exuberance more than offset her size. Those who liked her called her feisty, while those who didn't simply spat; or at least wanted to. Morgan fell in with the former crowd.

"Levi Morgan, welcome home." Even that short phrase betrayed her Southie heritage. His name sounded like a combination of 'maw' and 'gun',

He shook her hand. His green eyes mirrored the hue of his surroundings. At six feet, weighing in at two-fifteen, most people viewed him as average. Deb McDonnell had long ago recognized him as anything but.

She led him toward a briefing room that belied its subterranean nature, conveying, instead, the warmth of a sunlit office. "Good work yesterday, by the way."

He motioned toward several clusters of people in the corridor. "What's going on?"

"You're somewhat of a legend around here. These people want to see you."

He turned away from her as an assistant rushed down the hall with the chrome case.

"You might want to be careful with that," he called after the star-struck young man. "Plenty of C4 in there,"

McDonnell gave him a quizzical look.

"Nasjolay's weapons," he confided.

Bret Nasjolay had been a weapons dealer, a phantom they'd moved through a rendition several weeks earlier. The deceased Filipino assassin had arranged to purchase several special items for his hit from him. Morgan had assumed Nasjolay's identity to deal with the Filipino.

"Man, the NPO spent some money on this place." He grinned. "It's as good as the NSA, maybe even better."

"All courtesy of the White House's previous occupants." She smiled as she motioned him into a well-lit conference room. "They are nice digs. Now, let's get down to business, shall we?" She flipped on the LCD projector and a bearded man in his mid-fifties appeared on the screen. She pushed a dossier toward Morgan's side of the table.

Donning a pair of reading glasses, he flipped the folder open. A stranger might peg Morgan as an accountant or engineer from the owlish look he assumed, not a seasoned government assassin.

Deb hesitated, lowering her chin to give him a look over her own glasses.

He winked. "Things, they are a'changing."

"This is David Masters, founder and spiritual leader of the Ultraist Group; TUG for short. He's a Gandhi-like revolutionary. Over the last several years, the group's been picking up followers at an alarming rate, mostly through the Internet. Local chapters are springing up across the country and internationally. Their membership is in the millions. They espouse an insidious form of mutated Marxist philosophy."

"A new political party with millions of adherents." He scowled. "Where have I been?"

"It's not a political party. It's now the third largest spiritual movement in North America."

"Wait a minute; a religious communist movement? That's illogical."

"They're playing on people's frustration with everything from economics to politics to draw in followers. In their way of thinking, the more government screw-ups and scandals there are, the better."

He shook his head. "I can't believe I haven't heard about this."

"They're headquartered in the Tampa Bay area. Masters is a former evangelical missionary who now believes institutionalism is what's wrong with humanity. And with people like Demetri Peelee on the TUG board, they're a prestigious and influential group."

As one of the wealthiest men in the world, Peelee had made his fortune by cornering the market on computer operating systems prior to the PC revolution. In recent years, having noticed the growing gap between the have and have-nots, he'd become quite philanthropic. Many suspected he had ulterior business motives, but no one could deny that the less fortunate benefited from his charity.

"A number of wealthy business people are on the board; most notably, Michael Valley, founder of Valley Computers, and Golda Renfro."

"The TV mogul?"

"That's the one; richest woman in the world. These three appear to be the major sources of Masters's funding. TUG has various facilities in New York City, Philadelphia, Tampa, L.A., and New Orleans. These include free clinics, community centers, and other social programs. With these types of facilities and services, we estimate they would need an operational budget of $240 million a year."

"Doesn't seem to be much of a threat."

"Since philosophically and ideologically they claim to be pacifists, Masters and the Ultraist Group haven't been a concern. But Masters has been advocating radical government reform of a counter-constitutional nature. We know he has ulterior motives, but we haven't been able to get anyone close enough to find out what they are. For several reasons, we can no longer afford to wait.

"This organization takes in over two billion dollars in contributions every year. Since nonprofits don't have to be audited by outside groups, there's a growing concern in the administration about what they're doing with all that money. We suspect they're laundering money for terrorist groups. Intelligence indicates that Masters has pioneered a new age of cooperation in the international terror community. He's hit on a cord that's unifying diverse groups around a single goal." She paused, either for effect or to steady herself. "The assassination attempt you stopped yesterday was a diversion for a larger undertaking. We're hearing a lot of chatter around the upcoming economic meetings. Intelligence indicates there will be an attempt on the President's life during the APEC conference in Chile. Our analysis points to global cooperation among disparate terrorist groups brokered by TUG. They've realized the power of cooperating and they've found a way to beat Echelon."

Morgan sat dumb-founded.

From the Complex Number Calculators of the 1940's through Echelon Gen7, the NSA had driven computational device development. They'd always been ahead of the curve.

"Didn't The Times run an article a few years back detailing Echelon's capabilities?" Morgan interjected.

"But they only had information about generation six, which was still housed at Fort Meade.

"Echelon Gen7 represents a major breakthrough in quantum computing. It's not any faster than other supercomputers, but it has a distinct computational algorithmic advantage. It looks at computing in an altogether different way. With its radical programming approach, it leverages massive computing capabilities with a new perspective and philosophy. It makes Moore's Law irrelevant. No encryption program can withstand the computational onslaught of Gen7. All electronic communication is subject to its all-seeing eye."

The most powerful intelligence-gathering system ever devised had evolved over six decades. Now in its seventh generation, it could intercept and interrogate satellite, microwave, cellular, and fiber-optic voice and data transmissions. It managed a staggering level of information, including internet traffic and electronic communications. More amazing was its ability to filter and analyze data for the NSA's bureaucrats. Credit and debit cards, courier services, and a thousand other things passed through its sophisticated filters, which searched for patterns and potential threats. The NSA had realized its dream, a system that could connect the dots of human activity.

While it provided quality intelligence, Morgan didn't agree with the system's existence. He didn't see eye-to-eye with the bureaucrats charged with its oversight. They lived outside the law. In their minds, they were the law. Their push for a global agency that would act in response to Echelon data chapped his ass. He knew his agency and its British, Canadian, and Australian counterparts were the prime targets the NSA hoped to engulf through such a move.

Still, he couldn't imagine how anyone could defeat Echelon.

"In addition, a radical faction has arisen in the Ultraist Group," McDonnell continued, throwing another dossier onto his pile. The screen flicked to the image of an enormous strawberry-haired man in his late forties. He appeared to be six-six or so, weighing in around three hundred pounds, a mountain of a man. "This is Randall Hafley, the man who would be king. Literally. He's VP of Operations for the Ultraist Group, second-in-command behind Masters. We believe he's taking a small group toward armed rebellion. He's using Masters's cross-pollination idea to create a hybrid terror network with an independent ideology. They seem to be on the cusp of creating havoc. His goals are much clearer than Masters's are. They haven't become a splinter group yet, so you'll be dealing with a nonhomogenous organization. It'll be tricky. There's a man on the inside, but I'm not at liberty to divulge his identity yet.

"Finally, there's Steven Unger." The screen changed to the picture of a robust man in his late fifties whose dark hair was gray at the temples. "Unger was the architect of the space shuttle's computerized flight systems and the other reason why time has run out. He led the teams that developed and perfected the automated re-entry, descent, and landing capabilities for the shuttle. He's joined the Ultraist Group, and we believe he's aligned himself with the more radical faction within it."

"I still don't see your point. How can they leverage this against us?"

"In the aftermath of 9/11, everyone scrambled to make sure we couldn't be attacked by our own aircraft again. While the public focused on Sky Marshals and reinforced cockpit doors, the previous administration had a different solution. They began retrofitting commercial airliners with an updated version of Unger's GCCS software, the Ground Control Computer System. No aircraft comes off the assembly line without the technology that allows for the complete ground-based override of all onboard guidance and control systems. At this point, the entire commercial fleet has been refitted."

"How could they be doing that? The technology's not there. Scaling up the shuttle re-entry software would require too much computing power. Controlling one shuttle is possible, but not hundreds of aircraft. You couldn't string together enough supercomputers."

"The government leveraged the NSA quantum computing breakthrough and algorithms to create an exponential decrease in computing requirements. As I said, it's deployed."

Morgan jumped to the end game. "Shit, if that code gets into the wrong hands, it'll make 9/11 look like nothing."

"It already has. Apparently, Unger built a back door into his system; one that only he can hack. We suspect he's helping the Ultraist Group exploit that vulnerability.

"Yesterday morning, a plane in New Jersey skidded off a runway and plowed into a building. It was a Challenger CL-600 refit with Unger's flight controls. I'm not sure how the NTSB will rule on the accident, but the official story won't be anything close to what happened. They'll blame some poor ramp agent or frost, or God knows what. The pilot claims the plane wouldn't respond to any of his attempts to control or override the computer systems. Somebody controlled that plane and crashed it into a warehouse. We were lucky this time, no fatalities. But you can rest assured this is going to escalate. We've got to get inside the Ultraist Group, sabotage their systems, and take Unger out."

"What a fiasco," he said, shaking his head.

She looked tired. "It gets worse. The two largest air cargo carriers have also been refit with the system. They fly mass amounts of dangerous goods around the globe on a daily basis. In the wrong hands, those planes are flying bombs; potentially dirty bombs. And if that's not bad enough, in a few weeks, the military will have completed outfitting all transports and long-range bombers with a military version of the system." She continued with uncharacteristic gravity. "When that work is finished, every aircraft becomes a remote-controlled weapon."

"Holy shit, Masters can promise total anarchy and deliver it. But I still don't see how anyone could defeat Echelon Gen 7. Wouldn't it require a more powerful technology?"

"That's for you to figure out. It's as if they've blinded the damn system.

"Why me? I'm not a fit for this."

"We need to get someone deep enough inside the Ultraist Group to find the real answers; and that, my friend, is your next assignment. Unfortunately, your operating window is tight. We believe they'll move before the end of the year."

"But I haven't done this type of field work in years."

McDonnell waved him off. "We've signed you up for an associate membership in the group using this background information." The file joined the growing stack in front of him. "We've leased a house for you right outside the main gate of MacDill Air Force Base. You're a new professor scheduled to start the January semester at the University of Tampa. Given your security background and the location of the house, Randall Hafley should be interested in you." She hesitated and smiled. "Look at the bright side; you can use that PhD and spend some time with your son. Maybe you can finally achieve something better than your father."

He thumbed the pages of his cover story. "Yeah, that's great." Distraction prevented the full recognition of an opportunity to spend time with his child who attended the University of South Florida. He continued thumbing pages with a perplexed expression. "This looks pretty close to my real file."

"It turns out you're what they're looking for, and we know they're showing an inordinate amount of interest in MacDill. This may appear to be an innocuous group of intellectuals, but watch out for Hafley. He's vicious and driven. If he suspects you, he will terminate you."

He looked over his glasses and gave a fake smile. "I'll be careful."

She added a booklet to his pile. "Read this on the flight."

"What the hell is this?"

"It's the book that started this mess, The Ultraist Manifesto. It must be good reading; it made Golda's book club a few years back." She paused, waiting for some sort of acknowledgement. "Even you must have heard of the Golda-factor."

He grunted.

"Any questions before we move off that topic?"

"I'll let you know after I read the files."

She seemed somewhat uneasy. "Prior to your mission yesterday, you were briefed on who to take out and why. Now let me fill you in on details we've received within the past twenty-four hours. Those details relate the assassination plot yesterday to everything we've been discussing this morning."

"So Echelon is working."

"Of course it's working. But we're convinced they've found a way around it. We wouldn't have stopped that assassin if it weren't for an alert Customs agent at LAX three days ago. He notified the Secret Service that someone from the watch list was trying to enter the country. They passed him through in the hope of a larger round up. That's when we got the call. I briefed you on his movements and our intelligence about his target. Through bank records and Echelon, we traced his movements back to the Philippines to a contact we persuaded to talk. That's how we found the connection to Nasjolay." She rolled her eyes. "Thank God we had him in custody. Echelon hadn't picked up on anything or alerted the NSA about these guys. If the Customs agent hadn't recognized that bastard, the Filipino President would be dead and we wouldn't have a clue about the primary target, POTUS."

Morgan gave a pensive shake of his head.

"By the way, I'm on a nine-thirty flight to Dulles and you're on a ten o'clock to Tampa."

Deep in thought, Morgan managed a slight nod.

"You can tell me about your operation on the way to the airport."

That would be the high point of her day. She loved hearing about his work and the meaning he attached to it.

Chapter 11

Morgan emerged from one of the communal offices as McDonnell approached from a different section of the facility.

"All set?"

He started toward the elevator shaft. "Ready when you are."

"That's not our exit." She moved in the opposite direction. "Come this way."

They walked through another area of the complex.

"How's Thad doing by the way?"

"Okay, I guess."

"What do you mean you guess?"

Morgan could see the gnarled vein rise on her forehead.

"I probably know more about the kid than you do. I feel like his freaking grandmother."

"I haven't talked to him since right after school started. It's just so easy to focus on work. Before I know it, months have passed without a call or an email."

"God Levi, It's not that hard. Pick up the phone."

"I don't know what to say. Everything's a lie. Now I realize how my dad must have felt. He's probably laughing his ass off."

"I doubt that, you have a kid's view of your father."

Morgan stopped and stared at her.

She looked back and changed the subject. "How's your neck? I see you rubbing it and twisting it a lot."

"It's fine. It aches a little if I get a chill. The air-conditioning down here was bothering me. It's no problem though. I can do everything I used to, maybe even more." He chuckled. "My golf swing is better since the surgery. Can't swing as hard so I have more control."

"That's my concern. You're slower and little heavier. You could find yourself in a bad situation if you're not careful."

"It's not an issue."

A frustrated sigh escaped as she approached an access panel and keyed in a code. The door slid open, revealing another elevator. The unit whisked toward the surface, gliding to a stop inside a private parking structure on Fisherman's Wharf.

A Cadillac limousine pulled up to meet them. "Nice little setup you've got here." As he held the door for her, he noticed the armor plating and bulletproof glass. "This is some rig," he said sliding in beside her. The car exited the garage and wound its way toward Highway 101 and the airport.

McDonnell hit the intercom. "George, is the jamming equipment on and functioning properly?"

"Yes, Ms. McDonnell"

Turning, she pulled a bony leg onto the seat to face Morgan, smiling in anticipation. "Okay, let's hear it."

He wouldn't have been surprised if she'd bounced on the seat like a gleeful schoolgirl. He tossed a broken nylon tie into her lap. "Here's the weapon."

She smiled broadly.

For the last four years, they'd performed this ritual. After each kill, he'd present her with the weapon. It had started when he'd presented her with the weapon as a show of honor and respect. Since then, he'd given her every one. He assumed she kept a macabre museum of mundane, yet deadly, artifacts.

"The ruse was perfect. No one knew what Nasjolay looked like. The Filipino took the bait and met me at the buy location. The weapons never left the case. In fact, it was never even opened." He gave a strange crooked smile. "Short, sweet, and simple; no complications, no trail."

"Bret Nasjolay died of a stroke right after the interrogation yesterday," she said disappointedly.

He rubbed his face with both hands. "Hopefully, we got all we could out of him."

"We'll never know for sure. He was a worthless bastard."

George pulled the limo up to the curb at the airport departures area. The door opened and McDonnell stepped onto the sidewalk.

Morgan pulled his bag from the trunk and handed it to a waiting skycap. "Thanks for everything," he told her.

Years ago, through a cross-departmental blind program, McDonnell had been assigned to counsel Morgan through his marital problems and the ensuing divorce. Later as his boss, she offered a sympathetic ear and soothing words as Morgan fought to avoid the parental mistakes of his father.

In many ways he likened her to the mother he had lost. No vain promises or words of encouragement were necessary. A deep respect and trust had grown between them. "Have a safe trip home."

"You, too. It was great seeing you again. It's been too long." She gave him a quick, platonic hug. They blended well with the other family, friends, and business acquaintances at the curb.

Morgan took his boarding pass from the skycap and turned for one last wave before entering the airport lobby.

* * *

He joined the participants assembled at the *Theater of Safety Activity*—TSA for short. Congregants streamed through the one-act play known as airport security, carrying out the false impression of heightened safety. The checkpoints were a sham with one purpose, and that was to comfort the public and keep them flying. Al-Qaeda had spawned an industry, and a lucrative one, at that.

All manner of threats, real or fabricated, could pass through the charade, except for certain high-profile forbidden items. Creative people could find a way around the taboos. The *Theater of Safety* existed to make the innocent and law-abiding feel better. Every so often, it even intercepted a would-be terrorist, albeit a stupid one.

Ultimately, the pretense did nothing to stop anyone armed with information and will power. Even a member of the no-fly list could pass through security with a stolen credit card and a fake boarding pass generated on the Internet.

Recent screw-ups surfaced after a passenger had thwarted the latest bombing attempt. Everyone was clambering to connect-the-dots. How had the bomber gotten so far? Bureaucrats and politicians were in a feeding frenzy. The wrong heads would roll at some agency, probably the CIA. For all of their pissing and moaning over not being able to connect the dots, politicians would shit their pants if they knew what Echelon Gen7 could do.

Morgan's turn with the full-body scanner complete, he retrieved his shoes and moved toward the gate. He shuddered at the magnitude of the threat posed by GCCS. No plane or person would be safe once the military completed its refit.

He took in the news as he grabbed a bite to eat. A redheaded journalist in a lacey camisole beckoned his eye to her voluptuous breasts. She did a plug for an upcoming interview with the Secretary of Homeland Security.

"Mr. Secretary, isn't it true that security lines are the most dangerous place in an airport?" She interrupted her stilted reading with a theatrical pause. "Since they're completely unsecured, terrorists could paralyze the entire aviation system just by detonating a bomb at one of your security checkpoints. What just happened in Moscow is a perfect example."

"Valerie, this administration has a long-term vision for moving the checkpoints deeper inside airports, but there will always be some unsecured locations where travelers congregate. We want to avoid creating multiple unsecured gathering points."

The reporter pressed her point. "Isn't it true that the only things that have really made flying safer are reinforced cockpit doors and people's newly acquired willingness to resist hijackers?"

The secretary skirted her question. "If you're asking me if there's a way to stop a terrorist from carrying a bomb into a crowded location and detonating it, the answer is no."

Her head cocked to the side, her face assuming a confused, twisted look. With a slight squint and a scrunched nose, she asked, "How can we know we're safe then?" With an imploring tone of exasperation, she added, "What can we do?"

"Are we ever completely safe? Trust me; we have systems in place to protect the public."

The anchorman broke in. "Tune in tonight, at nine o'clock, for an interview that promises to scare and comfort everyone."

Morgan turned toward the gate, shaking his head. If the public only knew what protected them.

* * *

He maneuvered down the passageway, toward the rear of the aircraft. Analytical to the core, he sought to control his environment and eliminate the unknown. Mushin philosophy allowed him to be one-step ahead of his opponents; habit forced him to analyze and categorize the risk for each person boarding the flight.

A cultural melting pot streamed down the aisle, searching for free space to store their possessions. Mothers with babies in their arms, business people, tourists of various ethnic backgrounds: none fit the profile or manifested the physiological signs of a would-be terrorist.

The sky marshal came down the walkway and plopped into the aisle seat across from him, a talkative young man with a Texas drawl.

"Sure sucks bein' a business traveler these days." He took a pull on his Starbucks latte. "Everyone tries to bring their whole damn life in carry-on luggage."

Morgan just smiled and nodded, not wanting to encourage a five-hour rambling conversation. If he minded his own business, he'd be able to review his file and get some sleep before their morning arrival in Tampa.

His row mate arrived and took the window seat. The middle seat would be empty, purchased by McDonnell to keep him comfortable. He sat down, intending to get to work.

He began with a systematic review of each file, writing questions, observations, and analyses as he read. He survived on cold hard logic. Things always added up in his world. At least, until recently. His dreams of late were a growing cause of concern.

He began to read.

```
1. David Masters
   * Brief stint in the Navy; washed out of
     Navy SEAL training during week 25.
```

What the hell? No one washes out at that point. Week twenty-five is graduation time. No one would go through all that and quit. What was he up to?

```
   * Honorable discharge: September 1980
   * Dropped off the grid in 1981
   * Pops up again in Canada in 1984
   * Drops and resurfaces in Eastern Europe in
     1991
```

Was Masters doing non-official cover assignments? Did he have a change of heart through some religious experience?

```
   * Returns to the States late 1993 and begins
     TUG
   * Devised Hawala-type counter-intelligence
     system
   * Illegal contacts with Iran, Venezuela, and
     Cuba; as well as reported ties to Hamas,
     Hezbollah, the Muslim Brotherhood, Abu
```

```
        Sayyaf, the Revolutionary Armed Forces of
        Columbia, and MBR 200
2. Randall Hafley . . .
```

Hafley appeared mercenary in nature, but the report contained little information on him. If nothing else, he was the bully who ran the show.

```
3. Steven Unger
    * Computer systems architect specializing in
      aeronautical engineering.  Field
      operations have reported that Unger is
      assisting TUG in the development and use
      of wireless technology to seize commercial
      aircraft for use in terror attacks.
```

He was a geek, no surprise there. The type who loved playing with his gadgets and ideas.

```
4. Tommy Haddon
    * Brigadier General, U. S. Air Force
    * Access to Echelon
    * Access to Nuclear Armament codes
    * Member of the Ultraist Group
```

Why hadn't McDonnell mentioned Haddon in the briefing?

He reviewed his own background file for his cover. His uneasiness grew as he noted how it mirrored his actual life.

The review complete, he kicked back and read The Ultraist Manifesto. An interesting read, though more of a pamphlet than a book. It made TUG seem like just another innocuous head-in-the-clouds group of do-gooders.

When he finished with it, he settled back for a couple hours sleep before landing in Tampa.

Chapter 12

Sunday, November 17

"You're sure?" Randall Hafley let out a bullish snort. "He's been feeding the Feds false information. I can't believe we trusted him. What kind of evidence do you have?" He listened for several minutes, vacillating between affirmations and pissed-off grunts. "You're sure? I don't want to find out I'm not getting the full story here." His eyes twitched as he listened to the caller. "We don't have any choice, then. He's an ungrateful bastard." He paused and gave his full attention to the electronic litany. "I don't give a shit," he blasted. "This has gone far enough. Clear out his desk, confiscate his files, and revoke all his access immediately. Eliminate the problem."

Gillian imagined steam pouring from the massive redhead's nostrils as he slammed the receiver onto its cradle. Hafley stood in the executive boardroom; in silence he gathered his thoughts. Eternity passed as he gazed out the windows, toward the sun-drenched Gulf of Mexico. He turned and faced the room, studying the seven stunned faces comprising the operational managers of TUG's security team.

"Gang, we've got a huge problem."

Everyone around the table shifted in their seats, shuffled papers, and avoided eye contact. The emotional vortex had sucked the energy out of them. No one wanted to be entangled in Hafley's building hostility. They'd all seen him angry, but never anything remotely resembling this rage. For her part, Gillian just wanted to fly under the radar a little longer. Let someone else face this maelstrom.

"That was Mike Markus. It seems we have a serious security issue."

They all knew Markus. The stoic Deputy Director of Security for TUG had developed a reputation for being ruthless. A wise person would neither trust nor cross him, intentionally or otherwise.

Hafley shook his head in disbelief. "Markus tells me our own Director of Security, Ben Bradley, has been producing fake documents. Over the past several years, he's fed the FBI false reports on our movements, activities, and contacts." He paused, staring out at the skyline. "I've instructed Markus to cut Bradley loose before he can do anymore damage."

Gillian felt conflicted. Her daughter Maddie was six-months old when she started this assignment. During the ensuing eighteen months, Gillian had come to appreciate, even agree with the Ultraist's ideals. They lived a philosophy that she wanted to pass on to Maddie.

But Hafley's actions represented something altogether different. Markus was a sadistic killer who'd been released from Leavenworth just seven years after the brutal murder of a meter reader. He had claimed PTSD and received a light sentence. Trained by the military, he'd gone rogue years ago selling his psychotic services to the highest bidder. Letting his insatiable hedonism loose on Bradley would lead nowhere good.

She hated dumping Maddie on her mother to come to a Sunday morning meeting. No one should have to endure this tirade, even for money. If Hafley and Markus caught on to her, things could get dangerous. She couldn't expose her two-year old to harm.

Gillian had been ecstatic last year when David Masters had offered her a position as his aide. The plan that she and her handler devised had worked perfectly. In fact, a few months ago, under the pretext of giving her broader exposure to his organization, David had requested that she move into Hafley's area and study the activities there. Now, a maternal foreboding replaced her euphoria.

"Confiscate all of Bradley's files and lock down his accounts within the hour. No exceptions." Hafley glared around the room. "Do I make myself clear?"

No one spoke. Heads around the table nodded.

As David's former top aide, Gillian thought Hafley had suspected her of corporate espionage. She concluded that paranoia must have driven her to misinterpret his micro-expressions and comments. Guilt flavored the relief she felt upon hearing it was Bradley who'd been fingered as the Feds' inside man.

But he couldn't be sabotaging the Ultraist Group. Bradley believes in David's goals and philosophy. Shit, he's been with David from the beginning. Why would he feed the Feds false information about TUG? Markus's accusations don't make sense.

Markus knew how to eliminate the problem. Over the past several years, he'd dealt with a number of problems for his employers. He'd been well compensated for his loyal service. He would arrange for Bradley to have an accident, and that would be that—an instant promotion.

The next morning, a notation on page three of the Tampa Tribune's Local Section reported Director Bradley's untimely passing. The cause of death: asphyxiation. Police suspected suicide.

Chapter 13

As the plane taxied to the terminal, Morgan stretched out the kinks. His neck hurt like hell. He would never be without this daily reminder of his brush with death. The doctors were amazed he wasn't a quadriplegic; they said it was a miracle.

He noticed several messages on his cell and punched in his retrieval code.

Professor Morgan, this is Elaina, from the Ultraist Group. She spoke professionally. *Doctor Masters would like to meet with you on Monday afternoon, at three o'clock, if possible. Please call and let me know if you can make the appointment.* She left her phone number and the address of the meeting.

He made a mental note to return the call and accept.

There were two more perplexing messages. Both times, the caller had left muffled grunts and a dial tone. Instinct drove him to think something terrible had happened to his son.

The phone rang and he answered. "Hello?" Silence. "Thad, is that you?"

The voice on the other end choked out a word. "Dad."

"Are you okay? Where are you?" Dread crept into Morgan's heart. "Are you hurt?"

Thaddeus Morgan regained his composure. "Was it worth it?"

"Was what worth it?"

"Was it worth it to desert me and Mom to pursue your dreams? Was it that bad? Was *I* that bad?"

"Thad, what's wrong?"

"Mom's dead."

Morgan stroked his close-cropped hair willing his mind into action. "What? What did you say? What happened?"

"She killed herself, Dad. She killed herself." Thad broke down, his grief-racked lungs gasping for breath.

The phrase denied the laws of nature and gathered energy after its release. To hell with Newton and inertia, those three words slammed into Morgan like a freight train picking up speed. Liz had had issues, but Morgan hadn't seen this coming. He'd never imagined she could be so selfish. "What? How? Are you sure?" He sat stunned. "She can't be dead. There's some mistake."

"No," Thad murmured between stuttered gasps.

"Where are you? I just flew into Tampa. Let me grab my bag and get to you."

Thad pulled it together enough to say, "I'm at the house."

"I'll be there as soon as I can. A couple of hours, no more. I love you." Those words felt flat, one-dimensional, as he hung up.

Time had misbehaved during the call; most of the passengers had since deplaned. Uncharacteristically, he'd lost awareness of his surroundings. The sky marshal and a woman looked away, embarrassed for eavesdropping. His row-mate looked sad and helpless, and then mouthed the words, "So sorry."

His thoughts raced as he sought to pull together even a half-baked plan. He couldn't afford to waste time on feelings. This was too important.

In the terminal, he dialed one of the rotating numbers that constituted his office. The receptionist forwarded the call on a secure line to one of the NSA agents on duty for the area. "Please state your name for voice identification."

"Morgan, Levi."

"Please hold for verification." Several seconds later, the agent came back on. "Voice identification verified. How can I help you, Mr. Morgan?"

"I need to be transferred to Director McDonnell on a secure line."

"Please hang up, sir. I'll have the Director call your satellite phone on a secure channel. Hold one second." The duty officer shuffled papers. "Your vehicle is in the parking garage. You can collect the key at the rental counter under your name." The line went dead.

Morgan called the Ultraist Group to confirm his three o'clock meeting with Masters. He collected his bag at the conveyor belt, picked up the car keys, and moved toward long-term parking. Taking the elevator into the shadowy parking facility, he held up the keys and clicked the remote. A vehicle answered his call.

Shock prevented him from noticing McDonnell's personal touch, a specially updated 1953 Dodge pickup. He got in and flipped on the jamming equipment and scrambler. The engine roared to life, idling with the purr of a highly tuned street machine. Harsh sunlight glared through the windshield as he exited the airport and headed south toward the Skyway Bridge and home.

The truck trundled along with the rest of the pack through the winding curves leading to south. He felt no inclination to compete with the traffic around him. In fact, he felt nothing at all. Liz's death had opened a void, kicked through his armor, leaving him vulnerable. He could no longer use her as an excuse to avoid his parental responsibility. He didn't feel empty; he was used to that. This was something altogether foreign. He felt fear.

The call came in as the truck rolled along the Pinellas stretch of the highway. The secure channel light indicated an agency call. "Morgan here."

McDonnell sounded tired. "What's up?"

"I just spoke with Thad. Liz committed suicide."

McDonnell said nothing.

"He's a mess. I'm headed there now. It shouldn't interfere with the op, but I'll need some time for the services and to look after Thad."

"God," McDonnell said haltingly. "I'm so sorry to hear that. You all right?"

"I'm fine. I just can't believe she checked out on him. She was self-centered to the last." Anger replaced his initial dismay. This would have a devastating effect on his son's life.

"Don't be too hard on her. She'd been through a lot. She was never strong, and I think the empty nest was more than she could handle." Deb McDonnell spoke from experience. She'd seen dozens of Black Ops marriages go sour. "Do whatever you need to help Thad through this. Just keep me posted so I can move another operative in if I need to."

"Sure thing, boss. Thanks."

"Do you like the truck?"

"It's perfect, thanks." He smiled. "It screams quirky college professor."

The Skyway Bridge loomed on the horizon. The warm breeze, pregnant with salty moisture, blew through the open window. He never tired of seeing the magnificent structure with its towering steel sails.

His thoughts turned toward Thad and their reunion. He loved his son more than life itself, but he would never have been accused of spending much time with him—nor quality time, for that matter. His career and his estranged relationship with Liz had allowed limited family occasions through Thad's formative years. Things had gotten better when Thad had chosen to room in the college dorms. He'd been able to join the boy during school breaks. They'd even vacationed together during the past two summers.

He pulled off the highway and parked in a rest area along the northern approach to the bridge. Slipping from the truck, he wandered along the water's edge, until he stopped and stared out across the mouth of the bay.

The late morning sun burned fiercely. He performed a meaningless act of penance, allowing the heat to scorch his skin as he lingered in thought.

Thad's news reminded him of his failure as a husband and father. His perennial absence had been difficult for Liz. The walls he'd maintained to perform his job had sealed the fate of that relationship long ago.

He looked beyond the point, where the waters of the river began to mingle with the bay, beyond the coastline of the barrier islands, far into the Gulf, where great ships became specks and disappeared. He wished he could see that far into his future. Hell, he wished he'd had that ability twenty-five years ago.

Samurai masters maintained the physical prowess of the warrior but denied its deepest spiritual nature of Zen. Out of necessity, he'd built walls to protect himself from the distraction that kills. Intimate relationships, such as having a wife or son, could create a *suki*, an opening that might invite attack. Mushin theory had served him well in combat, but he longed to experience the reality of consciousness in every area of his life, without walls. He longed to experience *sartori* and become a Zen master—one with everything.

The walls had to come down. Only he could do that. He needed to clear the air with Thad, to let him know how he'd pursued the enemies of the State. But he couldn't; it was all classified—beyond top secret.

He pulled into the driveway of an unremarkable stucco home produced by the same cookie cutter used for every other home in the neighborhood, and every other house in the county. Overpriced and under-built, these developments had become the final resting place for the first wave of blue-haired baby boomers.

He squinted against the amplified sunlight as it leapt from the white sidewalk. At the door, he rang the bell, stepped back, and waited for one agonizing, eternal moment, wondering what would approach from the other side— friend or foe.

The door swung open to reveal a strapping young man. Thad Morgan's six-foot-three lean frame was loaded with bronze muscles. He dressed in the style of his generation, a logo jersey and long basketball shorts.

"I'm so glad to see you," Thad sighed. He stepped over the threshold and gave Morgan a hug, letting out a long pulsating breath.

Thankful he didn't have to face the foe quite yet, Morgan embraced his boy, breathing in the expensive cologne hawked in men's magazines. He wanted to hold him forever. "I'm so sorry."

Thad convulsed with spasms of grief, and Morgan held him in silence. Thankful that boy needed his presence, not words.

When the spell passed, they moved into the house. It had been years since Morgan had done more than wait in the foyer. He'd always felt as though an invisible fence barred him from the rest of the house after the divorce.

Thad slumped into a chair in the great room. He covered his face with his hands in a vain attempt to hide his grief. "She never said a word to indicate she might do this. I hadn't spoken to her in several weeks. Getting ready for finals took all my time. If I'd been around, this might not have happened. I thought she was doing fine. She'd been dating a guy and seemed happy for the first time in ages."

"There aren't any easy answers. I'm as confused by this as you are. I had no idea your mom had become so fragile."

"I loved her so much," Thad said as he wept. "Why wasn't that enough to keep her going? Now I'm alone in the world."

His words cut deep. Thad had felt isolated and alone because of his career. Morgan crossed the room and knelt to embrace him. "You're not alone. You'll never be alone again. I promise."

"You're full of shit, and I really don't like you," Thad said lifelessly. "But I'm glad you're here." Weariness and emotion drained the last of his energy. Exhaustion consumed him.

"I leased a place in south Tampa, but I can stay here if you want."

"Whatever."

"I'll make arrangements for the services in the morning. I've got a three o'clock meeting in Tampa."

"Maybe I'll come up with you. I need to pick up a few things at the dorm."

"Get some sleep."

Chapter 14

Aided by the rhythmic hum of the ceiling fan, a soft current of air flowed through the tiny bungalow. The stifling nights had given way to pleasant evenings, not unlike an Illinois summer. Deep in thought, Gillian sat twirling a brown lock of hair around her finger, a habit she'd acquired from her father.

Recollections of catching fireflies on summer nights and memories of hide-n-seek around the old neighborhood provided clarity. She recognized what she had lost; what she wanted for her daughter. She deserved a stable life, a life without evil people like Hafley and Markus in it. Maybe they could settle down here and she could work for the Ultraist Group.

There was one problem with that: she was a spy.

Maybe David could help. Why would he help me once he discovers who I am, my true reason for joining TUG?

The earlier meeting with Hafley had made it clear. Arrests were necessary. Gaps in the evidence made it difficult to create a comprehensive list of conspirators. Time was running out, an attack seemed imminent. If she waited, it'd be too late. Gillian's security role with TUG granted her access to internal memos addressing everything from missing nuclear waste to mass storage locations of hydrofluoric acid. In isolation, every item seemed aboveboard and explainable, but within a larger context, signs of espionage and battle preparation were evident.

There were plenty of credible risks but no corroborating evidence. The intelligence she reviewed puzzled her. Everything was circumstantial at best.

Whoever sought to control the Ultraist Group had discovered the leak and had wanted it plugged. She'd seen documents indicating an improvised nuclear weapons strike on the D.C. area. During their last meeting, her handler had requested that she dig deeper for signs of a decapitation strike against the government.

Conflict raged on every front ... in every person she knew. David seemed oblivious to the violent connections.

Although he proclaimed the virtues of anarchy, David Masters was non-violent to his core. He believed mankind could become responsible and humane enough to care for one another without all the rules and regulations of a society. He possessed a childlike optimism.

Gillian knew better. Life—real life—had taught her something far different. People rarely changed. The path they chose was the path they stuck to.

She never believed David's audacious hopefulness fronted anything sinister. He promoted a platform for change and established numerous mechanisms to help the less fortunate. He lived his philosophy. Randall Hafley, on the other hand, manipulated people and circumstances to achieve his goals.

Nevertheless, she had to consider the possibility that David had violent aspirations. She considered the labor strikes TUG advocated. Was the phrase "national workers strike" some type of code for a military strike? Had the Ultraist Manifesto been written as a codebook, a low-tech tool used to outwit the government's high tech systems of decryption? Was David using Hafley to insulate himself from prosecution. From me? Was Hafley his means of plausible deniability?

Her heart gave the answer. David was genuine, even if his head was in the stratosphere. Unlike her dad, David was a man to be trusted.

A different memory rushed in from childhood. She'd been visiting her father and had burst into tears when he'd dropped her off. "Please, please don't go. I'll be better. I promise, I'll be better. Just don't leave, Daddy. You and Mommy stay together."

She'd felt responsible for her parents' divorce. If she'd been a better girl, they would have stayed together.

Her father's drug-fogged mind hadn't been able to comprehend her sense of responsibility for his broken marriage. He'd never dreamed a ten-year old could feel guilty for his problems, though she'd said it out loud. The Bureau had forsaken him, claiming he'd gotten too close to the enemy. His disgrace had proven too painful and he'd fled everything and everyone.

Getting to know David Masters had taken the sting out of those painful memories. David had helped her realize she could be happy if she focused on the positive. She felt free of her past, experiencing the ability to make new and different choices in life. Instinct informed her that David had brought about all of that change in her life.

He was a good man. But not everyone in TUG was altruistic.

Just a few short months ago, it would have been impossible for her to conceive that TUG was involved in international terrorist activities. Today's events had given birth to a full-blown conviction in it, albeit unsubstantiated. The Bureau needed to act soon. She needed to file a report requesting action before this thing matured into something hellish.

Someone had tapped her phone and monitored her email accounts. They were capturing all her electronic communication and, according to her handler, eavesdropping on many of their face-to-face conversations. Most troubling of all, she didn't have a clue who held her leash.

Only ties to high-level government intelligence agencies could explain that type of surveillance. She needed to report to her superiors face-to-face in a controlled environment. But how, with such constant scrutiny? She'd have to hide Maddie and her mother before they were dragged into this mess.

Once she did that, her anonymous assailants would know she was their leak.

Chapter 15

Monday, November 18

Morgan was on the lanai having coffee when Thad appeared. Against his better judgment, he'd already decided to make a haphazard attempt at providing his son with a legacy, resolving to come clean about his career. He wanted him to know why he'd been away so much.

"Hey, have you got a few minutes?"

Thad poured a cup of coffee and retrieved a doughnut from a box in the middle of the table. "If it's going to make you feel better, go ahead. It's not going to change anything between us. You can't make the past go away."

"I thought we could have a simple service for your mother this Friday morning and scatter her ashes over the Gulf," he said, diverting the conversation in the face of Thad's intensity. "I was wondering . . . do you want to buy a plot somewhere and set up a marker to visit her?"

"She'd like the idea of spreading her ashes over the Gulf. It was one of her favorite places. As for the marker, I don't think I need that. I can go to the Gulf anytime. Besides, her spirit is elsewhere, right?"

"She's moved on to paradise and is waiting for us there."

"You're so full of shit. She might be waiting on me, but I think she'd rather see you in Hell."

"Don't you mean you'd rather see me in Hell? Your mom wasn't that vindictive." He loved his son's candor, but he wanted to bring the subject back on track. "Yesterday, on the phone, you asked me if it was worth it. I've been asking myself that same question for months."

"Don't worry about it. I was just pissed off."

"No, you were right. We need to talk about things. If we hold on to old pains, we'll never know each other. That's been my problem for too long. I need to let you into my life."

Thad slumped in his chair, pushing his gangly legs under the table, arms crossed. "Go for it."

A shiver ran up Morgan's spine; his tongue turned to cotton. He wanted to vomit. In the face of Thad's dour attitude, he couldn't risk the truth. The whole story would have to wait.

"Your mom and I got married young. I had to make difficult decisions. I don't regret my choices, but I regret some of the consequences. I regret the effect those consequences had on you and your mother." He paused. "Was it worth it for me to sacrifice my relationship with you? Hell no, it wasn't worth it. But, I was right to leave a failing marriage because of incompatibility. It was a marriage that hurt the both of us. It seemed right. We were young and stupid. We didn't understand the consequences of our differences. Puppy love and hormones drove us to get married."

Thad scowled.

"Don't get me wrong," he continued. "I wouldn't go back and change anything. I got the best thing in the world from that relationship: you. Your mother felt the same way. But I knew something bad would happen if your mother and I stayed together."

"Something really bad happened anyway, didn't it?"

Morgan ignored the comment. This time, he shed the tears. "I regret being away from you all the time. It wasn't worth it, not even close to it. I love you and I'm sorry."

"I'm not ready to forgive you. I love you and I'm glad you're here right now, but this isn't over."

In his son, he saw all the virtue that had been overshadowed in his own formative years. "Can I stay here with you for a while?"

"Sure."

"It'd be better if we drove up to Tampa separately. I don't know when I'll finish up there. I'll meet you back here tonight."

"I meant to ask you what brought you to Tampa anyway? You didn't come because of Mom."

"I'm here to teach at the University next semester. Today, I'm going to meet with David Masters of the Ultraist Group."

A flash of recognition crossed Thad's face. "How does David Masters tie into your *career*?" The word sounded comedic as Thad stuck out his tongue, rolled his eyes, and jogged his head like a bobble-head doll. "A bunch of my friends are members of the Group. From what I've read, it's interesting."

"Just be careful around them." He dug into his wallet. "Here's some money for gas."

Thad took the money and growled disgustedly. "You're too weird." He pushed away from the table and went inside.

Morgan sat back. "I think that went pretty well."

Chapter 16

Morgan found the swiftness of Masters's meeting invitation perplexing. He hadn't contacted the University of Tampa yet to discuss his role as a visiting professor of philosophy. Why would Masters already be interested in him?

He parked his pickup in the garage and made his way to the lobby.

Masters wouldn't be an easy mark. His persuasive powers rivaled some of the greatest orators in recent history.

He'd have to be careful. He couldn't afford to be exposed; or worse, fall under the man's influence. His op was to discredit and dismantle TUG by whatever means necessary.

Masters's assistant escorted him into a simply furnished Tibetan-style office which conveyed an aura of reverence. Masters rose from a floor cushion behind a low teakwood table supported by large polished stones. The simple yet elegant piece was bare except for a closed laptop. Masters moved toward him with his hand extended, a pleasant smile on his face. The room felt warm and inviting with a circle of pillows situated to take in the Tampa skyline.

Morgan sized the man up. Six foot, medium build, mid-fifties, with well-defined forearms. He had a commanding, yet not disagreeable, handshake. His casual tropical attire disguised any further opportunity for evaluation. Still, he assumed David Masters was in relatively good shape and actively kept himself that way.

"Ah, Professor Morgan, so good of you to come on such short notice. I'm David Masters. Please, have a seat." Masters motioned him toward the circle of floor pillows. "Being a student of philosophy, I love to meet the local influences whenever possible. When the Chancellor told me UT was getting a new professor, I wanted to meet with you. Then, when we received your application for membership in the Ultraist Group, I couldn't wait." He repeated his offer, "Please, sit down. Can I offer you something to drink? Would you care for some iced tea, water, anything?"

"No, thank you, Doctor. Please, call me Levi." With a hint of surprise, he asked, "You're Buddhist?"

Masters looked up and gave the assistant a slight shake of his head. She left the room and closed the door. "Zen, actually."

Morgan glanced at the desk as he passed. There was nothing on it, not even a to-do list.

He sat on one of the pillows and soaked in the manmade beauty of the skyline gleaming in the midday sun. The entire setting gave him a deep sense of relaxation and peace; things he hadn't known in quite some time. "I've studied yoga blended with the way of the sword for years."

Masters motioned toward the windows. "Isn't it amazing?" He seemed to meld with the view, soaking in the peace. "Zen is lightning that comes in a heartbeat but remains for a lifetime."

Intrigued, Morgan pursued that line of thought. "What does it bring?"

"No one can explain. A person must experience it; and even then, he can't explain it."

"It's a mystery like all religions, meditating or praying in pursuit of a mystical experience."

"Zen does *not* meditate," Masters insisted. "It acts."

His words had an odd empathetic quality, as though a work of art were trying to explain itself.

Masters moved toward a side table and poured himself an iced tea. "How are you finding Tampa so far?"

"I barely have my feet on the ground. I leased a house sight unseen and I still haven't been to the campus."

Masters was relaxed for someone trying to overthrow the American government and alter the global economy. He didn't manifest any of the obsessive/compulsive behaviors normally associated with megalomaniacs. He radiated a palpable inner peace. He didn't seem the type to force a movement, but rather, to wait for the swell and ride the wave as the opportunity presented itself.

Their conversation meandered off in a casual direction. Eventually, Masters brought it around to the point of the meeting. "Tell me a little about why you're interested in associating with the Ultraist Group."

Relieved to end the small talk, Morgan launched into his script. "I'm a man in transition. I'm nearly forty-four and in the process of a career change. I broke my neck about three years ago and took advantage of my convalescence to earn my PhD in Philosophy from New York City University. After reading your book, I realized my transition could be a lot more than a career change. Your theories resonate with me. I'm looking for more purpose in life. Improving society seems a great place to start."

"You understood my meaning." Masters let out a long sigh of relief. "Maybe there is hope for humanity. Sometimes I find myself doubting. I wonder if we'll ever attain Elysian or if we'll wallow in the domain of Hades forever."

"I'm sorry; I'm not sure I follow the leap from your manifesto's philosophy to your remarks about Elysian and Hades."

"That's because they aren't mentioned in the Manifesto." He continued. "Ever since mankind had the capacity to dream and communicate, there's been a vision of Elysian. But it isn't a dream; it's a possibility. A possibility that will become a reality when we're ready."

Morgan knew the paradise of Greek mythology all too well. The Romans had borrowed the idea, changing it to Elysium—a place where all valiant heroes went when they died, their families either waiting or joining them. Male-dominated societies had adapted the myth to guarantee family support for freedom fighters. The matriarch passed on values and ensured the children honored their father. They gained access to Elysium as a family then.

His father had drilled the same philosophy into him throughout his formative years.

"In our ignorance, mankind has associated Elysian with the afterlife and our longing for perfection and paradise," Masters continued. "But it's a divine revelation embedded deep in our selves. Elysian is part of what makes us human. It's a vision that's been in progress for thousands of years, spanning the predatory phase of humanity. Now, as that age draws to a close and mankind prepares to make its evolutionary leap, the divine revelation of Elysian becomes clearer. It's the goal we strive toward—a living, growing global Elysian Community in this life, not the next.

"We live on the brink of a brave new world, Professor Morgan. It's a world of unlimited possibilities if we stop preying on one another and walk together in the Elysian Fields. Jesus of Nazareth pointed to it, as did Gandhi, King, Einstein, and Thoreau. The path is non-violent. Non-predatory.

"Donne wrote, 'Any man's death diminishes me,' meaning that we share a common fate and inheritance, which can't be achieved individually. Through solidarity we will reach our full potential as a race. Humanity moving to the next level as a whole is Elysian."

The room—the whole world—seemed to drop away from Morgan at the utterance of those words. *Any man's death diminishes me.* The thought pounded away at the walls of his life. An uneasy feeling of déjà vu crept across his psyche. Masters had tripped a dormant trigger deep within his soul.

Intimidation crept over him, so real he could almost smell it. Adrenalin-generated enzymes filled his mouth, creating a metallic taste that set his teeth on edge.

A recurring nightmare had leapt into his waking life. The dream had been coming with increasing frequency, yet he hadn't been able to recall the details until that moment. His skin crawled as the taste in his mouth and the tingle in his spine evoked the vision of a murderous supernatural slayer dragging him along on an absurdly macabre night of carnage. He wanted to escape the homicidal rogue—the ghastly metaphor of wall-to-wall slaughter that constituted his life. He and the homicidal rogue were the same person. His true nature fought to break free.

He knew what had led him to that life. Like an absentee voter, his father had run his family from afar. He'd stood as the great provider but had done little to earn such reverence. He'd lived on glory, never realizing until it was too late that a father's glory was in making his children feel safe and loved.

In spite of that, he'd assumed his father's role and had sought to best him at every opportunity. He both hated him and craved his approval. But his obsession with pleasing and trumping his father had cost him a marriage, as well as the love of his son. He'd sacrificed it all for honor and valor in a vain attempt to follow his father's warped legacy.

Masters approached with a glass. "Have some water. It may help. Many people flying in to this climate feel faint. I'm sure it'll pass soon."

Shaken, he sat dazed, disoriented, and troubled. How long had they remained in silence? He hadn't a clue. Had time and space been altered in the room? His confusion and concern grew by the second. For the first time in memory, he felt as though panic might overtake him; yet, he experienced an odd peace within his being. Was that Masters? How could it be him?

Masters moved the conversation toward its conclusion. "Based on the information in your membership application, my Director of Operations wants to meet with you as soon as possible. He's impressed with your security background and wants to offer you a short-term contract to do a security review for us. I hope you don't mind. I've taken the liberty of arranging an interview today. Do you feel up to it?"

He'd regained his composure "Of course. I'd be delighted to meet with him."

"It's no problem for Elaina to reschedule."

He shook his head. "No, I'm fine, really."

"You'll find Randall Hafley to be quite competent. I don't concern myself with any of the operations with him in charge." Masters eyed him with concern. "Are you sure you're okay? Feel free to stay as long as you need."

"I'm fine now, sir. Thanks for meeting with me." He rose to leave.

"It's been a pleasure. I look forward to spending more time together. Elaina will show you to Mr. Hafley's office."

As Morgan waited in the vestibule for the assistant to guide him to his next meeting, he noted something timeless, almost ancient about David Masters. It demanded further investigation and analysis.

Chapter 17

Randall Hafley's domain personified masculine control. Every aspect designed to give the impression of power and wealth. The rich aroma of leather, expensive cologne, and cigars filled the air. By comparison, Masters's office seemed unpretentious, even Spartan. Hafley's plush suite comprised a southwest corner of the Ultraist's building. The west windows revealed a view of the Sunshine Skyway Bridge far across the bay. The south-facing ones looked over the sleepy runways of MacDill Air Force Base.

Hafley rose from a high-back leather chair. He didn't come around the desk; but rather, leaned forward, planting one plump paw on the desktop, while extending the other. "Welcome, Professor Morgan."

Morgan sized him up. He couldn't afford a repeat of what had just happened in Masters's office.

Hafley was an imposing forty-something man with bushy red hair. His large frame was big-boned and overweight, but not grossly so. He moved like a man used to getting his way.

"Nice digs," Morgan said, "This must have set TUG back a few bucks."

"We have to maintain an environment conducive to wooing our primary audience, America's intellectual elite." Hafley chuckled. "That would include you, Professor."

"Hardly. I'm just a man making a career change."

"Why don't you tell me a little about your interest in the Ultraist Group?" Hafley said, coming straight to the point. "You've read the manifesto. What did you think? How did it strike you?"

"As I said, I'm a man in transition." He began with a version of the same spiel he'd given Masters. "I broke my neck several years ago and took advantage of my convalescence to earn my PhD in Philosophy. I'm here at UT to fill in for a tenured professor who's on sabbatical.

After reading the book, I realized my transition could be a lot more than a career change. To be honest, it didn't break my heart to see the previous administration replaced by something a little more for the people."

"Well, Professor, I'm thrilled to make your acquaintance."

"Please, call me Levi."

Hafley nodded. "I won't beat around the bush, Levi. Our computer system flagged your application because of your security background. My staff forwarded it to me, and after reviewing it, I was eager to meet you."

"That's intriguing. These days, I'm just a quirky college professor who hasn't even made tenure."

"Come now, no one appreciates unwarranted humility. You may not be a tenured professor, but your resume is impressive. I'll admit; you're a bit of an enigma." Hafley moved to a bar near the west windows. "Join me for a drink? How about a glass of bourbon?"

"I'll have Woodford Reserve if you have it." He needed it after his encounter with Masters.

"Isn't this view stunning? Few people understand the true capability and significance of what lies outside these windows." He passed a heavy lead crystal glass to Morgan. "Here you go, double Woodford on the rocks."

Morgan was puzzled by his statement. "I don't know." He paused and sipped the pungent drink, allowing it to soothe his tension. "MacDill is hardly a bustling hub these days."

"I'm not talking about air traffic. I mean the city under the bay, with its access via the Skyway."

Morgan knew what Hafley meant. "The city under the bay" was the code name for Echelon Gen7. A large underground complex spread halfway across Tampa Bay to the west of MacDill. Most people who'd been in the facility hadn't even realized its true size or location. They just thought they were in a top-secret section of the base. The sprawling complex housed technologies used to track and destroy terrorists at home and abroad. Echelon tracked and manipulated every human on earth from that bombproof facility.

He didn't take the bait. "I know CENTCOM runs out of there, but I'm not sure I would call it a city under the bay."

"Let's not quibble over size here. I know it's there; you know it's there."

"So, why am I an enigma to you?"

"Let's review your file. You've earned a PhD in philosophy but you're in black ops. Or, at least you were up until two years ago. If you hadn't broken your neck, you'd still be tooling around the world for Uncle Sam. Or is that for Big Brother? I can never keep them straight?" Hafley drained his glass. "Need I go into your participation in the Alberta incident or your work in the Balkans? How about your trip to Panama that ended just ahead of the American invasion? Or there's my personal favorite—your work with your father in Grenada. You do get around."

Morgan's voice turned flat and fatal, "What do you want?"

"You must be conflicted," Hafley said, almost fatherly. "What with pondering the meaning and value of life while acting as the Grim Reaper for a shadow government."

"Not at all. I try to look for the bad in everyone I kill. Then I just kill the bad. I'm doing humanity a favor."

"Ah, the Mushin way, and in the present tense. You're still in the game, then?"

"If I need to be. Besides, no one ever really leaves the game." Once again, he lost his emotional footing and slipped toward panic. SAP security had been breached.

Two *sukis* in one day. How the hell did he know about Mushin philosophy? Who was he? Was he someone McDonnell had handled?

Morgan knew everyone on the Mushin team, everyone who'd been trained, successfully or otherwise. Had someone been compromised and turned?

"You spoke of doing humanity a favor. I have a small favor to ask. TUG just lost its Director of Security. I'll be starting a search for his replacement this week. In the meantime, our security could stand a thorough review by an expert. Would you consider taking the project? I can make it worth your while. Professors do consulting gigs all the time."

"How did you acquire all of that information on me?"

Hafley smiled. "I'm an old farm boy, Morgan; I can dig some dirt."

He didn't know how Hafley fit into the overall picture. Accessing Sensitive Compartmented Information meant he was a problem to be removed, but was he *the* problem or just *a* problem? He needed to get closer, convince Hafley that he supported his cause and its effects.

"You have some grave concerns about your organization. I'd need to know more specifics."

"Does this mean you'll take the position?"

"Let's just say that I'm considering it. After I get the details, I'll give you an answer."

"It seems someone is feeding the Feds information about our operations," Hafley said. "About our capabilities and, to a lesser degree, our goals. I need to find this leak and remove it."

This was even better than he'd hoped. McDonnell's inside man would be the leak. If he could locate him, they could hook up, while throwing Hafley a bone or two. Together, they could decapitate the Ultraist Group.

"So, the Feds are trying to prevent Doctor Masters from encouraging people to take back their government. Something doesn't seem quite right about that. It doesn't fit. What haven't you told me?"

"The Feds believe the Ultraist Group is capable of creating a grass-roots movement that could topple the current government. We've been designated as a national security risk. As a result, they've infiltrated us with the intent to discredit TUG. I believe they want to take us down a radical road that will disillusion a majority of our members and cause them to walk away. Several seemingly isolated incidents support this. As you're well aware, the status quo is the only acceptable situation for our government."

Morgan ran through his list of action items. "I'll need details of those incidents, as well as a list of all the Ultraist Group security personnel, along with their records. I'll need computer access to TUG membership databases and files for queries and background reviews. And a couple of assistants to sift through data and create reports."

"You're free to access whatever you need."

"I'll need to see the data before I can give you a fair estimate of how much time this project will require. Now, let's talk price."

Hafley grinned. "Everyone has their price. Name yours and I'll pay it."

"I'll need at least a hundred and fifty an hour, plus expenses."

"Done."

"Just one question, Mr. Hafley. What was that talk earlier about the city under the bay?"

"Another time, Professor, another time." He waved his arm dismissively. "I can promise you, if this assignment goes well, we'll discuss the city under the bay in great detail." He pressed the intercom. "Karen, could you show Professor Morgan to his office and get him set up with the proper IDs and biometrics?"

"I'll be right in."

"Pretty sure of yourself, aren't you, Mr. Hafley?"

"Please, call me Randall." He smiled once again. "Yes, I am."

Chapter 18

Tuesday, November 19

Two men entered the conference room, Hafley and a man Gillian had never seen before.

Something about the newcomer called a panther to mind. He seemed relaxed, even at ease, but with a sharp animalistic aspect to his mannerism that said he could pounce at any second. He didn't strike her as threatening, but rather comfortable with his ability to control everything around him. He was well dressed but she thought he would look good no matter what he wore. Like a one-man anti-marketing campaign, everything about him screamed that the man makes the clothes. *God, how do guys get away with that?*

Hafley crossed the room and took a position near the window. "Good morning, everyone. I want you to meet Professor Morgan. You'll be reporting to him for the next few months." His tone felt upbeat and energetic, completely out of character for the ne'er do well man Gillian had come to know and distrust. He seemed almost gleeful, like he was up to something. "Professor Morgan has had a distinguished career in the security analysis and troubleshooting industry. He'll be leading us in a staff-assessment initiative. Levi, would you like to say a few words before I leave?"

"Sure, thanks for the kind words." Morgan turned to the group with a grin that made Gillian's heart flutter. "You'll be joining me in a fact-finding project that could take a few weeks or a few months. It involves a specialized type of analysis. We'll be looking for signs of corporate espionage. I think you'll find it challenging and interesting. You might call it spy hunting. TUG's leaders are concerned that the government is trying to sabotage its work." He stepped to the white board and began to write.

Several females in the room cocked their heads to check him out with brazen looks of lust.

He called over his shoulder as he scrawled the last of his notes. "No trying to sneak a peek." He turned back with a devilish smile and blocked the board. "Just like our government's top counter-terrorism agencies, we'll use technology to map complex sets of relationships and activities indicating what a person might gain from undermining our mission. As we sift through data, we'll extrapolate information about our potential attackers. We'll assign a priority rating to each credible threat. Our final product will be a threat matrix that we'll present to Mr. Hafley and his security team for further evaluation. It'll be fun." He stepped away from the board, revealing a list. Name, birthplace, education, expertise, and favorite thing. "Now it's your turn to talk."

Like a wizard deciding who to zap first, he waved a marker around the room, ultimately pointing to the nearest team member, a well-proportioned blonde with an infectious smile. "Let's start with you, miss. Where are you from; tell us something about your education, aspirations, and what's the most important thing in your life?"

She laughed. "Hi, I'm Nancy. Are you sure you don't want my weight and measurements, Professor?" She made the word 'professor' sound like a delicious morsel, and everyone laughed.

Morgan didn't miss a beat. "I was going to get those later." He winked and smiled. "Please, everyone, call me Levi."

Nancy continued, naming her college, degree, and hometown. "I'm an administrative assistant looking for a good husband," she said with another laugh and a toss of her shoulder-length hair.

"Thanks, Nancy." He pointed to a young man with long mousy hair and thick glasses. "Sir, you're up."

The guy fidgeted as though his bones irritated his skin. He spoke with an odd nasal tone, stammering the words out as fast as he could. "Dick, University of South Florida, Lutz, I'm a database administrator. The Ultraist Group is the most important thing in my life." All the while he spoke, he seemed to look for a place to throw up.

"Thanks, Dick. Welcome to the team."

Several long-time staffers introduced themselves, no doubt there to make sure Hafley received regular reports on the progress and direction of the analysis.

Morgan opened his hand toward the final team member. "And last but not least . . ."

"Gillian Anu, I grew up in Chicago and graduated from the University in 1993. I was on the six-year program. My expertise . . ." she paused gathering her thoughts. "Well, Doctor Masters has helped me turn my life around. I hope to help people have the same opportunity. What's my favorite thing? That's easy. I'm a single mom and my two-year-old daughter is my life."

"Thanks, Gillian," he paused.

Gillian thought he must have taken note that she had avoided talking about her area of expertise. She always jumped to the worst possible conclusion.

"Thanks, everyone," Hafley interrupted.

Several people jumped in their seats having forgotten he was in the room.

"It's nine-thirty and I need to be going. I'll leave you in Professor Morgan's capable hands. Levi, I believe you know how to find your office. Your team has been relocated to the desks around you. They should be able to assist you with anything you need. If not, just contact my secretary. Good luck, everyone. I look forward to hearing your reports." He walked out of the room.

Morgan didn't waste any time moving forward with his presentation. He flipped on the LCD projection unit. "This is the tool we'll use to correlate data and reveal hidden relationships. This sample chart details the activities and movements of the 9/11 hijackers."

A detailed chart of staggering proportions appeared on the screen with tiny type.

"Dick, I have a gentleman coming in later to help you set up the database."

Dick nodded. His hair pulled into a tight ponytail gave him an oddly feminine quality, almost matronly in appearance.

"These tools cut analysis time from weeks or months to just days. I expect to wrap up phase one by the first of December. I know that's a tight timeline, but it's critical that Mr. Hafley gets this information as soon as possible. Unfortunately, that means I'll need all of you to work the day before and possibly the day after Thanksgiving. I'll let you know about that as soon as I know."

Groans throughout the room.

"I've arranged for hands-on training sessions this morning on the use of the e2 suite. Are there any questions?"

Nancy piped up. "Can I get your home number?"

Everyone laughed.

"I'm afraid I'm not the kind of man you're looking for," he deflected. "Gillian, did you have a question?"

"What kind of data will we be looking at and how will you divide the workload?"

"Good question. We'll be looking for aliases, phone numbers—both current and past—post office boxes, addresses, vehicles, cell phones, anything we can find to tie someone to things they might want to hide. We'll use criminal background and credit checks. You never know if someone is being blackmailed because of bad credit. Maybe they have a debt with a loan shark. Maybe an unknown third party has traded or purchased that debt. You'll be surprised how quickly a computer search and a good relational tool can give you a trail to follow.

"We'll be looking for emotional bonds that would indicate enduring relationships. Those relationships are susceptible to exploitation by various parties—the mob, governments, or anyone who's motivated to manipulate circumstances against TUG. We're looking for any and all threats. That is, anyone who's tied to an individual or organization that's opposed to the goals and ideals of the Ultraist Group. For example, maybe someone's tied to a radical right-wing religious group that's gathering information to assassinate Doctor Masters."

The ladies squirmed in their seats. No one had ever thought anyone would want to hurt David Masters.

"Anyone else with a question?" Silence. "No? Does this make sense?"

Everyone nodded.

"All right, then. Let's make our way down to the training room."

Chapter 19

Morgan spent the rest of the day with the team in e2 training. As part of his cover, he'd been supplied with access to e2 investigative analysis software. The integrated suite of tools used by military, law enforcement, and intelligence agencies provided a storage structure that allowed quick access and analysis of incredible arrays of data.

At the end of the day, he sat in his office reviewing staff dossiers. To a person, the team was well educated, bright, and experienced. Everyone seemed legitimate, on the up-and-up. Just normal stiffs who worked for an up-and-coming nonprofit agency. Everyone except Gillian Anu.

She didn't fit. Her background seemed too perfect, as though it had been designed for undercover work. He couldn't confront her without more information. He had to get closer to find out why she was working for TUG.

His encounter with Masters had started something strange. The event intrigued him. Had Masters triggered the thoughts about his father and his childhood, and the repressed dream? He'd claimed to be a follower of the Zen ways. Could he have achieved *sartori*, the ultimate revelation? Was he one of the masters who'd overcome separateness? *Could Masters lead me from Mushin warrior into the liberating experience of an enlightened state?*

The phone snapped him out of his thoughts. "Levi, this is David Masters. Can you come by my office at four o'clock?"

The sound of Masters's voice brought back the odd metallic taste. The encounter troubled him more than he was ready to admit. "Yes sir, I'll be there at four."

* * *

Morgan made his way up to Masters's office, his hands stuffed in his pockets, his shoulders slumped. Masters's middle-aged assistant looked up from her work. Her demeanor spoke volumes. She was the gatekeeper. No one entered the monastery, as some called it, without her permission.

Her face brightened, "He's expecting you, Professor. Go right in."

He pulled himself up to his full stature and entered Masters's dim monastic quarters.

"Do you believe we create our own reality?"

The words came from out of nowhere and everywhere at the same time. In vain, Morgan peered into the shadows.

Masters stepped from the window. The light streamed around him like an aura encasing his silhouette, blurring the boundaries between the man and his world. He seemed both ancient and young, transfigured by the luminous backdrop.

"I . . . I'm sorry, what did you say?" Morgan stepped back and scratched his head. "Where were you?"

Masters crossed the room and brought up the lights. The transfiguring effect diminished only slightly. "Would you and your son join me for dinner tonight?"

What the hell is going on with this guy? His thoughts raced to find answers that didn't defy logic.

He gave up and addressed the question. "I don't know his schedule, but he would be excited to meet you."

"Let's call him right now." Masters held out a wireless phone. "Can you dial his number for me? And would you join me regardless of his answer?"

Morgan finished punching in the numbers. "Sure. And my son's name is Thad."

"Great, it's a date then."

The phone rang. Masters held up a finger to hold Morgan in place as he answered the line. "Hello, is this Thad Morgan? . . . Thad, this is David Masters. Your father works with me. I'd like you to join us for dinner tonight here in Tampa. Can you make it? . . . Really? Great. I'll transfer you to my assistant and she'll give you the details. I look forward to meeting you."

Masters pressed a few digits to transfer the line and hung up. "He'll meet us at the restaurant. It's going to be a nice evening. Thanks for stopping by. Elaina will give you the dinner details."

Morgan stood stupefied in the hallway. Around Masters, he felt like a flat-footed, scrawny kid in a gym full of professional athletes, outplayed by a superior opponent.

Chapter 20

Morgan paced the sidewalk outside Pedestals, a high-end restaurant on the Gulf Coast. He watched the comings and goings of the rich and famous, and the indebted. Several minutes passed and a limousine sidled up to the curb. The driver came around to open the door. Morgan called out and waved.

Thad strode toward him, the personification of youthful confidence, yet not quite the real-world equal of his father. "Hey Dad."

His son's apathetic mumble let Morgan know his punishment would continue. How he dealt with the last remnants of Thad's adolescence would determine their future relationship. "Nice ride."

Thad perked up. "Doctor Masters sent it by to pick me up." His voice rolled with laughter. "It was cool to see everyone watching as this baby picked me up."

Morgan felt a twinge of envy. Or was that resentment? He wasn't sure. Thad should be feeling that way about him, not a complete stranger.

He felt like giving up. He was busting his ass to win Thad's approval, but to no avail. Masters wasn't even trying and he'd already hit it off with the boy. Like the samurai, maybe he wasn't cutout for intimate relationships.

The restaurant's exterior doors slid open as they passed into the building's thermal barrier. Cooler air greeted them when they walked into the main air-conditioned lobby.

Pedestals was a recent renovation of an abandoned warehouse complex. The foyer looked more like a mall than the waiting area of a restaurant. The enormous facility contained a traditional waiting area, several gift shops, a coffee shop, bar, and an art gallery.

Morgan looked Thad in the eye. "This is a tough situation, but we need each other right now."

"How long does it take to get over a lifetime of rejection?"

Morgan stood silent, recalling how Liz had always demanded answers to what he'd considered rhetorical questions.

At Morgan's uncertain silence, Thad said, "A lifetime, Dad. It takes a lifetime."

"We've never really discussed the past but I think it's time we do. I think it's time we start to be open and honest with each other. We need to see if we can have an adult relationship."

"I'll choose who I have an adult relationship with." His muttered remark did nothing to deaden its viciousness. He leaned toward his father, his voice just above a whisper. "I have relationships with people I care about and who care about me. People who are willing to show love and interest. They're not *afraid*." His hand sliced the air as though cutting off the conversation.

Morgan's temper flared. Had Liz taught him how to push his buttons? One sure way to piss him off was to call him a liar or a coward.

He bit back angry defensive words and sighed. "I know you feel ignored."

Thad cut him off again. "Look, I accepted this invitation out of curiosity. It had nothing to do with you."

Masters approached from the far end of the foyer, his hand extended and a broad smile on his face. "Hello, Levi." Pivoting, he said, "You must be Thad. So pleased to meet you. Did your ride work out okay?"

"You bet; it was amazing," Thad beamed. "You should have seen my friends' faces when your limo pulled up. I have several who are members of the Ultraist Group. When I told them it was your limo, they were blown away." He seemed enamored with this new father figure. "Thank you so much, Doctor Masters."

"No problem. It was my pleasure. I thought you'd get a kick out of it. I think we have a reservation. Let's go on in."

Thad's amazement grew as they entered the main dining area. He looked around in wonder. "Whoa, this is really something."

The developer had raised the ceilings eighty feet. The company that had reproduced Venice in Las Vegas had once again brought Mother Nature to life within the air-conditioned space of Pedestals. They'd created a dome to tower over the entire dining area and then transformed it into the firmament, making it wide open and spacious. An amazing masterpiece of architecture and human ingenuity, the sky showed a perfect shade of blue that was more an amalgamation of violets, purples, and reds. The clouds appeared not as part of the ceiling, but as if a goddess had hung them in the air. The combined effect of the dome, the ambient lighting, color choices, and the application techniques created an environment that tricked the mind into believing it was experiencing an outdoor summer afternoon. It was a work of pure genius.

Thad seemed to awaken to new possibilities and thrills. "This is the most amazing thing I've ever seen."

A massive chamber was filled with vine-covered trellises around U-shaped booths for privacy. Once seated, the illusion of dining in a secret garden took over. Each booth was situated so one couldn't see into another, and each was furnished with chairs and pedestals. Some contained a single pedestal, providing an intimate, romantic setting for two. Others were arranged for parties of four, six, or eight.

A hostess led them through the labyrinth of booths. As they approached their table, Morgan noted all observation points were cut off within the maze. Direct line of sight required standing on a chair to look over the trellises. An assailant could stay low and avoid detection.

The hostess seated them in a two-pedestal booth. Each pedestal was large enough to set a few drinks.

The air, rich with the aroma of garlic and spice, compelled a relaxing impression. Scents of various meats evoked primal memories of sacrifices to the goddess.

"Each course will be brought out on a tabletop," the hostess said. "Don't worry; the tops are made of light-weight clear acrylic polymers and no wait staff will be harmed during this production." She smiled and winked. "At the end of each course, the staff will remove the top and bring out the next one. When they come through, please pick up your drinks, slide your chairs back, and keep your feet under the chairs, so as not to trip anyone. Your utensils, serviettes, and water glasses will be replaced with each new course. May I take your drink order?"

A large man with a bushy mustache approached the table after she left. "Welcome Doctor Masters."

Masters stood. "Buona sera, Mr. Mangione. How are you tonight?"

"I am well; and you?"

"I'm terrific." Turning to his guests, Masters said, "Mr. Mangione is the owner." Turning to the restaurateur, he completed the introductions. "I'd like you to meet Levi Morgan and his son, Thad."

"Pleased to make your acquaintances."

Levi and Thad both stood and shook his hand.

"Enjoy your dinner, gentlemen." Mangione turned to greet his other guests.

"He's a nice man, one of the charter members of TUG in the Tampa Bay area."

"I hope you don't mind, but I've taken the liberty of inviting one of our staffers to join us tonight. Here she comes now."

Thad and Levi turned and followed Masters's gaze.

Gillian Anu radiated an air of coiffed wildness. Though pulled back, strands of her golden brown hair fell to her shoulders. Her olive skin and high cheekbones heightened the beauty of her light green eyes. The blue satin fabric of her blouse accentuated the curves of her torso, while the black mid-length skirt revealed shapely calves hinting at an athletic lifestyle. She was a classic beauty who needed neither make-up nor fashionable clothes to make her the most attractive woman in the room. She didn't have a supermodel shape, yet she possessed a down-to-earth solid beauty unshaken by age or circumstances. In just one day, she'd carved a place in Morgan's psyche. In his mind, she was every man's *suki*, the distraction that kills. Every man who met her would fall in love after some fashion.

"Gillian, it's good to see you." Masters's affection couldn't have been clearer. He gave her a warm embrace. "You know Levi; and this is his son, Thad. Where's Maddie? I was hoping to see her."

Masters's rapid-fire remarks revealed his excitement at seeing her. There was more to their relationship than met the eye. It made sense; Masters was charismatic and caring. What a combination they made—the perfect couple.

Chapter 21

"Sorry I'm late. Maddie has the sniffles and I had to get her settled in with my mom before I left. Wouldn't you know it; I got caught in traffic on the Skyway." She laughed as she sat next to Thad, across from David. "That bridge is so beautiful, but I hate driving it every day. If anything happens, the backups can be incredible."

David turned toward Thad. "Gillian lives on the river, south of the Skyway, not too far from you."

"Cool," Morgan jumped on the conversation. "I had a place down near the river." Then, with a pang of conscience, he added, "well, uh, my son, Thad, and my ex-wife have a place there."

Like a wounded warrior, Morgan hobbled through his thoughts. He looked chagrined but couldn't stop. In spite of David having already introduced them, Morgan did it again. "Gillian, I'd like you to meet my son, Thad. Thad, this is Gillian Anu. She works on my team at the Ultraist Group."

"Pleased to meet you, Thad."

"Likewise."

He flashed a winning smile that Gillian misinterpreted as boyish interest. In reality, the boy was savoring the spectacle of his dad falling over himself.

The panther has a weakness. Gillian had never thought of herself as a distraction, but she had derailed Morgan's train of thought.

As if compelled by some mysterious embarrassing force, he continued to speak. "I've leased a house here in Tampa, but I'll be staying with Thad for awhile."

Mercifully, David changed the subject. "So, Thad, how's college life?"

Thad waved the last foie gras finger sandwich. "It's great. I'm in my last year of pre-med at USF. I'm hoping to start med school soon, but I may take a short break and join the military to help pay for it."

Morgan looked perplexed. "When did you start thinking about that?"

Thad brushed him off, continuing his conversation with David while munching the last morsel.

The headwaiter appeared, "The soup is now served—roasted chestnut with candied pecan."

They obediently retrieved their drinks, and a pair of white-clad servers moved the soup table into place. The settings were immaculate, everything perfectly positioned. It smelled wonderful.

David turned toward Gillian. "I hope you don't mind; we ordered the seven course fall menu."

"No problem, I'm happy not to think about ordering. I just need food." She let out a relieved laugh.

"I'm sorry to hear about your mom," David said turning to Thad. "What was she like?"

"She was nice," Thad replied. "My fondest memories are of her in the dirt." He gave a slight laugh. "She gardened as an art, and we went to the botanical gardens a lot. She loved to steal their ideas. We acted like spies when we went there. I was the lookout, making sure no one caught her scrawling in a tiny notebook. Sometimes, when I was younger, I thought we'd get in trouble if we were caught." He had a faraway look. "One spring, while we were driving in North Carolina, she pulled over just to take in a field of wildflowers. She enjoyed the simple pleasures in life. Those moments were peaceful for her." He paused to look at David. "Do you believe the human spirit lives on after the body has stopped functioning?"

David turned to Gillian. "I apologize for the oversight. Thad's mother recently passed on."

"I'm so sorry, Thad." She felt guilty. This boy's mother had just died and she was attracted to his father.

He spoke to Thad. "Life in this physical body is just the first step in our spiritual journey. As we evolve, at some point, we'll be reunited to pursue magnificent goals and exploits, conquering time and death."

After that, the conversation meandered from topic to topic.

"Tell me, Thad, do you follow politics?"

"I'm not as involved as some of my friends are, but I am politically concerned. I think we need to give more tax breaks to fuel economic growth. We could do more to support fledgling democracies around the world."

As the waiters came to remove the salad course, Gillian noticed they worked in fixed groups.

"This is like a choreographed dance," Thad said. "Sort of like art you become part of."

David smiled. "It is enjoyable."

During a lull, Morgan looked at Gillian. "Tell us more about your daughter."

"She's wonderful, although not always understood or appreciated."

"Isn't she quite young yet to be misunderstood?"

"Maddie is precocious in the truest sense of the word. She can be a handful. She's active and moves from one thing to the next quite quickly."

David grinned. "That might be an understatement."

"So people don't like her because she's inquisitive?" Thad asked.

"A lot of adults just want kids to behave, teachers included."

"Ah. She's not well behaved," Thad said, appreciation in his voice.

"People felt that way about Thad," Morgan said. "It drove us crazy. I think they knew he had a good heart. Some even told us that while they were bashing him." He shook his head. "People who've never had an exceptional child think of us as bad parents."

This guy gets it.

"You have to be incredibly strong to raise an exceptional child by yourself."

"I've got my mother who helps out a lot. She loves Maddie, but even she struggles with my parenting philosophy.

Morgan laughed. "You can't beat ADHD or precociousness out of a child. I wish I'd been there more. Thad's mother did her best to give him the skills to manage his life."

Wow, this guy really does get it.

"Why do people judge each other so much?" Thad threw in.

The approaching smell of lobster distracted the group.

"The first main course is served. Poached live Maine lobster with fennel ravioli and homard sauce.

Ah, real food.

David spoke as they ate, directing his remarks to Thad. "What do you think of the moral and ethical decay within our government and big business? I'm curious what your generation thinks we need to do about the economic collapse and the pandemic of corruption."

The boy put his fork down and looked him in the eye. "People vote and select their representatives. The majority rules society. How can that go wrong? Worst case scenario: the American people suffer for their mistakes for a few years."

"Life has taught me that the majority view is rarely the right view." David's words were gentle not condemning. "The truth—the right thing to do—hardly ever enjoys a majority opinion."

"That was delicious," Morgan said, having inhaled his meal. "Thank you for inviting us."

Gillian wasn't far behind him in finishing.

Shortly after the intermezzo, the second main dish arrived—prime tenderloin of beef with morel mushrooms and saffron potatoes.

"A girl could get fat on a steady diet of this food."

Everyone laughed.

Ever the rebel, David diverted the conversation back to the earlier topic. "What about corporations that lobby Congress to strengthen their profits at the tax payers' expense? Do you and your friends talk about that?"

"Most of my friends talk about the war and what it means for them after college. They're worried about the draft."

"How about you? Are you worried?"

"No, I'm thinking about joining."

Morgan leaned forward a little. "Over my dead body."

"What the hell does that mean? You were in the military."

"It's too dangerous."

"Coward."

Morgan's face flushed.

Gillian changed the subject.

"The other day, Maddie's teacher accosted me. She said Maddie won't stay on task or do the things the other kids are doing. When they're in their discussion circle, she gets up and goes to the playhouse."

David chuckled. "She's two years old. How long is her attention span supposed to be? Good God, there are adults on our staff who can't sit through a whole meeting."

Morgan steered the conversation back to the war. "What's the connection between the Ultraist Groups and the Muslim Brotherhood?"

Gillian looked shocked by the bluntness of his question. She had wanted to ask it herself many times. *Why would he ask? What was he really doing at TUG?*

"TUG isn't funding terrorists," David said. "We want humanity to evolve into what it was intended to be. Hassan al-Banna, the founder of the Brotherhood, wasn't a violent or a political man. He established a network of non-violent interfaith groups cooperating for the betterment of his people. He focused on addressing local needs and concerns. He chose not to exclude or shun the followers of other religions. Each allowed the other to embrace his own way of life. That model worked amazingly well in Egypt until the occurrence of politicization after the Arab-Israeli conflict began."

"JFK gave a speech about the fight against communist insurgencies in Latin America," Thad chimed in. "He believed the real South American enemies were hunger, ignorance, and inequality, not communism."

"Excellent point," David said. "Kennedy understood Hassan's model and thought it worked beautifully. People need hope and opportunity. If we give them those, they won't become radical. They'll start giving back instead of blowing themselves up."

David avoided Morgan's question.

The wait staff removed the second entrée. David shifted noticeably and pulled out his cell phone. "Sorry, I have to take this call." He stepped out of the booth and out of earshot.

Gillian took advantage of his absence to put Morgan on the spot. The Bureau had little information on him. Somehow, he'd lived off the grid. "Professor, you seem to know quite a bit about TUG's connections. What's your story?"

"Please, call me Levi. I like to know what I'm getting into when I join something."

"I can appreciate that. I can't believe how many people get involved in half-baked schemes and crazy causes." She let it go.

David returned. "Sorry all, but I need to take care of some business. Nice meeting you, Thad. Good night, Gillian. Give my love to Maddie. Levi, if you're interested, I'll have Elaina contact you to help sublet that house if you want to stay with your son. I'm sure there's someone associated with TUG who'd love to have it."

"That'd be great. Thank you, sir. Have a good evening."

"I'll see you in the office tomorrow."

The dessert arrived as David walked away.

As they enjoyed their pumpkin mousse cake and cranberry almond, Gillian leaned toward Thad. "That's an unusual earring. Does it have some special significance?"

"My mom had it made for me as a welcome-to-manhood gift. It's weird, but it's one of a kind." He soaked in the attention.

"Is there some symbolism associated with it?"

"According to my mother, the circle symbolizes unending life. The heart stands for persistence and courage, and the wings represent man's ability to soar above all obstacles. She worked with my crazy aunt to design it." He smiled.

"That's beautiful. What a wonderful keepsake, especially for a doctor."

"Thanks."

She looked at her watch and fidgeted. "I'm sorry, but I left my daughter with my mother and I really should get going. It was so nice to meet you. I hope we can spend time together again." She started to stand and then sat back down. "David is giving a talk this Saturday. Would either of you like to join me?"

"Thanks, but count me out," Thad said. "I'm cramming for exams before the Thanksgiving break."

Morgan looked across the table. "I'd love to hear more of what he has to say."

Chapter 22

Hurricane season had ended weeks ago, yet the sultry night air lingered in the city. Storm clouds blanketed the sky, holding the heat close to the concrete and asphalt. An easterly breeze mingled the rancid low tide bay air with the stench of garbage.

Humidity clung to Morgan's face as he parked in a public garage several blocks from the Plaza. Perspiration rolled down his torso and soaked the clothes under his coveralls. He shoved an external card reader into his pocket, along with several data cards, and clipped on an employee ID he'd lifted earlier in the day.

He performed one final audio test on the digital recording system. "November twenty-first, zero-one-thirty hours; Ultraist Group security and systems penetration test. The Plaza, Tampa, Florida." He pressed PLAY to confirm that the device was working.

Headlights glared against the concrete as he armed the proximity sensor on the truck and headed toward the stairs. At street level, he raced down the sidewalk, just another janitor late for work. He moved along the deserted sidewalk, reviewing his plan one last time. TUG's security monitored all activity inside the server room through video and data monitoring. The only means of getting in and out without raising suspicion was to leverage his security-consulting role.

Inside, he walked straight to the lobby security desk and addressed the duty officer in broken English. "I'm fill-in for Jose tonight. *Sí.*"

"Goddamn it, can't you guys do anything right? Yeah, yeah, go on through. Why don't you fuckers get this shit approved before you just show up?"

"Sí, *gracias, señor. Llamaré adelante el próximo tiempo.*" His accent perfect, he assured the guard he'd follow his advice, then started toward the elevators.

"Hey, use the other elevator," the guard yelled, jerking his head in the opposite direction. "You dumb wetback son of a bitch. And speak English, goddamn it."

Morgan turned and threw up his hands. With a confused look on his face, he headed in the other direction. *"Eres un hijo de puta y quizás te matere esta noche."*

The guard shoved his chair back. "God*damn* it. I bet you don't have a key for the freight elevator, either, do you?"

He shook his head, trying to look pathetic. "Key? No key."

The guard pushed past him, inserting his key and calling the elevator. He stormed back to his desk. "You'll have to get someone up there to help you down or walk."

In the elevator, Morgan muttered, "That was easy enough."

Every good hacker knew security breaches happened all the time. With a bit of good timing, a dash of frustration, and some old-fashioned tension, he could duplicate nature.

He checked track two on the recorder to make sure it had caught his conversation with the guard. "The breach of initial security occurred at zero-one-forty-nine hours with little effort. I stashed the coveralls and stolen ID above the ceiling of the freight elevator. The penetration testing of TUG security continues."

During his tour of the facility, he'd focused on the TUG server room and had inquired about various topics. How did they maintain physical security? What technology did they use for access control? He'd been surprised to learn that the server room was staffed twenty-four hours a day. It seemed extreme.

Hafley had affirmed that TUG produced a product—global change. People joined the movement through the website all the time, downloading information outlining how to improve society and human relationships. Those catch phrases seemed like hollow platitudes coming from Hafley. Morgan was confident he'd find a more sinister reason for the server room coverage the deeper he looked.

He held his employee ID up to a plate glass window overlooking the servers and knocked. When the night operator looked over, Morgan pointed at the door. The man jumped up and scurried over to it. He hit the intercom button. "Can I help you?"

"Yes, Mr. Morgan to check on processes and procedures for System Security."

The door swung open, revealing a cheerful young man. "Hello, sir, I was told you might stop by sometime. Come on in, have a seat. What can I do for you?"

Morgan inwardly groaned at the prospect of enduring a hyper-caffeinated conversation. "What's your name?"

"Larry, sir, Larry Callahan." He motioned Morgan to an ergonomic rubber-mesh chair. "Please, have a seat. I don't get many visitors on my shift. What's up?"

"Pleased to meet you, Larry. I'm performing a vulnerability assessment; looking for security risks; anything that might create exposure." His strategy to hack into the server involved the use of social engineering to learn more about TUG's systems and security. To crack systems and sneak the data out for NSA analysis, he would need to overcome the monitoring of it. "Mr. Hafley has already made a catalogue of assets and capabilities available to me. He's indicated which infrastructure and data resources have the most value and importance. My job is to identify the potential threats to each resource and mitigate the most serious vulnerabilities. I understand the Ultraist Group employee and membership databases are the most valuable assets we have. Can you tell me a little bit about how they're monitored and protected?"

Larry moderated his rate of speech, speaking in a more rational manner. "I've only been up to the security area once. They've got these cool dashboards for all kinds of things. They monitor network and processor activity, as well as read and write to the databases. They use Nessus to audit the devices and applications. It provides great security-event management that updates their dashboards on a real-time basis. It's so cool. You can't touch these boxes without security knowing what you're doing."

"Why don't you go ahead and log onto the database server for me?"

"I'm sorry, but that's against policy."

"Look, Larry, I have a job to do. We can do this the hard way or we can do it the easy way. You don't want me to raise your name with Mr. Markus as someone who stood in the way of this assessment, do you?"

Larry's eyes darted apprehensively at the mention of Markus. "I don't know, Mr. Morgan. I could lose my job for logging you into the servers."

"Don't worry about it. They can tell I'm here. You even said so yourself; you're just taking orders. Grease the skids for me on this and I'll put in a good word for you. Maybe I can even get you transferred to the security team."

"Well, okay, I guess it'll be alright."

Seated at the terminal, Morgan continued to ask questions with an air of nonchalance. He fired them off and recorded the answers as if he was doing a legitimate analysis. Larry gave him everything he needed to crack the system.

Morgan stretched his shoulders and sat up straight. His neck made a loud pop as he rubbed it and slowly twisted his head, then stood up. "Hey, I'm going for coffee. Would you like one?"

"Sure, can you get me a double mocha cappuccino?"

"No problem. I'll be right back."

Leaving the server logged on, Morgan headed to the cafeteria on the third floor. He bought two coffees the same. At the condiment area, he made a deep mark on one cup with his thumbnail and emptied a small vial into that cup, giving it a quick stir.

Back in the server room, he handed the marked cup to Larry. The server session had timed out. "Can I get signed back on here. I need to check the user profiles and verify that we're using one-hundred-twenty-eight bit encryption on the passwords."

"Sure, no problem."

"I see you're a Bucs fan."

"All the way. I think we can win it all again this year."

Morgan rose as Larry's head started to dip. He caught him just before his face slammed into a monitor, and gently laid his head on the desktop. About Thad's age, Larry was just coming into his own. Morgan wanted to take care of him, hated to use him, but had a job to do. He would keep an eye on the kid, keep Markus from swooping down like a giant bird of prey to devour him.

He hurried to attach the card reader, search for the correct tables, and download the information. When finished, he switched his coffee for Larry's laced cup, then, after double-checking everything, he administered an antidote.

"Hey, wake up. You ought to get more rest before you come to work."

"That's weird. I never doze off at work. I must be getting sick."

"Do you need me to stay? Should I call someone to check you out?"

"No, I think I'll be fine. Sorry."

"Okay, I have to go. I'll put in a good word for you."

"Yeah, thanks. It was nice meeting you. Good night."

Morgan walked out of the server room and headed for the main bank of elevators. His next moves would be critical, nearly every inch of the Ultraist facility was under video surveillance. On the way up to his office, he feigned checking the card reader to make sure it had worked properly. In reality, the custom card reader had high-speed copy capabilities. He transferred data to another card and updated his audio record of the event. "Exited the server room and now moving to my office, where I'll secure the stolen files until they can be returned to the Ultraist Group security team. This ends the penetration test. The time is zero-two-forty-five."

When the doors opened, he rushed to his office and locked the card, along with the voice recorder, in his desk. He headed back to the elevator and exited at the lobby, where he passed the smart-ass guard watching the third overtime of a west coast basketball game. The guard didn't even look up.

Mike Markus stood beside the security supervisor as Morgan exited the building. The monitors had provided a blow-by-blow account of everything he'd done and said while he'd been in the building.

"Good job. That's exactly what I wanted. Now I've got him."

The security supervisor seemed puzzled. "Why would he crack the system if he knew he was being monitored? It doesn't make sense. He could see the video cameras."

"When someone cracks a database or a network, it's an ego trip. They get what they're after; they don't care who knows. In fact, many crackers want publicity. We still don't know what he'll do with the data."

Morgan drove from the garage and wound his way from downtown to Ybor City, driving the deserted streets

Around the turn of the Twentieth century, this area of Tampa had been known as The Cigar Capital of the World. It had prospered well into the twenties and thirties. But the combined pressure of the Great Depression and America's growing infatuation with cigarettes had brought on hard times. The "spit campaign" of mechanized cigar manufacturers tolled the end of an era for this historic section of Tampa. Modern man had fallen prey to the lie that saliva was a major component of the hand-rolled Havana-style cigars.

Morgan turned onto Seventh Avenue. Warehouse-like factories, empty for decades, waited patiently for some entrepreneurial developer to turn them into the next grand masterpiece.

Over the years, Ybor had suffered through the stages of urban blight. In the last decade and a half, it had moved from a simple artisan community to a commercially gentrified area packed with restaurants, bars, and nightclubs. People flocked there to experience the nightlife with a carnival atmosphere. Along with that came a disproportionate amount of late-night crime and violence.

He passed the normal glut of local police and sheriff's cars trolling for drunks and troublemakers, and wound his way through the borough long enough to know he wasn't being followed. Convinced, he jumped back onto the highway and headed south. Traffic remained light; just normal bartender and wait staff traffic. He would easily spot a tail if one existed.

Pumped with adrenaline, he pounded the steering wheel. "Fuck yeah!"

It felt good to create a plan and execute it. It had been ages since he'd done anything other than kill a would-be assassin. This was invigorating; it revived his love for the business. This particular op was flawless; he'd timed it just right.

He leaned over and fumbled through the glove box for the satellite phone and the connector for the card reader. The truck swerved slightly as he leaned over. "Shit, don't get pulled over for DUI now."

He dialed the secure number he'd arranged yesterday. The on-duty NSA agent answered. "Please state your name for voice identification."

"Morgan, Levi."

"Please hold for verification." After several seconds, the agent came back on. "Voice identification verified. How can I help you, sir?"

"I need a secure uplink for data transmission. Reference special operation, Baker-Alpha-three-five-nine-zero-zero-four-Levi-Morgan."

"Yes sir, any special instructions?"

"Have the initial five names from the special-op instructions back to me by EOD Friday. Have the rest back to me by EOD Monday."

"Yes, sir, we'll do that list of five by the end of the day tomorrow and you'll have the rest by EOD on Monday."

Morgan verified the secure uplink, and began transmitting the data.

Chapter 23

Thursday, November 21

Hafley rubbed his fleshy digits over his chin, then took a draw on a cigar. "I know what she says. But I can't give him a chance to join us. I want him dead."

In contrast to the brilliant sun-washed Tampa morning, the luxurious suite consisted of shadows. Lush red velvet drapes overlaid the tinted corporate windows. They combined with the dark wood and leather décor to subdue light and sound. During the early part of the day, the drapes stood open along the west windows, presenting a muted view of the bay, but long before noon, they closed. Accent lights highlighted the somber effect.

"I know this guy," Markus volunteered with a shake of his stogie. "He'll balk at the offer; too much integrity. We'll pressure him, but he'll rebel."

Hafley sneered. "Then we'll make him the patsy for the whole thing. Fuck the bastard; we'll let his SAP-ass take the blame for everything if we fail."

"Not that I believe we need a fall guy, but it's nice to have one."

Hafley had a faraway look that flashed sadistic. "I'm going to love paying off that old debt." His thoughts drifted toward another life, filled with mud, jungle sounds, and torture. His thoughts drifted toward revenge.

The door opened after a quick knock, and Morgan's face appeared in the crack. "Your assistant left a message that you wanted to see me."

"Oh, Morgan, come on in." Hafley picked up a pen, and with surprising dexterity, twirled it through his plump fingers. "I wanted to let you know that we've sublet your house."

Morgan drew back astonished. "That was fast. Thanks."

Hafley waved his cigar. "Turns out it was exactly what someone was looking for."

"I thought you might want to know; things are going well with the project. The team is working out well. Progress is excellent. I'm hoping to have an initial report and recommendations right after the Thanksgiving holiday."

"Glad to hear it." Hafley let the pen drop loudly on his desk. "Anything else?"

"I'll be taking tomorrow off to be with my son." Morgan shook his head. "It's his mother's funeral."

"No problem, take whatever time you need. Anything else?"

"No, I need to get back to work." He backed out of the office. "Thanks again."

Markus puffed his cigar when Morgan closed the door behind him. "Do you think he has any idea?"

The corner of Hafley's mouth drew back as he shook his head. "He's oblivious."

Chapter 24

A warm breeze moved unseen through the dense jungle. Massive tangled vines ripped at mud-caked fatigues. The team labored toward the location where cocaine flowed from Columbia into the western hemisphere.

Just after midnight, six shrouded figures had dropped through a cloudy moonless night onto the pampas. The subsequent hours of tortured travel took them into a different time and place. Their assignment: seek and destroy those who caused humanity to rot even as it lived.

The constant smell of dank earth and decomposing vegetation suited the area terrorized by lowlife scum profiting from atrocity. These "revolutionaries" bullied the poor locals, creating a chaotic state of greed-induced grief and fear.

The sun had just appeared over the mountains as the six began to fan out along the western edge of the guerilla camp. There, along an animal trail, fate appeared in the form of a young man. No more than twenty and dressed in a guerilla uniform, with the standard Soviet-issue Kalashnikov rifle slung over his shoulder, he searched for a place to relieve himself. He glanced back up the path, shouting something in Spanish while unzipping his fly. He stepped off the trail and walked straight into Morgan.

The boy spun in horror as he came eye-to-eye with death. He attempted to backpedal, yelping incoherently. Morgan pounced, covering his mouth. He slit the boy's throat and drove his knife through the carotid artery with one fluid motion.

As Morgan cleared the trail, a girl in her mid-teens came around the bend, laughing and singing. That song died on her lips and her eyes darkened as she staggered back in horror, then raced toward the young corpse.

Morgan sprang, clamping his left hand over her mouth while pinning her to the ground. He held her there with tears in his eyes as he listened for the sounds that would force him to take her life. His true nature struggled against his training; he wouldn't hurt her anymore than he had already.

He heard movement and shouting. Revolutionary guerillas moved through the area, doing their normal morning reconnaissance. He glanced up; confident his ghillie suit would conceal him.

The girl took advantage of his shift. She bit down, exerting a vise-like grip on his index finger. He pulled his hand away and she screamed.

The guerillas opened fire. The patrol sprang into action.

Morgan released the girl but used his weight to keep her pinned to the ground. He returned fire with the systematic efficiency and accuracy of a Navy SEAL. He swept his rifle to his left, toward the heat of the skirmish.

A wall of knotted vines and intractable brush separated one of the team from the rest. The guerillas concentrated their fire against that man. Out of the corner of his eye, through a spyglass tunnel into the impenetrable undergrowth, Morgan saw his teammate go down in a spray of gunfire.

"Skip!"

Morgan bolted up, tears streaming down his cheeks. He looked around the bedroom he'd shared with his wife in a long forgotten age. The room was perfect, just as she'd left it a week ago.

Through a sleepy fog, his mind re-introduced him to the events of the preceding week. His past seemed determined to visit him in the present. "Don't tell me I'm going to start having this fucking dream, too."

He recited a line from Donne's Meditation XVII. "Any man's death diminishes me . . . what happens when any man turns out to be your best friend?"

He'd loved Skip Hutchins. They'd been childhood buddies, gone to school together, joined the Navy, and had become SEALs together. They'd been more than family, virtually inseparable.

SEAL Team Six had dropped into the Santander province of Columbia. In a fierce firefight, Skip had been cut off from the team and killed. The lieutenant had signaled a withdrawal and the team had moved toward the extraction point under heavy fire. That was, everyone except Morgan. With a passion-induced mania, he'd pressed forward to recover Skip's body. A teammate had to render him unconscious and carry him to the extraction point. Skip Hutchins had become one of the few Navy SEALs ever to be left behind in battle.

Through his training, he'd fooled himself into believing he'd eradicated that shame from his soul. While true in his waking thoughts, guilt lurked as a constant predator through his dreams. Nightmares didn't lie; he felt responsible for Skip's death.

His subconscious was a subliminal safe haven for the dark awareness of failure. He'd failed everyone important in his life: his father, his closest friend, and now the mother of his child.

That's when it hit him. There were those who could never come back home.

He broke down and wept, remembering his mother, Skip, Liz, and countless others he'd killed. It was too late for them, but he wouldn't fail Thad. He couldn't face such a failure.

Chapter 25

The doorbell heralded a new and dismal day.

A deliveryman fidgeted as he stood hoping for a tip. Thad signed for the package and opened the card. It read, "With deepest sympathy. During this difficult time, my thoughts are with you. Please don't hesitate to contact me." It was signed David Masters and a phone number was under the name.

Thad closed the door and wilted against the wall. The reality of his loss came like a flood. Grief wracked him in uncontrollable convulsing waves. He slid down into a squat and wept, clutching the flowers to his chest.

Wonderful memories of his mother rushed forward in a cascading torrent of bittersweet sentiment. She would never welcome him home again. He would never enjoy her company in the future. That realization dominated his consciousness.

Demons of guilt pounced on him, obliterating those precious memories. She must have felt like he'd deserted her. He'd moved out to the dorm and had spent more time away. He'd become self-absorbed over the last several weeks. He'd loved her beyond expression, but never told her. Now it was too late. All those thoughts and sentiments were futile.

His father emerged from the master bedroom suite, his own tear-stained face misshapen by a deep awareness of failure. "Hey, buddy, it's . . . it's, uh . . . it's . . . um . . . It's getting close to the time to go to the service. Is there anything I can do to help you get ready?" The tender words felt hollow, imbalanced.

Thad wiped the tears with the side of his hand. "Nothing's going to help me get ready for this." He pulled himself together and stood up. "Let's just get this over with."

Morgan tried to ignore Thad's cell phone conversation as he backed out of the driveway. It was hard not to be curious when he heard Thad's side of the conversation.

"Doctor Masters? Thad Morgan. How are you?" he said as though it were a normal day. "Thank you so much for the card . . . I'm doing fine, really. I was wondering, can I get together with you sometime next week? . . . Yes, next Saturday night would be great. Thanks. See you then."

"So, is this guy your mom was dating planning to attend?"

"I couldn't get a hold of him. Besides, I can't imagine he'd want to come with you here."

The next ten minutes passed in cruel silence. Morgan wanted to yell out his fury. The boy was driving him crazy. And what the fuck was Masters up to? It sure as hell looked like he was insinuating himself into Thad's life. That couldn't be good. He'd bury the fucker before he'd see him hurt Thad.

He swung into the Marina Jack parking lot and took a space reserved for Enterprise Sailing Charters. "Thad . . ."

"Don't," That one simple word made it clear. He didn't want to talk. As they approached the boat, he moved away to join his friends.

It was good that Thad's friends had shown up. They'd serve as a deterrent to some of the other invited guests that would make this a difficult occasion. Liz's parents had passed away several years ago, but her two sisters would be onboard. He'd gone out of his way to invite them even though they hated him.

The captain welcomed everyone with a somber manner worthy of the occasion. His khaki shorts, boat shoes, and bronze skin didn't detract from the solemn duties he was hired to discharge.

Morgan stepped under the bimini and headed toward the transom. His eye caught a flash of movement in the passageway leading below deck. As he turned, he caught the left hand of his attacker, but not the right one, which thumped against his chest.

"You fucking killer," Irene accused. "You killed her. You might as well have fed her the pills yourself. I can't believe you have the nerve to show yourself here."

He wasn't ready for the outpour of emotion. Everyone turned toward the sparing pair. "Irene, I'm so sorry. I know this is hard."

"Hard, hard?" veins on her neck pulsed as she screamed the words. "You don't know hard, you fucking coward."

Morgan stood stock still, a picture of discomfort. His mouth moved but no words came out. He was not used to so much attention.

Everyone watched as she stalked off in tears, her emotional stores depleted.

Like the second act of a tag-team wrestling match, Liz's older sister spoke to someone on the forward deck. It had always amazed Morgan that a psychologist could share information so indiscreetly with relative strangers.

"Elizabeth had suffered from debilitating depression for a number of years," Theresa said. "Recently, she'd been doing better. Her new medicine seemed to be working and she had a new man in her life." She looked around, locking eyes with Morgan. "I'm not surprised the guy's not here. Who would want to face her ex?"

The engines changed from an idle murmur to a deep throb as the crew used an aft spring line to ease the boat from the slip. The tide headed out as they entered the deep channel and began bearing north. Million dollar homes and glimmering high rises created an upscale parade route for Liz Morgan making her final journey between the mainland and the barrier islands.

Gulls flocked as they crossed under the Ringling Causeway and passed through the last vestiges of Sarasota Bay, heading toward the Gulf of Mexico. The beauty of the area struck Morgan. For the first time, he realized why Liz had wanted to settle here.

The boat made a gradual arc to the west and left the Intracoastal Waterway via the cut. The drawbridge stood at attention as the boat chugged through. The key islands created the barrier between the calm waters of Sarasota Bay and the more animated Gulf of Mexico.

He looked up in wary surprise when Thad joined him on the transom.

The boat slipped into the Gulf, gliding by Liz's favorite beach. On cue, the sails unfurled, as if setting her spirit free to enjoy the scene forever. The forty-one-foot double-mast ketch must have looked magnificent from shore. Under full sail, the captain stopped the fuel flow to the engine. The powerful thrum gave way to the breeze, the gulls, and the slap of waves against the hull.

"She loved this place."

Thad wept in silence.

Morgan placed his hand on his shoulder.

"I don't need you to reassure or encourage me," Thad bellowed. "Can't you see it's all fucked up? I fucked up."

Perplexed, Morgan struggled to understand his son's ordeal. Thad's feelings came from his love for his mother. His own feelings came from his love for his son. The father spoke from his heart to the son. "I can't say what love is, or why it causes so much pain. How can something so great bring so much devastation? To love is human, and humanness is love."

Awareness rose on the horizon of his understanding. Love involved agony, pain, heartache, and sadness. It was far more complex than he'd ever thought. He'd never been good at affection because he hadn't experienced it for decades.

When the shoreline had all but disappeared on the horizon and the buildings shimmered as points of light in the late morning sun, the captain barked the order to heave-to. The crew backed the jib and eased the mainsail, and the boom swung out over the water. With the sail doused, the boat drifted leeward. The jib pushed away from the wind and the rudder nudged the boat along.

The captain herded the group to the leeward side. The rhythmic slapping of water against the hull was all that could be heard as the service began.

"Death is not our enemy." With a look of compassion, the minister scanned the faces in the crowd. "Fear is our enemy." She paused, allowing the idea to soak in. "Fear causes us to hold on to what has been liberated. Fear creates denial, anger, and guilt. Fear creates pain and robs us of joy. The dead don't ask us to suffer when they move on. We create our own pain. We have a choice. Is this a tragedy or a transformation? Have we lost or gained through knowing Liz? Has Liz lost or gained through moving on to the next phase of her existence? Must we judge in these situations? Can we accept that she's moved forward in her spiritual journey?"

The words of the minister reflected the Ultraist philosophy.

"This event represents a choice—an unavoidable choice. Don't be a victim of these circumstances. Will you wallow in denial, anger, and guilt, or rejoice in the life and future of Liz Morgan? To do nothing is to embrace fear. Acceptance is the only means of experiencing the joy of Liz's continuing life.

"Some will say that to rejoice rather than suffer is the ultimate denial, but you won't be denying the pain of separation. Deny fear and ignorance in order to enjoy your memories. Don't give fear a foothold in your life. Choose to continue your relationship with Liz beyond this physical life. She has transformed. All things are possible. Believe."

The minister looked radiant as she held out her arms in benediction. "Would anyone care to say a few words in memory of Liz?"

Theresa, the "new age" psychologist, stood up. "We're here to celebrate a life and to remember a mother, a sister, and a friend. I'd like to say something to the man in her life." She paused for effect. "Thad, your mom was a good mother and a fine person. She had her struggles, but we all do. Remember, this didn't happen because of you. There aren't any easy answers, and I don't want to feed you platitudes or clichés."

She appeared to be gaining momentum yet remained clinical. "Your mom had some personal issues she either wasn't aware of or couldn't express. Sometimes life overwhelms us. We become confused and spun around, disoriented. Our world becomes dark and we can't verbalize our feelings. The subsequent loss of perspective leads us to conclude that there is no way out. With no hope of relief, we despair. Rather than burden others, we seek a way out; not realizing that we're placing the ultimate burden on those we leave behind.

"We must go through pain and heartache in order to begin cleansing the toxic waste from our psyches. Our pain comes from love."

Morgan couldn't help but think that she was right, even if she contradicted the minister Masters had sent for the occasion.

Thad stood to speak. He breathed out a low pulsating sigh; devastated, he swayed near exhaustion. "I loved her so much." Spasms of grief gripped his body. "Over this past week, I've vacillated between feeling crazy—like I might join her—and wanting to escape from all of this guilt and fear. Forgive me if I've lashed out at you." He looked to his friends. "I'm numb with emotion. I've lost my best friend, and I admit; I failed her. I hope that she'll forgive me. I know her spirit has moved on. I want to believe the human spirit lives on after the body has ceased to function."

His words rang with the hollowness of doubt rather than confidence. Taking several steps, he slumped onto a bench.

The captain handed the ashes to the minister, who in turn, passed them to Irene, who looked as though she might vomit. She pushed the urn toward Theresa. "I can't bear to part with her." She ran below deck.

Theresa stood. "Elizabeth Rose, we commend your spirit to the universe from whence you came. May you find peace in the universal consciousness that eluded you on earth and guide us spiritually so we may join you when it is our time." She gave a more or less regal look toward her audience and dumped the ashes over the side of the boat.

Morgan sat on the lanai, working on his laptop. Thad appeared, face taut and pale, and dropped into a chair. "Thanks for making the day special."

"You're welcome."

"I think Mom was pleased."

It was the first positive statement he'd made about his mother. "I think we should both stay here a little longer. What do you think?"

"I have to finish a few more exams before the Thanksgiving break, but that'll work."

"Hey what can you tell me about this guy your mom was dating? I'd like to see if he's all right."

Thad shrugged, "His name is Mike. We only met once, I didn't catch his last name. I'm going to lie down for a while." He went back inside.

Morgan sipped his bourbon and thought about Mike. Who the hell was he?

His satellite phone ordered him to attention, "Morgan here."

"Phase one analysis complete and ready for review, sir. Please provide the security pin for download."

"Affirmative."

He hung up and settled into his staff review. He would call Deb in a few hours to discuss his findings.

Chapter 26

"I love this place. Who did you say it belongs to?"

David smiled and winked. "I didn't."

"Come on . . ." Gillian gazed through the massive French doors at the Gulf of Mexico. An infinity system created the illusion that the pool flowed into the Gulf.

"Seriously, I can't say. It's part of the deal. They provide this home and transportation for me. Their one requirement is that TUG doesn't disclose their identity."

She followed him into the pool area. Royal palms towered above the pool like ancient columns supporting the sky.

"Doesn't that make you nervous? I mean, what about questions of ethics and conflicts of interest?"

Maddie sat down and kicked her feet in the water, squealing at the effects.

David motioned toward a poolside table, "Churches don't disclose their donors, especially those who don't request a tax deduction."

"This house isn't a tax deduction for someone? Don't you think that's odd?"

"Why? Someone thinks I deserve a peaceful place to relax."

"But why does it have to be so extravagant? It seems so out of character for you."

"I like it. The donor understands how taxing the passions of others can be for me. Along with every blessing comes a curse. Strong emotions, tension, and passion often hit me with exceptional force."

"It must have been incredibly difficult for you at city hall the other day."

"Not all. Sometimes people come up to me and ask how I could control myself when so-and-so said this or did that? In public or in business meetings, I don't notice people's antagonism. I just get into a zone and do the right thing."

"So, what's the house about?"

"It's in personal relationships where my heightened awareness is a curse. With those closest to me, I feel their emotional stress and turmoil. It can be overpowering. This place provides a retreat for me. It's a monastery of sorts. And the long commute without driving allows me to meditate."

Maddie pulled on the cuff of Gillian's shorts. "Come, Mommy, I want to swim."

David held out a bottle. "Do you have suntan lotion?"

"We put some on at home."

"Come here, Maddie; put on these swimmies. This one looks like it'll fit." He tugged a floatation vest from a storage area.

Vest fastened, Maddie launched herself into the refreshing water.

David sat across the table and leveled his gaze at the young mother. "I know who you are and why you're here."

Gillian panicked and sputtered.

He raised his hand. "It's not important. What's important is that we're running out of time. I need you to do a job for me."

She regained her composure. "Name it."

"Keep an eye on Levi. He's at a vulnerable time in his life. He's on dangerous ground."

Hope and fear rode on those words. Maybe he had no idea who she was.

"There are things you don't know about him. Life-altering things. He needs guidance, maybe even a nudge or two. He needs help to understand his choices."

"How can I guide him? I'm not even sure I'm changing myself. I'm not sure I get what you're teaching."

"We're all on a spiritual journey. We're just in different places. An open heart moving in the right direction is a powerful thing. I have no doubt you can guide Levi away from the negative."

"I think you're better qualified to guide his metamorphosis."

"You underestimate yourself. And my time will be consumed with other endeavors."

Maddie got out of the pool and ran between them, her golden locks muted to a buttery brown by the water.

"I can't do it."

"Hmm, that's not like you."

"Maybe I've learned something." She couldn't tell him that she was too busy investigating him to baby-sit.

"What's that?"

"I have control over what I say no to."

"Sounds like the beginning of a good lesson. Just don't let it rob you of living." He smiled as he rose and went into the house.

She contemplated his words as she watched Maddie paddle about the pool.

She rubbed a dime-sized scar on her wrist, a memento she'd acquired a decade ago in a minor motorcycle accident. Along with a couple of steel pins in her wrist, it gave her a new perspective on an old boyfriend. That event had been the genesis of her independence. From that point forward, she was determined to take charge of her life. She made sure that she had control.

It was a constant reminder that good things could come from bad events. She was a survivor, someone who learned from life.

She hoped destiny had bestowed that same gift on her daughter, *the* good thing in her life.

David's request to mentor Morgan was flattering, but Gillian wasn't comfortable with getting close to him. She'd exorcised her demon for picking the wrong kind of man. For the first time in her life, she was comfortable without one. She felt significant, secure, and confident on her own—just her and Maddie. Still, she couldn't deny that she was attracted to him. They seemed kindred, sharing an unseen bond. It was undeniably comfortable—natural— being with him. That scared her more than anything.

Chapter 27

Saturday, November 23

David Masters was already speaking when the couple slipped into the back of the auditorium.

The scent of Gillian's perfume was intoxicating. Morgan sensed that she was hiding something. She seemed innocent and caring—genuine. The NSA report Morgan had received revealed a tainted past. Maybe she was just another fortunate person Masters had helped.

Gillian had arrived ready to take control. There was no way she was going to fall for this guy.

She reached into her purse, pulled out a notepad, and scrawled, *What do you think?* She passed him the pen and paper.

Morgan thought for a moment and wrote, *Reminds me of church, minus kneeling and praying.* He pushed the pad back, grinning.

She smiled and wrote. *LOL.*

"Take an ancient manuscript, proclaim it the perfect word of God, interpret it beyond its historical and cultural context and you get religion," David said from the podium. He looked around the room. "To the novitiate, such dogma is the ethical and moral standard of a drone-like existence."

Morgan took the pen and paper and scribbled furiously. *Okay, so not like church.*

Not like any church I've ever attended, she replied.

"If knowledge brings power, the maintenance of ignorance preserves power. Science discovers new truths to help humanity grow in understanding and capability. Yet ancient religious institutions refuse to modernize. Could it be they fear losing their hold over us? Zealots dwell at the heart of religion, not God. Religious leaders hold on to power by enslaving the masses in the ignorance of the past."

Gillian leaned over and whispered, "Let's go for a walk afterward."

Morgan nodded.

David closed the homily and dismissed the crowd.

"Wow, that went fast," Morgan exclaimed as they exited the building. "I can't believe he's done,"

"Maybe it had something to do with our passing notes." She gave him a playful jab in the ribs.

"Could be. I'd prefer to think it was because he's such a great speaker."

They strolled along the edge of the river, then stopped to look across at the golden dome of the University. "Tell me a little about your wife."

He looked surprised. "Not much to say really. Our relationship had become a catalog of wrongs she couldn't let go. She put up with it for ten years. When Thad was about eight, Liz and I divorced. After that, I wasn't around much, maybe a few times a year until Thad graduated from high school." He paused and leaned against the heavy concrete balustrade overlooking the river. "When I broke my neck, I took stock of my life, of what has lasting value. I rearranged my priorities and spent more time with him. But it was too little, too late."

"You broke your neck? Unbelievable. I would have never guessed."

He raised his chin and pointed to a scar just above his collarbone. "That's a story for another time." He looked at her, his face filled with pain. "I wish I had those years back, knowing what I know now. I would have been a better father, a better husband."

"Don't we all? It seems you've learned a few things about life and love. Who knows, maybe you'll get another chance."

"That would be nice, but love isn't so easy to come by these days."

She gave him another jab. "That's pessimistic view even for a guy with a PhD in philosophy."

With a look of pain, he pulled himself away from their conversation. "I'm sorry, but I need to run and check on Thad. Can we meet at the bookstore on Cortez later? I'll buy you a coffee. You can bring Maddie if you want."

"That would be great. I'll meet you there around six-thirty."

"See you then. This has been great." He walked away.

They both felt something they hadn't experienced in quite awhile: leaping hearts and fluttering stomachs.

Chapter 28

Gillian pulled into the plaza and saw Morgan pacing the bookstore sidewalk like a nervous school boy about to bolt. He executed an about-face, making eye contact with her. He marched into the lot as she parked in a vacant space.

"Hello," he said arm outstretched as though worried she might not have seen him. Gillian felt the flush of infatuation in her body.

"Been here long?" She asked, stepping out of the car.

"Just long enough to annoy the hell out of everyone at the sidewalk tables." He bent down and looked into the car. "Where's Maddie?"

"Oh . . . I decided to leave her with my mother so she could get to bed early."

The aroma of coffee mixed with pastries enveloped them as Morgan opened the door. "Coffee?"

"Sounds great."

They walked to the counter, and he asked rather oafishly, "What do you like to read?"

"A little of this, a little of that; I'm not picky. A good romance novel isn't beneath me."

They ordered coffee and wandered the literature, aisle cups in hand, browsing aimlessly through the shelves.

"I'm not much of a reader. I think studying for my PhD burned me out. It just feels like work these days. Typical I guess."

Gillian gave him an impish smile. "I'm not so sure about that."

He just looked at her blankly. She punched him, a friendly shot to his muscled shoulder. "Hello?" she said, flirting more than intended.

He kept staring like he was from another planet—a dense one at that. She turned and faced him full on, hands on her hip. Nothing. No indication of what she was talking about. Exasperated, she threw up her hands, arched her brow, and said, "I seriously doubt you're typical."

She thought he was anything but typical. Strong, but sentimental about his family; aloof with women, yet naive about his appeal to them; and truthful with himself. Her only question was how deep did it run?

"Oh," he said. "I guess I need to keep up with the conversation better."

They strolled the aisles and made small talk about various books. Gillian enjoyed his company. She relaxed for the first time in ages.

"Mind if I give Thad a quick call? I've been trying all afternoon, but I haven't been able to reach him."

"Not at all."

He punched in the numbers and waited for an answer. A look of anxiety crept over his face. "Thad, it's Dad. It's about seven-fifteen. I just wanted to see how you're doing. Call me and let me know if you want me to bring you dinner."

Seeing this man care so genuinely for his son touched her deeply. It was refreshing. She remembered her own absentee father and wished he'd been more like Levi.

"I'm really starting to get worried. I've tried to contact him all afternoon. He needs to be more responsible. He needs to pay attention to the people who care about him."

"He'll be fine. I'm sure he's just out with friends. Or maybe he just turned his phone off to cram for exams." She laid her hand on his shoulder. "It's great that you love him and you're willing to show it, but he is an adult."

"You're right. I need to stop trying to protect him. But I'm worried. This thing with his mother was a huge trauma. He's a lot like her, and I know that scares him."

"He seems well-adjusted. As long as he can talk about things with someone, he'll do just fine."

"He's been through a lot over the years." His voice tinged with emotion. "I've put him through a lot."

"I've only met him once, but he seems pretty normal for a kid his age. You know they have their own ideas about family, and they tend to lean more toward friends than relatives."

He laughed. "He more or less told me that the other night." He's created huge walls to protect himself from pain—and from me. I've built some serious walls myself. I just hope it isn't too late to knock them down."

She looked at her watch. "Speaking of walls, I'm not big on exposing Maddie to strangers—men, in particular. If I'm going to date, I want to get to know the man before they meet her."

"I respect that." His lips spread into a massive smile. "You can't be too safe these days. There are a lot of creeps looking to take advantage of an unsuspecting and vulnerable woman."

"Why don't you follow me home? I'll check on Maddie, and we can go for a walk along the river."

"Sure."

They wandered out of the store.

"You love Thad and you show it. Trust me; that has a far greater impact than people think. It's the greatest thing we can give our children."

He opened her door. "I'll follow you to your place."

She watched as he walked to an old Dodge pickup. It was gorgeous and quirky, and suited him. She lowered her window. "Is that your truck? I love it."

Gillian drove toward downtown, passing through a seedy area of cheap motels providing hourly and monthly rates. A trained eye could pick out the drug dealers and prostitutes getting an early start on the night. In a few hours, the area would be crawling with sleazy men making sordid deals at the expense of the misfortunate.

The two-car caravan followed Tamiami Trail, the old highway that stretched from Tampa to Miami. In bygone days, it had been the only effective means of making that trip. It had been the final leg of the old Dixie Highway, which ran from Ohio all the way to Miami.

Gillian turned right and followed the river east, passing under the new bridge. At the hospital, she made a left, and then a quick right, entering a quiet neighborhood with a traffic circle ringed by towering royal palms. Morgan followed her into a driveway a couple of blocks up from the river. The house was a modest 1950's ranch on a big lot.

"Come in and meet my mother while I check on Maddie."

She dropped her keys into an old chrome art deco ashtray just inside the door. A little black cat lay relaxed and cozy in a large bowl on the cluttered hall table, head down, eyes closed. Gillian rubbed her head.

"Hi, Mom," she called. "Looks like we've got a bowl full of kitty."

Jean Anu looked up from the TV and laughed. "I didn't even notice. That cat is something."

The cat began to preen herself. Morgan scratched her, gently rubbing the tips of her ears. She purred as though high on catnip and rolled over in the bowl, exposing her belly.

"Don't fall for that trick." Jean called out. "She only tolerates a scratch on the head. Touch her anywhere else and you'll get scratched."

The cat stretched long and deep, her front paws outside the bowl. She jumped to the terrazzo floor and trotted off toward the back of the house.

Gillian followed her down the hall. "I'll be just a minute."

When she returned, she stood in the kitchen out of sight but within earshot. Her mother had gotten up from the couch and turned off the television. She was speaking to Levi in a sing-song voice that Gillian adored. "Pleased to meet you. Levi. That's a lovely name. Is it Jewish?"

Her mother was a spry gray-haired woman who'd overcome many obstacles during her seventy years. She'd triumphed yet somehow retained an air of timidity.

Gillian peaked around the corner.

"I like it myself, ma'am. To tell you the truth, my father named me after his favorite kind of pants."

The mother tossed her head back and gave musical laugh. "Now that's funny."

Gillian smothered a laugh so as not to interrupt.

"He was a character," Morgan admitted, a little uncomfortable with the admission. "I miss him now, but it's been a long time." Gillian noticed that Morgan stumbled through awkward moments and remembered the restaurant. *A possible pattern that might come in handy.*

"Thanks for watching Maddie so Gillian and I could spend some time together."

"It was my pleasure. I love being with Maddie, and it was no inconvenience. I live just across the street." She smiled, a picture of gracious hospitality.

Gillian walked in with two bottles of water. "Mom, do you mind if Levi and I take a quick walk along the river?"

"Not at all, dear. Take your time and enjoy yourselves. It's a lovely evening for a walk."

They walked along the river, toward the Gulf and crossed under Highway 41. A 1920's hotel stood to their left, while half of an old bridge reached out toward them from the Palmetto side of the river.

"Every time I see that place, I think of Hotel California."

"I love this place," Levi said. "It reminds me of my childhood visits to my grandmother's. It hasn't changed much since I was nine. My brother caught a rainbow trout off the old bridge over there where it ends." He gazed toward the bridge, now a fishing pier. "Maybe it's radically changed and I just haven't noticed."

They walked on in silence, boats bobbing in the small marina. Gillian picked up their earlier conversation. "You're a philosophy professor. Do you think love has an opposite? Is hate the opposite of love?"

He simply shrugged and shook his head. He was deep in thought. Then he went somewhere unanticipated. "My father was one of the original members of Navy Special Operations. I always thought he was a real son of a bitch. I could never please him, no matter what I did." He shook his head. "Ours was a love-hate relationship, minus the love. God, I hated him. In my mid-teens, I planned ways to kill him. He was never around, but when he was . . ." He paused, searching for words. "He just seemed to be this big prick who expected everyone to meet his needs and standards.

"It was just my mom and me in base housing. My father was always off on an op. She died during my senior year in high school. He was off doing something classified and didn't show up until after the services. Something snapped inside me. From that point on, I just wanted to be better than him, to make him realize he wasn't so great.

"My best friend and I joined the Navy and became SEALs. I was determined to best my father at everything he'd ever done. Still, I was never good enough to impress him or make him proud. Hating him became all-consuming at that point, and it's ruined my life ever since. He died on the battlefield in Grenada. What a fiasco."

He shook his head as if trying to wake up. "Wow, where the hell did that come from?"

She pursed her lips and looked down, not out of embarrassment, but habit. "I'm not sure, but it was awfully powerful."

"To answer your question, hate may not be the opposite of love, but it sure destroys it." He gazed toward the horizon. "Check out that sunset. It's absolutely gorgeous. No hate there."

They stood in silence, absorbing the revelation as it extended toward them. The breeze lifted a pleasant scent of salt with a hint of fish from the Gulf. The sound of gulls returning with the day's final meal added to the glory and beauty of dusk. As the fiery ball winked goodnight, they turned back toward the house.

Gillian but I treasured the time.

"I find David to be an amazing, but confusing man," Morgan said.

"What do you mean?"

"I don't know exactly. He makes me feel . . . well, strange." He watched the ground as though it might provide the words he searched for. "It's kind of paradoxical. After I've been around him, I feel comfortable and relaxed; but, at the same time, I feel invigorated. Does that make sense?"

She took his hand as they walked on. At the door, he leaned down and kissed her on the cheek. "I had a wonderful time today. The best time I've had in years."

"Me, too. It's been lovely. Would you like to come in?"

"No, I need to get going. I've got work to catch up on; and I really should see if I can track Thad down."

Again, he kissed her cheek and gave her a hug. "Thanks for everything. I'll see you Monday." He turned and walked slowly toward his truck.

"Bye."

He turned and waved. "Bye."

Gillian was thankful for that one single word.

Chapter 29

Monday, November 25

Morgan stopped by Hafley's office and spoke to his secretary. "Morning, I'm Professor Morgan. I need to arrange a meeting with Mr. Hafley." As an afterthought, he said, "If possible, today."

"Hang on; I'll check his schedule, Professor." She was an attractive twenty-something woman with natural red hair caressing her shoulders.

"Please call me Levi. What's your name?"

She gave a shy smile. "Karen."

"Pleased to meet you, Karen."

"Nice to meet you. Let me check the calendar."

He surveyed her immaculate work area. There was a place for everything and everything was in its place. A picture of her with a young man sat on her desk.

"Mr. Hafley is available at nine this morning."

"That'll be fine. Please make sure Mr. Markus is invited. Thanks." He paused. "You two make a handsome couple."

"That's my brother. We're twins."

"You seem close."

"We were," she said.

She had muttered the answer thoughtfully, and he sensed there was a tragic story behind it. "I have to run. It's nice to see a cheerful face. Have a good day."

He thought about his time with Gillian as he rode the elevator to his floor, her floor. For the first time in ages, he'd been himself: anxious, vulnerable, sad, yet happy. With her, he'd been able to throw off his robotic existence, to abandon the façade of indifferent perfection and compliance. He'd become himself with her.

He drifted down the hall toward his office. Mike Markus passed, forcing him back to the reality of his assignment. He had to sell Hafley and Markus on why he'd cracked TUG security. His clandestine penetration test would either be a huge success or a bonehead mistake.

He reviewed the trail of evidence he'd planted: the coveralls on the roof of the elevator; the digital recording locked away in his desk, along with the card containing the downloaded data. He'd need to present the test results in such a way so as not to undermine Markus's position with Hafley.

It had to happen today. He couldn't wait for the complete NSA analysis. The rules of security analysis dictated speed and surprise to capture accurate data about systems and process flaws. He'd play his cards and take his chances.

***

Hafley rose as Morgan entered his office. "Morning, Levi. You remember Mike Markus from your tour last week."

Markus stood and shook hands with Morgan. Indeed he remembered him. Instinct told him that Markus was a ruthless, dangerous man. Someone to keep an eye on. "Morning, Mike, Randall."

"So, what's on your mind?" Hafley asked.

"I've begun my analysis and I need to share a few critical findings with you. Normally, I'd wait for a formal presentation, but several items are so serious it wouldn't be prudent to wait." He tossed the electronic card on the table. "This card contains the list of all Ultraist Group personnel, as well as the unabridged membership list. Names, addresses, birthdays, social security numbers, etc. I obtained this early Wednesday morning."

"We know; we watched you steal it." Markus's baritone voice reverberated through the room; he looked as if he'd tasted something awful. "Our security is a little better than you think."

"I'm not trying to undermine you. I'm being paid to do a job and I'm doing it to the best of my ability. Your security measures seem impeccable to me. Everything I achieved Wednesday, I accomplished through social engineering, not cracking. As far as I can tell, the TUG systems are impenetrable." He hesitated, hoping for an exchange he could parley into an uneasy truce. But his adversary sat motionless and mute. "Check the maintenance hatch in the northwest elevator number three. You'll find the coveralls and employee badge I used to gain entrance into the building. I'm sorry, Mike, but I couldn't let you know what I was doing."

Markus muttered several unintelligible curses, scowling at Hafley. "We fucking saw everything the dumb son of a bitch did." He sat, shaking his head.

Hafley's face twitched as Morgan turned back toward him. He'd seen that mannerism but couldn't place it. "By the way, if you don't mind, I'd like to meet with you Saturday to do a formal presentation of my phase one analysis."

"It's Thanksgiving week . . . but if you'll be ready, I can give you a few hours in the morning. Set a time with my secretary."

Morgan started to leave the room and then stopped. "Randall, have we met before?"

"Not to my knowledge Levi."

* * *

"Hey Dick," Morgan said, rapping gently on the cubicle's metal edge. "I'm heading out for an early lunch to beat the rush. Can I get you anything?"

Wrestling his gaze from the monitor, Dick looked up without actually looking Morgan in the eye "No thanks, I brought my lunch today."

"How're things going? Is there anything I can do to run interference for you?"

Dick Mattel removed his glasses and massaged the bridge of his nose. "No, everything seems to be going well. I've been able to get all the data extracts I need to set up the databases." He made a slow side-to-side motion with his head as he spoke. "I've had to explain things repeatedly to the HR/IT folks, but that's par for the course. They're usually more HR than IT. They don't understand that data has to be in a certain format before it can be loaded into a database." He hesitated, pursing his lips in a childish way. "I've done most of their work for them, but it's no big deal. I enjoy it."

Dick spoke more right then than he had the entire previous week. A conscientious worker, he took pride in seeing things done efficiently. He was a nice guy whose issues of significance and self-worth had turned him into a seemingly one-dimensional character. On the other hand, it might only be his professional persona. He probably lived in his mother's basement among old pizza boxes and half-eaten cartons of Chinese takeout.

"Thanks for all of your hard work on this project. It isn't going unnoticed. Let me know if there's anything I can do to facilitate it."

"Thanks, Professor. Enjoy your lunch."

"You too, Dick." He smiled and moved toward the elevator.

Chapter 30

Morgan pulled the old Dodge off the highway and parked in the rest area at the North Skyway Fishing Pier, where he kicked off the data download. He hoped he hadn't screwed up with Hafley and Markus by meeting with them before he received the analysis of the full Ultraist data set. He needed this data to identify his targets and resources.

This new role frustrated him. His handlers had always given him the targets. Now he found himself in unfamiliar territory, thrust into a nebulous scenario with no program or playbook to go by.

The download completed. He perused the analyzed data. The information didn't jibe with his intuition. It couldn't solve his problems. It wouldn't tell him who to kill.

He started the truck and headed back to the office. He could review the files there as long as he stayed off the network.

The phone was barely audible as the tires hummed over the concrete road surface. "Deb, it's me. Can we talk?"

"Where the hell are you? You're really muffled. Speak up."

"I looked at the NSA analysis of the TUG staffers. I thought it would make things clear, who to kill, who to trust. Fuck!" Morgan looked in the mirror as he swerved to avoid a car cutting him off from the right.

"What the hell is going on out there?"

"Some asshole just cut me off."

"Would you be careful?"

"I'm alright. It was nothing."

"It didn't sound like nothing."

"Who is your inside man?"

"Analyze the data. He's there."

"Just tell me."

"Not over the phone." She hung up.

***

He settled into his desk and opened the encrypted file, hoping the full data set would reveal hidden elements, activities, and goals.

```
    REPORT   CLASS  TOP   SECRET  WARNING  NOTICE—
SENSITIVE   INTELLIGENCE   SOURCES   AND   METHODS
INVOLVED—NOT RELEASABLE TO FOREIGN NATIONALS—NOT
RELEASABLE   TO   CONTRACTORS   OR   CONTRACTOR   /
CONSULTANTS  — CLASSIFIED  BY  RECORDED  REPORTING
OFFICER—XGDS-2.
    CIA Trace Report
    Report Class: Top Secret
    DOI: 22 November 20XX
    Subject:  Possible  plans  of  extremists  to
commandeer and  crash  airliners;  possible  plans
to assassinate POTUS
    Source: Field Operations, NSA, Echelon
    1.   This   agency   has   conducted   an
investigation of the names of persons suspected
of involvement in terrorist activities designed
to overthrow the American government and destroy
both   civilian   and   military   targets.   The
following represents the primary threat threads
based on numerous factors:
    * Operational and technological fact-finding
    * Key indicators (hostile counter
      intelligence activities / motives /
      involvements)
    * Hostile nexus information
    2. David Masters, Brief stint in the Navy,
washed out of Navy SEAL training . . .
```

Nothing new except that the intelligence on Masters felt wrong. Could Masters be complicit in the terrorist plot?

And the growing relationship between Thad and Masters, what about that? Masters had invited Thad to dinner and had sent a car. He'd sent flowers and had offered his time to the boy. He was drawing closer to Thad, but why?

Thad's aggressive behavior toward him was making it difficult to protect him and do his job.

He read on:

```
    3.  Michael   Markus,   Deputy   Director   of
Security  TUG,  formerly  known  as  Brian  Wilcox,
ex-Green  Beret,  served  7  years  in  Leavenworth
for     manslaughter,     dishonorable     discharge,
mercenary  services  available  to  highest  bidder
since  1993;  enduring  relationship  with  David
Masters  since  the  mid-1980's;  presumed  hostile
nexus
    4. Steven Unger, Computer Systems Architect
specializing in aeronautical engineering . . .
```

He skipped down.

```
    5.  TUG   has   a   private   security   force
consisting  of  2500+  ex-special  ops  and  military
personnel.  This  force  takes  care  of  everything
from      physical      security      to      electronic
surveillance.  They  are  extremely  high  tech  and
well  endowed  for  a  private  security  force
possessing  comprehensive  technical,  operational,
and  administrative  capabilities.   Field  Ops
assumes  this  team  will  protect  TUG  leadership
and  seek  to  establish  the  main  point  of
operations during any assault.
    6.  The   following   members   of   the   TUG
management  team  appear  to  be  clear  of  any
involvement in covert terror operations:
    * Randall Hafley, EVP of Operations TUG
```

It didn't make sense.   Hafley had to be involved. Something wasn't right.   Someone was covering for him, erasing the trail.

```
    * Benjamin Bradley (deceased), Director of
      Security TUG
```

Morgan dropped to the next section of the report.

7. The following government-aligned personnel are currently participating in non-operational activities with the Ultraist Group:
* James Meyer, Tampa Police Department, Badge 79849, volunteering at TUG Tampa Free Clinic

8. The following government-aligned personnel are currently on active operations within the Ultraist Group:
* Thomas Black, DEA, undercover, details of operation unknown
* Mark Holter, ATF, undercover, investigating illegal firearms activities within TUG
* Gillian Anu, FBI, Field Agent, deep cover, TUG Security Team Tampa

So Gillian is FBI. She must be McDonnell's inside man.

He made a list, shoved it in his pocket, and headed toward the elevators. A flood of relief accompanied the knowledge that Gillian was FBI. He couldn't reveal the nature of his mission, but at some point, he might be able to solicit her help in bringing TUG down. He could relax, confident that their goals were similar.

Chapter 31

"Dick, I have some errands to run," Morgan called. "I won't be back today."

"Sure thing, boss. I'll let the others know."

"Call me on my cell if you need me."

The elevator doors slid open and Masters stepped out. "Levi, just the man I was coming to see."

Morgan stood dumbfounded, his hands fidgeting. They felt dirty for some reason. "How can I help you, sir?"

"Would you and Thad join me for Thanksgiving dinner?"

Relief and shame flushed his face. "That would be great."

"Perfect. I'll have Elaina contact you." Masters headed down the hall, toward Gillian's cubicle. "See you around," he called over his shoulder, then stopped and turned. "By the way, Gillian and her family will be there as well."

"Okay." Morgan hesitated. "Thank you."

This guy was no terrorist.

***

His sat-phone rang as he approached the Skyway.

"Morgan, what's going on down there?" McDonnell asked, sounding unusually distressed. "We can't screw around with this forever. A lot of people could die if we don't straighten it out soon."

"Things are convoluted. I think someone in our organization altered the report I received today."

"Goddamn it, just take Masters out, will you?"

He'd never heard her so out of control before. Something didn't add up. The briefing she'd held with him ... her uneasiness concerning Echelon ....

"Deb, what the fuck is going on?"

143

He calmed down. "This is a secure line, but I'm not in a secure location. I can't tell you why, but we have to wait. Masters isn't the issue here; I don't even think he's involved. This thing is larger and more dangerous than we ever imagined. I'm not sure how far it goes up in the current administration, but we can't strike now or we'll be fighting an unknown enemy."

"What the hell are you talking about?"

"I need more time to identify the nucleus."

"You've got a week and that's it."

He grabbed his doodled notes from the laptop bag. "I was looking over the report. Who did the field operations? Who do you have on the inside?"

"I can't divulge that information."

"Who's involved in this conspiracy? The analysis doesn't add up. What are their real goals? How do they plan to accomplish them? Come on, Deb, be straight with me. Crashing a bunch of planes and killing the President won't establish a new world order. It won't even cause anarchy. What's really going on?"

"You know everything I know." She snapped. "Keep digging. I'll talk to you in a few days."

The line went dead.

Someone deep within his group was complicit in the TUG affair. It could be anyone, even Deb. He had to report to her, keep her informed. But he needed someone to trust—someone objective.

Chapter 32

Thad had just left for the day when the doorbell rang.

"Who the fuck could that be?"

Morgan banged his bare foot on the leg of the dining room table as he rushed to answer. "God damn it!" He stooped to rub his reddening toe. The bell rang several more times.

"Hold on I'm coming," he shouted as he hopped toward the door.

Morgan couldn't register what he saw as he pulled the door open.

"Deb, what are you doing here?"

"Well happy Thanksgiving to you too," she exclaimed.

"Come on Deb, you didn't come here for Thanksgiving. You gave me another week."

"Are you going to invite me in?" She looked pissed, and tired.

Morgan turned and walked into the house. "Come on in."

"Nice place you've got here."

"You must have gotten on the plane right after we got off the phone yesterday."

She shrugged. "I have some business here."

"You didn't mention it."

"I know everything you're doing. You don't need to know everything I'm doing. How's Thad?"

"How do you think?"

"Wow, you really can't stop competing with your father. Can you?"

"Leave my father out of this. He was a fucking idiot and none of your business."

"You'll never be half the man your father was."

Was that sorrow in her gaze?

"I didn't know you two knew each other."

Deb turned a deep red and looked out the window. "We met before his tragic death."

"Deb, don't step in on this assignment. I have it under control."

"Well I'd hate to see it out of control. Like I said on the phone; you've got one week from yesterday."

"So why are you here then?"

"I'm here to meet with Haddon over at MacDill. I have to finalize arrangements for another operation. I'm leaving tomorrow night."

"It must be some op if you have to be here in person. If you have time I can see about you joining us for Thanksgiving dinner."

"Where would that be?"

"Thad and I are joining David Masters and a small group of friends."

"Oh," the word sounded ominous. "You have friends now. That could be dangerous—*for them*. I won't have time. You should be careful around Masters. He's not what he seems to be."

"What can you tell me then? Everything I've observed tells me he is not involved."

Trust me on this.

"Deb, what the fuck is going on? The DEA, ATF, and the FBI all have ops going on in here. If we make a wrong move, we could be fighting each other unwittingly.

"You never answered me yesterday. Who did the field ops for that report; who blessed it? Who could have altered it before I received it? Who do you have on the inside?"

"I told you yesterday. I can't divulge that information."

"Come on the analysis doesn't add up. Morgan was turning red now. Be straight with me. You want me to take out a cell that can't be identified. What's really going on?"

"God damn, are you nine-years old? Get a fucking life, you never asked these questions before."

"You never gave me shit intel before."

"You just crossed a line."

146

Morgan looked fierce but did not try to hold her gaze.

"It's hard to believe you are your father's son. Do your job."

She turned and walked out the front door.

Morgan stood staring as she climbed into the waiting limousine. *What the fuck just happened?*

Chapter 33

Thursday, November 28

Morgan rang the bell of a modest modern-Greco home. He turned from the door to gaze into the reflecting pool in the courtyard. He was a mess—the mission, Thad, Masters, and Gillian. *God what am I doing? I've got to get out of here.*

He could hear muffled words and the latches rattling. A woman's voice said, "Careful."

The door opened to little Maddie Anu, who stood with beautiful ringlets of golden hair and a wide-eyed precious smile. Her mother crouched behind her, beaming.

"Maddie, this is my friend, Levi. He's Thad's daddy."

Maddie gave a belly laugh, rich and full of wonder. "Tat's silly, Mommy. Tad's too big to have a daddy."

Morgan smiled broadly. Kneeling, he held out a blue cornflower. "Here you go, sweetheart."

The girl's eyes widened. She took the flower and gave him a quick hug. "Tanks."

"You're welcome."

She tore down the hall, squealing, "Gramma, Tad, look what I got."

Morgan stood up. "I guess that was a hit. Things should go so easily with Thad." He handed Gillian a bouquet of wildflowers, giving her a kiss on the cheek. "Happy Thanksgiving. From Maddie's reaction and the cars in the driveway, I take it I'm the last one here."

"Yeah, come on in. Tad, I mean Thad, and my mom are already inside, helping with the food." She slipped an arm through his. "Thanks for the flowers. David's in the kitchen cooking. He's dying to see you."

"It was nice of him to invite us all over."

The pleasant aroma of turkey, dressing, and sweet potato soufflé filled the house. He couldn't remember the last time he'd been in a holiday setting.

"Are you kidding? He lives for these things." She hesitated. "I can't imagine how lonely he must be since he lost his family."

Morgan turned to face her. "I had no idea." He shook his head in disbelief. "Wow."

"They were killed in a tragic accident overseas working as missionaries. From what I heard, Hafley saved David's life. That's how they got together."

"Interesting. Go figure; I guess fate does make strange bedfellows."

Masters came out of the kitchen, wiping his hands on an apron. "Levi, so glad you could come." He rejected Morgan's handshake in favor of a hug.

"You know Jean."

"Hello Mrs. Anu."

"She and Thad have been here slaving away with me for hours now."

"Hi, Dad. Happy Thanksgiving."

"I see you've already met the guest of honor." Masters winked at Maddie as though they shared a secret. She giggled. "Make yourself at home. We'll eat in about an hour. Right, Thad?"

"That's right, boss."

Morgan plopped on the floor of the great room next to Maddie and her blanket. He smiled in her direction. "I have an idea."

"What?"

"Let's play 'you can't find me'."

"How do you play tat?"

"You get under the blanket and I try to find you."

A look of sheer amazement crossed her face. She looked at her mother, who nodded. "Okay." She quickly threw the blanket over her head and laid down, squirming.

"Where's Maddie?" he called as he wandered around the room.

Maddie giggled when he looked under chairs and tables. She snickered and waved from under the blanket. "I'm over here."

He feigned ignorance and moved toward the adjoining kitchen. "Thad, do you know where Maddie went?"

Thad made a face and threw up his hands. "I don't know. She was here a minute ago."

The giggling blanket rolled on the floor.

Morgan went to the entertainment center and looked in the cabinets. "Maddie, where are you?"

The blanket rushed into his arms. "Here I am."

He pulled back the cover and dropped his mouth in pretend surprise. "There you are." He gave her a big hug and spun her around. "You're really good at hiding."

She squealed with delight. "Can we play again?"

"Sure."

Several games of airplane and horse ride kept him and Maddie occupied for the next hour.

"Dinner's ready, everyone," Jean called. "Come to the dining room."

"Wow, Jean," Masters said, choked up. "This is lovely. I haven't had such a beautiful setting in years. Thanks."

Jean gave him a hug. "You're welcome. Thanks for everything you've done for our family. Please, everyone, sit down; let's eat while it's hot."

Morgan wondered about Masters's family. *What had happened? How has he coped and remained so normal? How was Hafley involved? He seems like such a dick. Maybe he isn't as bad as I think.*

Masters gave a quick blessing. Comments abounded as plates passed over the table, filling up with the traditional holiday fare. The room went silent as everyone settled in to gorge themselves on tryptophan.

Thad waved a fork of potatoes toward his father. "Remember that time we built the Lego ship together?"

"How could I forget? You just looked at the picture and built it without instructions. Pretty amazing."

Thad smiled and shook his head. "Remember when we built the air traffic control tower and flew the plane down a string on the runway? That was so cool." He flew his fork toward Maddie, made a loop and landed it in his mouth. "We should do that, Maddie."

"We did have some fun when you were growing up, didn't we?"

Thad nodded.

For a moment Morgan caught a glimpse of the life he had never fully enjoyed.

Maddie began to fidget and fuss.

"What's wrong, sweetheart?" Masters asked.

"She's fine," Gillian said. "It's just past her nap time; she's tired."

Maddie started to cry.

Gillian frowned regretfully. "I'm sorry, David, I think we need to go. It's been wonderful. Sorry to leave you with the dishes, but she needs her nap."

Maddie wailed as if to emphasize the point.

"No problem. I've arranged for the cleaning lady to take care of all of this tomorrow. Thanks for coming."

"Can I help you out to the car?" Morgan almost knocked the chair over as he rose to help her.

"Thanks, but Mom and I can manage. See you tomorrow."

Morgan's ears felt suddenly hot as he helped gather Maddie's toys. "Yeah, see you tomorrow." He hoped his disappointment wasn't too obvious.

Jean took Maddie to the car as Gillian said a hurried goodbye.

Silence descended on the house as the door closed behind them.

"Poor kid, I hope she can sleep," Masters said.

"Sorry, guys, but I'm going to have to get going, too." Thad flashed a sheepish look. "I promised a friend I'd would stop by later."

"A friend, huh." Masters nudged Morgan. "What's her name?"

"Maybe another time. Thanks for everything, David. This has been great."

Morgan felt a twinge of jealousy. *That should be me.*

"My pleasure. Come by any time."

"Thanks for coming, Dad. This has really been a terrific day." Then the unexpected happened. Thad gave him a warm embrace. "I love you."

"Love you too, son. Drive careful. I'll see you later." Morgan's heart pumped with a ferocious joy. His son loved him after all they had missed together.

As the door closed behind him, Masters asked, "Can you stay for awhile and have a drink?"

"I'd love to." Morgan couldn't stop smiling. He felt an energy he'd not experienced in years.

They picked up several plates and moved into the kitchen, then drifted toward the back of the house with drinks. The two men sat silently by the pool overlooking the Gulf, a scintillating sunset providing serene entertainment. Morgan felt something that he could only describe as peaceful exuberance. It was strange but not unpleasant.

"I guess a legacy is a lot like a sunset," Morgan said, sipping his drink. "It's there every day but not always appreciated."

"Damn, that philosophy degree wasn't wasted on you."

"Thanks for taking time with Thad. He seemed like a new person today." It wasn't a grudging thanks. Morgan realized that Masters had no ulterior motives; he cared enough to act and encourage.

"We just spent time together talking. Nothing special."

"Thanks all the same. It sure helped him realize we have had some good times together."

"You did that; not me. When he saw you with Maddie, being *yourself*, he remembered."

"Nonetheless, I think you helped him realize some of what I've tried to give him."

"My father taught me how to write an impressive signature," Masters said, drifting into a melancholy tone. "I imitated the sweeping capital letters he'd used in his name. The 'M' was majestic. I learned to mimic his style for the 'D' in my name. His first name was Lowell. The 'L' always looked like a monarch's pen had stroked the page. He got me to believe in myself. I was blessed beyond measure by a simple man who gave his children all that he had: love, confidence, and integrity.

"I always felt like I'd been created for a purpose that I was destined to discover. That idea shattered when I was nine. My father died." Masters didn't elaborate. He merely paused in silent observance, speechless. His face contorted as though a nightmare had grasped his throat. "Then Del Daisin entered our lives. Daisin was a greasy low-life. An abusive alcoholic. He manipulated and controlled my mother through her heartbreak. He raped my sister and beat my brother with a board."

Masters's account of his history was as though it had happened to someone else, someone he didn't know or care about. Morgan knew that lack of feeling well. He'd built numerous walls to avoid ugliness and pain.

"When my mother died a year later, Daisin disappeared. My brother and sister and I moved from foster home to foster home. Eventually, my brother ran away and my sister married her high school sweetheart. I prowled the area in the hopes of fulfilling my burning desire for revenge. At seventeen, I caught up to Daisin. He'd been in and out of prison. He was then homeless and destitute. I put him through mental and emotional hell. He knew who I was. He knew how we'd suffered. I made him relive every moment of our torment."

Masters's face took on a faraway look. "Then I hung him from a beam in an abandoned building—after forcing him to write his own suicide note. His hands were a bloody mess from using an iron bar to engrave the word into the concrete floor. 'Sorry.' No one ever suspected it was anything but the suicide of a mentally disturbed ex-con. I'd avenged my family, yet I felt no satisfaction. My heart was filled with darkness and malice. I became the same man I'd tortured and murdered.

"Then I joined the Navy," he went on confidently, "determined to make something of my empty life. That's when I discovered the worst part of my brutal crime. I wanted to kill again. I wanted to excel at killing. I entered SEAL training."

The story was a slap, a wakeup call. *Whoa, we're not that different.* Morgan hoped his face had not revealed his astonishment. *Shit, if he could overcome his love of killing then he might be able to help me. But he didn't say he'd overcome it.*

Masters shook himself as though waking from a dream. "Then God stepped in."

"You mean Jesus?" Morgan asked curiously.

"More of a black-haired beauty," Masters smiled. "I mean my wife; Jesus would come and go later." He suddenly changed the subject. "By the way, have we sublet your house yet?"

"Yeah, Mr. Hafley informed me late last week that someone had leased it."

They clinked their glasses.

"How did you overcome your thirst to kill?"

"My wife was a doctor who specialized in Post Traumatic Stress Disorder. She recognized it in me while we were dating. She could needle with the best of them. 'Something happened to you I know it. Tell me.' She would always say.

"For a couple of years I kept feeding her my boilerplate answers. You know the stuff we make up to lie to ourselves. But she just kept digging. 'Something happened to you, something shocking or traumatic.' She recognized the telltale flashbacks and the anesthetized state.

"Finally I broke down and let it all out. For me, the memories came as an ephemeral feeling, like a vague sense of being diseased. I was terrified that I would never find who I could become. The nightmares were horrific, old demons from childhood, Daisin torturing my family. I could meet someone and experience a waking nightmare, a flashback that I could taste, that made my skin crawl. They were so vivid, just like reality. It frightened her, but she understood.

"I felt guilty and embarrassed. She brought me out of that fog. She helped me see who I could become and walked with me there."

"Now that Anahita is gone my biggest problem is knowing who to trust. Since her death, I've withdrawn. I've spoken more with you tonight than I have in years."

"Why is that?"

"I see we are a lot alike."

"How did she die?"

"We were in Lebanon working with a Christian medical relief organization. The world had gone crazy. No one felt safe in Europe or the Middle East. Terrorists struck everywhere—Paris, Lisbon, Ireland, Greece, two-hundred-forty-one Americans and fifty-eight French soldiers had been killed in Beirut."

"So why did you stay?"

Masters shook his head. "We were spiritually inclined and followed the teachings of Jesus. If we didn't help who would? We didn't necessarily agree with the church but they were a means to an end—helping poor Palestinians."

"But you could have brought your family back to the States, to safety."

"For years I regretted not leaving. I did enough soul searching for two lifetimes. In the end, I realized that it was right for us to stay there. What would leaving have taught my son? He was nine-years old and already in love with the idea of helping people. How would Ana have felt if I denied her the right to live how she wanted—caring for those who no one else cared? *Ahura Mazda.*" Masters spoke those final words with great reverence.

"The uncreated creator of everything from Persian myth—the good and wise god," Morgan could only assume Masters was calling on the ancient deity.

"It was my son's name, a wonderful name for a wonderful boy."

"A good name is more desirable than riches." Morgan spoke the words while his heart began to break.

"The name of god is a strong tower." Masters nodded.

"We had gone to the market in Beirut on a crisp March morning. My family and I were buying fruit and vegetables for a dinner with friends. The falafel, the spices, the bread—the gritty air, and animal smells—there is nothing quite like a middle eastern market. Animals and people press uncomfortably close for western sensibilities arms flailing voices rising in negotiation. I had wandered a few stalls away to look at some tools. I didn't notice that they were drifting through the crowd in the opposite direction.

"I'll never forget the smell and the sound of those next few minutes. It is beyond reason—beyond hatred.

"I heard cheering and looked up the street toward my family. Flags made it clear that Hezbollah leadership was somewhere nearby in the market. I tried to push through the surging crowd.

"A dirty white sedan came screeching around a corner. I heard screams and the crackle of gunfire. People began pushing against me looking for shelter from the attack.

"The car erupted in a ball of flame. The concussion flattened the crowd in a deafening roar. As I pushed myself upward, I heard nothing, my eardrums still concussed from the explosive pressure. I looked toward the spot where I had last seen my family. A man was moving through the wounded doing what looked to be triage. It was Hafley. I staggered toward him through the debris, falling over bodies, dragging myself along to save my family. Shards of glass and twisted metal were everywhere. I saw pieces of cloth that used to be clothing, a shoe with part of foot in it. And toys, oh my god, I saw toys. How could anyone do such a thing to babies?

"The closer I got to Hafley the more horrific the scene became. There were no longer bodies but only grisly pieces of flesh and bone. I'll never forget the stench of blood and death mixed with burning diesel."

"I remember that," Morgan interjected. "Buckley was taken eight days later."

Masters nodded. "The fucking CIA murdered my wife and son along with seventy-eight innocents. Buckley got what was coming to him. I would kill them all if I could— Hezbollah, the CIA, all of the fucking terrorists and spies.

"Eighty people died and Hezbollah walked away without a scratch. They are animals."

"And what about Hafley, what was he doing there?"

"He didn't seem nearly as stunned as everyone else. Like I said, he was moving through the victims doing triage. It was odd though, he seemed to be searching for someone. When he saw me, he waved and started toward me. Gunfire broke out and he dragged me kicking and screaming into a nearby shop where he promptly knocked me out. That was the last time I saw that street. Not even a glimpse of my beautiful Ana or my boy. *Men Anahata*." Painfully Masters's breathed the words and thumped his chest, rocking ever so gently. A single tear slipped down his cheek into his beard.

Morgan felt embarrassment in the incredibly private moment. "I'm so sorry for your loss. I don't know how you've managed to stay sane."

"Sometimes I wonder if I have. Then I remembered the saying, the night hides a world but reveals a universe."

"Was your wife American?"

He nodded. "Naturalized citizen, she was born in Iran."

"Had the CIA or the State Department ever contacted you? I mean prior to the bombing?"

"No, why?"

"Just wondering." *Hafley was looking for Masters. They must have thought he was working for the other side.*

"So after that you and Randall teamed up to start the Ultraist Group?"

"Well not exactly, Randall helped me with funeral arrangements and got me out of the country. He must have had some powerful connections."

"Yeah, I would agree with that."

"Anyhow, I came back and did quite a bit of soul searching and started the Ultraist Group to honor my family and to carry on our vision. Randall showed up right when I needed a chief of operations with international experience. Fortuitous I think."

"I couldn't agree more. David, I'm touched that you have opened your home and your life to me. Sorry to say I have to go in to work tomorrow."

"No problem. We don't want to disappoint Randall. Don't work too hard. Thanks for coming. I haven't had such good company in years."

Chapter 34

Friday, November 29

Levi sat at an expansive conference table as the team drifted into the room. The smell of fresh coffee and bacon did nothing to placate the malcontents. Even Levi had a tired it-is-what-it-is expression. He took a long pull on his coffee washing down a bite of doughnut. "Help yourselves to breakfast."

"Coffee, just give me coffee," Nancy squealed with characteristic melodramatic humor.

"I really appreciate you all coming in this morning. If we work hard, we'll be out of here by ten-thirty. We just need to wrap up a few things so I can prepare an update for Mr. Hafley."

The group divided according to the natural selection process. Cheerful utterances about the pay and food mixed together with groans and moans about bed. Overall, they were focused, ready to finish their work and leave.

Levi wiped the coffee from his lips. "Just to be clear, you can take a comp-day in place of today. And I've arranged for an additional compensation day." He paused. "And you're being paid time and a half for eight hours today."

"Cool!" Nancy spouted as she moved toward the table. "I told you we were going to love this guy."

As the others made their way to a seat, Levi began the meeting. "Dick, I want to thank you for all your hard work and the extra hours you've put in to get this project off to a smooth start. We couldn't have made this kind of progress without you."

As always, Dick simply nodded in acknowledgement and continued munching on a Danish.

"Each of you has done an excellent job. The start-up of this project couldn't have gone any better, and I couldn't have asked for a better team. Jan, would you give us your overview of the phone record research?"

Jan flashed through the facts as they displayed on the overhead. "We performed basic scans of all employees, doing further research on the red flags and TUG insiders." Her presentation was succinct. She pointed out a few figures along with several interesting facts. "All of the pertinent data was extracted and given to Dick for upload into the data cube. It surprised me that this level of work could be done with so little manual effort. It's a great tool."

"Thanks, Jan. How about you, Nancy? Tell us what your analysis of email and flat files has turned up."

Nancy gave a report echoing Jan's in both content and length.

"Michelle, can you pull up the Analyst's Note Pad and give us a first look at the relational data map?"

The screen filled with an extensive diagram. "As you can see, through correlating all of the data, we've identified numerous potential threats. If anyone wants to read the details, this binder contains a compendium of reports." She pointed toward a four-inch ring binder innocuously labeled 'Read Book.' "Three of the most dangerous threats have been designated as threat threads." Three boxes on the diagram turned red. "Based on their backgrounds and activities, we'll recommend that Mr. Hafley move quickly to investigate them. For the sake of time, we'll just briefly look at those three. I'll hand it over to Gillian for that."

"Thanks, Michelle," she said. "Given the dual criteria of searching for signs of corporate espionage and government saboteurs, we've come up with the following three possibilities." Three pictures flashed on the screen. "Jim Meyer, Tom Black, and Mark Holter. Each has his own unique story."

God, I'm glad I didn't show up on this report. She thought. That would have been a disaster.

A scruffy haired guy in his late twenties popped up on the screen. "Jim Meyer is employed by Tampa PD. He's an undercover cop. He's openly volunteering at our Tampa free clinic. He has no family ties and was extremely hard to research. Which is probably one of the reasons he was red-flagged."

"He's just a cop who's volunteering his time," Nancy quipped. Obviously, she didn't like where this could lead. "We can't prove that he's doing anything other than volunteering."

"I agree," Gillian replied. "He's the least likely of the three, but that alone may mean that we need to keep an eye on him.

"Mike Walker is an agent with the DEA whose real name is Thomas Black. Mr. Black's actions have made it clear that he's trying to infiltrate TUG at the highest possible level. Unfortunately, his goals aren't clear. It's possible that he's part of an interagency operation. Any questions?"

The room remained silent.

"Finally, we have another TUG member operating under an alias. Mark Holter is an undercover ATF agent going by the name Pete Banyon. Holter is the most interesting of all, since TUG is a pacifist organization. However, his presence, combined with Tom Black, gives credence to the idea that there's some sort of interagency operation underway. That's about it."

Jan shook her head. "This seems crazy to me. I don't see how there's enough of a thread here to determine anything."

Levi responded. "I know it feels that way, but remember, we're not saying these guys have done anything wrong. We're simply saying they bear watching and further investigation." He paused. "Are there any other questions or comments? No, okay. Thanks, everyone, you've done a great job. Your analysis has allowed us to identify potential threats. As I said before, Mr. Hafley will use the maps to determine the credibility of these three and to decide what action he may want to take."

Gillian sat listening, thinking about Hafley's recent tirade and Bradley's suicide. She had a bad feeling about these three men and wanted to work out a plan to protect them.

Levi closed the meeting. "These are definitely the prime candidates for our security leak. I'm sure Mr. Hafley will be pleased with your work. Have a good weekend."

Chapter 35

Shadows stole across the lawn, preparing for their final sprint to the east. Color-coordinated perfection mocked Morgan as he sat on Liz's lanai. Ghosts spoke from every leaf and petal whispering, *You are a failure.*

Why had Deb shown up? Why had she said all that bullshit comparing him to his father? Why could he confront her about the mission but not his father. Months of discontent gave birth to realization. He was conflict-avoidant.

Absurdity of absurdities, a man who could kill without remorse, fled from turmoil. Killing was a job to him. Angst gave him the heebie-jeebies; but death, no problem.

Since boyhood, he'd excelled at school, sports, everything. His father had demanded perfection. Morgan saw excellence as the road to love and affection. In his father's world, unhappiness was the result of failure. Failure sprang from a lack of effort and execution.

After his mother had died, relationships had become a relentless cycle of demand, capitulation, and finally, defeat. Experience had led him to suspect he would never find anyone to accept him, warts and all.

True to form, he didn't erect simple walls, but ramparts to battle against imperfection and failure. In his mind, a life of loneliness was better than humiliation. His walls protected him from the distraction that kills and kept him in the mushin way. If he dropped his guard, he might drown among the limitless humiliating possibilities of life. His imperfections would become apparent to all.

What had seemingly kept him safe during his formative years now imprisoned him in oblivion. His efforts hadn't led him to enjoy his father's love and acceptance. He prayed his own son would never feel such rejection, but he knew it was too late.

He'd become what he hated, his father—the one thing he'd sought to avoid. David Masters had gotten beyond that, and he could, too.

There, on the patio of a modest Florida home, Morgan began his journey toward true humanness.

He couldn't blame anyone but himself for where he was and what he'd become. The responsibility was his alone. He'd gotten into this line of work to please his father, but no one had forced him. He'd made the choice. He'd also made the choice to be a people-pleasing, conflict-avoidant jackass who'd tried to keep his family in a test tube, like an OCD scientist.

Storm clouds loomed on the horizon. Aches and pains, trouble seeing fine print; all described him more than he cared to admit. For about a year, he'd operated on borrowed time. The end of the game would soon be upon him. They'd push him to a desk job, or a younger, faster version of himself would kill him.

Something gave inside.

He needed a complete and absolute change. This was it, his last assignment. He would retire and begin to search for the soul he'd offered up on the altar of patriotism and duty.

For the second time in a matter of minutes, he uttered a prayer to the divine for help and guidance, knowing a simple prayer wasn't enough; he needed to do the next right thing. He had to finish this assignment; he had to establish his willingness to work with the rogue members of TUG. The easy way to win Hafley's confidence would be to eliminate the three threats identified through the employee analysis.

Yet he sensed something wasn't right with the operation. Hafley had inside information that clearly came from the National Program Office. He thought about his time with Masters. David had more than ample cause to hate and attack the government. *Why had Hafley sought him out in Lebanon? Who was Hafley?*

His job demanded deception, but honesty would be his only hope with Thad. He was determined to stop living like a machine. Yet brutality was necessary to convince Hafley of his complete cooperation. Caught between two worlds, he felt like a sacrifice to both. He didn't care; he'd start to do the right thing.

Inspiration struck. *Deb wouldn't like it, but fuck her.*

He made all of the necessary arrangements. As he killed the lights on the lanai, he felt invigorated with the idea of *not* killing.

Chapter 36

Saturday, November 30

The security pad beeped as Thad opened the front door. "I'll be spending the weekend with friends on campus. I'll talk to you later."

Morgan peered through the master bedroom doorway. "No problem. I'm going in for a meeting this morning, and then I have a number of errands. I'll be up that way later. Maybe I'll give you a call."

Thad started to pull the door closed. "Don't bother; I'll be in Ybor with my friends."

"Hey, I love you, buddy." The term of endearment seemed hollow and forced.

"Yeah, me, too." The door clicked shut.

He listened as Thad's dilapidated G20 left with its mufflers howling. He smiled, remembering his own Pontiac Lemans with glass-pack mufflers. Those had raised the neighbors' hackles. They weren't so different, he and his son.

He headed to the office for his meeting with Hafley. For the first time in recent memory, he felt nervous.

Chapter 37

Gillian entered the auditorium contemplating that this precious period of her life might end soon. Instinct told her that Levi's presence signaled an end to the status quo. She was troubled in spirit. This had been her Camelot, her awakening. She longed to make it last forever.

She struggled against her attraction to Levi. David was clearly maneuvering them toward each other. Her training and background led her to believe that David was naïve where Levi was concerned.

Gillian's feelings for David were platonic. Romance and fiery passion didn't figure into it. It was something deep, abiding, and pure, the love of a pupil for the master. His ease with the universe and his expressions of reality brought a satisfying intimacy. His bewitching descriptions and demonstrations of the evolved life created a tender yearning in her soul, not a yearning for the man but for his reality. She'd seen firsthand his strength of character and dogged determination as he moved toward the realization of his dreams. Yet his meekness made her constantly worry for his safety.

The thought panicked her. Time was running out. She could feel it. Once this operation was over, She'd have to make a decision. Her life couldn't remain the same.

Dread enveloped her racing heart. She forced a change of focus.

I need to know Levi's plans soon; today, if possible. What is he doing? Is he an ex-Navy SEAL, a government agent gone rogue? That's what her supervisors said. It didn't feel right, but it was the only concrete report she had.

David began to speak as she took her seat. "This morning, I'm calling for action. The human race is at a critical juncture. National and global events force us to examine our way of life.

"Humanity is racing toward failure. I'm not referring to a cyclical financial slump brought on by poor economic practices and execution. We're facing an irreversible global calamity brought about by the confluence of resource depletion, environmental degradation, and overpopulation. Our oil and coal won't last another century. The use of fossil fuels has set off an unstoppable chain reaction in the environment. The global population stands at a fulcrum, which, once crossed, will plunge our ecosystem into overload."

Chapter 38

Morgan stood as Hafley and Markus entered the conference room for the briefing. Enigmatic and unreadable, Hafley baffled him. The intelligence he'd received on him was inaccurate, at best. The man's life was an abyss, devoid of information. Hafley seemed to know everything about Morgan's past, while appearing to have lived an unsullied life. Hafley held all of the cards from an intelligence perspective.

Nothing from the most recent report matched what McDonnell had stated about Hafley at the operational briefing. A mole had manipulated data in support of the radical faction within TUG. But who was it?

He didn't waste time. "Morning, gentlemen, thank you for taking time to meet. I think you'll be pleased with what we've accomplished so far." He turned on the projection unit and began his summation.

He quickly reviewed the TUG concerns and the reasons for commissioning the study. Afterward, he gave a brief overview of the processes used in the analysis.

Hafley became antsy and grew increasingly agitated. "Morgan, surely you've brought us here for more than an overview of things we already know."

"Yes, sir, I simply gave the background as a means of supporting the findings. On this next slide, you begin to see the results of our work." He displayed the relational data map. The screen contained several hundred boxes filled with fine print and crisscrossing lines of various colors and styles, along with a multitude of cross-references and footnotes.

Hafley gaffed. "Good God, man, who could possibly understand that monstrosity? I've seen eye charts that were more readable."

Morgan ignored the theatrics. "This detailed view indicates the existence of numerous potential threats to

TUG. Should either of you want to read the details, they're in this Read Book." He pushed a thick white binder toward the center of the table. "Three of the most dangerous threats have been designated as threat threads."

The next slide provided a first look at the unlucky designees.

"Now, that's more like it, Morgan."

Chapter 39

The G20 labored heavily as it ascended the northbound span of the Skyway. With its air conditioner broken months ago, music blared through the open windows in a vain attempt to gain precedence over the squalling muffler. The only cool thing about the car was that it had no payments, a fact wasted on nearly everyone but Thad Morgan.

Thad paid no attention to the traffic as he descended toward the St. Pete's side, until the clunker next to him jolted his driver side door.

"What the fuck?" He leaned out the window. "You fucking idiot, where did you learn to drive?"

The driver made a face as if to say 'sorry', and signaled him to pull off at the fishing pier exit.

Thad pulled over at the bottom of the ramp. He might have actually enjoyed the sight of Tampa Bay sprawled across the horizon if hadn't been for the collision.

The guy from the clunker parked weird, pinning him against the bay with no way out. As the man got out of the car, he realized something was wrong.

He'd been so upset about the accident that he hadn't noticed the other cars pull off with them. One blocked his route up the causeway, while the other kept would-be intruders at bay. The driver of the clunker had opened his trunk and was searching for something.

I'm being robbed by drug addicts.

"Hey, man, here's all my money and credit cards. Please, just take it. I don't want any problems." He held out the items but there was no response from any of them. The driver mumbled, as if he'd lost something important.

Forgetting the other cars, Thad shifted from self-preservation to rescuer as he realized the man might be mentally ill. He moved toward the back of the car with a purpose. "Hey, are you okay, man?"

No sooner had he cleared the end of the trunk than powerful arms restrained him from behind. The world began to melt as potent drugs flowed into his system via a well-aimed needle. The last thing he remembered was being sucked into a trunk-like black hole.

Chapter 40

Hafley took on an odd, excited expression as Markus's phone vibrated across the conference table.

"Markus here." He held his hand over the mouthpiece. "This will just take a minute. Okay, report." Markus sat nodding and listened to the caller. "Perfect, well done. Secure the package and report back in." He snapped the phone closed. "Sorry for the interruption, but that was important. Please continue, Professor."

"We believe that these three men, Jim Meyer, Tom Black, and Mark Holter are all potentially involved in espionage or sabotage. Jim Meyer is an undercover officer with the Tampa police. We believe he's hiding in plain sight. Tom Black, known to TUG as Mike Walker, is an agent with the DEA. And finally, Mark Holter, operating under the alias of Pete Banyon, is ATF. The presence of these three indicates some sort of interagency operation aimed at crippling TUG." Morgan paused for affect. "Any questions?"

The room remained quiet and non-committal.

Chapter 41

David paused as if deep in contemplation. Something was different about his speech this morning. A strange sense of urgency permeated the message and the audience.

A shiver ran down Gillian's spine and the hair on her arms rose as she listened. *Was David calling for a revolution now?*

"Perhaps I'm being melodramatic. Have I 'gone off the deep end'," he made quotations with his fingers, "and become a conspiracy wacko? I'm gravely concerned for you, your families, our nation, and our planet. Unfortunately, global economic growth is faltering in nearly every sector. But the condition of our planet represents an opportunity. Solving our problems can revive the economy, but first, we must find a new economic paradigm.

"We must act now to rein in socio-economic principles that deny our intrinsic human value and dignity. We must rise up and say enough to economic folly and oppression."

Chapter 42

Thad woke to muffled sounds and a throbbing pain in the right side of his skull. As he touched the side of his head, he felt sticky gauze and a sudden searing pain. He passed out again.

Chapter 43

David continued his homily.

"Look to old money and look to new money. That's where you'll find the generational leaders of America. Do you honestly believe that the President can stand against the likes of the controlling interest of Halliburton or GE? These men know money gives you power, and power is far more lucrative than money. Rockefeller, Ford, Carnegie, Morgan, Whitney, Astor, Rhodes, and Rothschild—these created both the Federal Reserve System and the Council for Foreign Relations. They run America, and with it, a global empire.

"We, the people, must topple the old guard and shift the economic paradigm. We must create a system that honors the intrinsic human value and dignity of every individual. We must rise up and say enough to economic and environmental folly."

Gillian's mind fought against the torrent of words and revolutionary philosophy. Something powerful was happening. The message seemed as though it went beyond politics or eloquence. Masters's speech felt like the warm glowing embers left after the bonfires of passion had been spent. Such embers drew people forward to partake in hidden knowledge, wisdom, and truth.

"The history of the human race is one of oppression. Can the cycle be broken? Can we, as a race, align ourselves with the divine to the degree that we can be freed from the cycle? Equal justice for all, equality of all, and tolerance must become the hallmarks of human society. Let us unite and ensure that educational opportunities are truly provided to all, adequate housing is provided to all, food is provided for all, and healthcare is provided for all. These are basic human needs that should be met based on our shared human dignity. We can't stand idly by while humanity self-destructs. We must forsake the fear of losing what we've accumulated.

We must think of future generations who'll have nothing if we don't change our thinking and behavior.

"Native Americans made decisions in light of their affect on the seventh generation. If left unchecked, what will our current human crisis do to our grandchildren's grandchildren? Will they be on the brink of extinction? Will we deliver them an unlivable environment? Will the earth be capable of supporting our grandchildren's grandchildren? Are we the most selfish generation in history? Are we the generation that saw what should be done but wouldn't do it because the cost was too high?

"Who will not act on behalf of their progeny? Who will stand against corporate and government abuses and call for a redress of grievances."

Chapter 44

Thad had lost all concept of time. How long had it been since the accident? What day was it? Where the fuck was he?

Thunk, ca-thunk, ca-thunk, thunk, ca-thunk, ca-thunk.

He wasn't sure if the rhythmic pounding came from inside his head or if it originated beyond the four steel walls of his prison.

Chapter 45

Morgan moved his presentation toward its logical conclusion. "All right then, let's move on to recommendations."

The next slide simply had the word RECOMMENDATIONS printed on it. "Before I begin, due to the nature of this topic, I won't give recommendations in writing. In addition, Mike, I need to know how often these rooms are swept for electronic surveillance devices."

Markus seemed perturbed. "The room is clean as of eight o'clock this morning."

"Then I'll speak plainly. We need to get rid of these three men as quickly and as quietly as possible."

"Do what you need to, said Hafley. "I want them out of the organization by the end of the day." Without another word, Hafley and Markus stood and moved toward the door.

Even if he'd recorded the conversation, it was ambiguous enough and could be interpreted in numerous ways.

On his way out, Markus picked up the Read Book and once again flashed a broad smile. Morgan found it disturbing.

Chapter 46

Gillian left the auditorium and staggered toward the car, her mind a demolition derby of conflicting thoughts. She never noticed the sedan that slid into traffic behind her.

Chapter 47

As he skidded the seventeen-foot Whaler onto the trailer, Jim Meyer reflected on the rest of his weekend. He'd given up on modern fish-finders in favor of his new Zen fishing technique. His buddies on the force had said he'd gone crazy, but he felt better just enjoying the environment rather than conquering it. He could put up with less fish and being called a loser if it made him less irritated and uptight. He enjoyed the sun and solitude while he reflected on his newfound spirituality.

He'd discovered a profound sense of purpose and belonging by helping Tampa's less fortunate citizens at the free clinic. He was little more than a gopher, but it gave him great satisfaction.

He looked up from the wench and noticed several suits approaching. As he straightened, he felt a hard cylindrical object press against his clavicle.

A dark suit wearing sunglasses spoke across the trailer hitch. "FBI, Mr. Meyer. Come with us."

"What the fuck is this? Show me some ID."

The suit dutifully presented a badge, giving him a nice long look.

"You guys are so fucked; I'm a cop, for God's sake."

"We know. Just come with us quietly, please."

As a straight cop who played by the rules, his instinct screamed for him to run, but circumstances dictated otherwise. Wedged between the trailer and the truck, with a gun in his back and two armed men in front, his escape options were limited. If he dropped, they'd only pounce before he could even roll. He slowly raised his hands. "Okay, okay. You care to read me my rights?"

"That won't be necessary." The handcuffs clicked. "You're not being arrested."

"What?"

"We just need to speak with you in private."

They patted him down, spun him around, and walked him toward a waiting panel van.

"Hey, what about my truck. My boat?"

"Don't worry. We'll impound them."

"Great, you guys are so fucked."

"We know. Just get in the van."

Morgan watched as the van drove away. "And that makes three."

To complete the illusion, he dialed 911 and reported an abduction at the Picnic Island Park near Port Tampa.

The old Dodge pickup rolled to a stop at the park entrance. He could afford a loose tail. After all, he knew exactly where the van was headed.

Thunk, ca-thunk, ca-thunk, thunk, ca-thunk, ca-thunk.

Several ships stood at the pier. Only one showed activity on it, moored next to a ten-story conveyor system. The ship's hold unceasingly belched loads of gravel destined for a nearby pre-stressed concrete plant.

Thunk, ca-thunk, ca-thunk, thunk, ca-thunk, ca-thunk.

There appeared to be no other activity, just one lonely tug berthed at the wharf. He turned onto West Commerce and headed toward Gandy Boulevard.

The van drove into the desolate rural farmland east of Tampa, passing abandoned orange groves waiting to be bulldozed in the name of progress, then turned onto the nearly deserted main street of a nameless town. Before tourism had demanded a new highway, the town had been on the main route from Tampa to Orlando. Paint peeled from the white clapboard buildings lining the street. The drug store had closed in the wake of big box deployment. Gas pumps stood forlorn before a mom-and-pop store and diner, with GONE FISHIN' scrawled in white shoe polish across the filthy windows.

The van pulled onto a hard-packed sand path and wound its way toward an abandoned warehouse near the CSX tracks.

Firmly planted in a chair, Jim's assailants removed his black hood. Despite the halogen floodlights pointed at his head, he blinked. He recognized what appeared to be an interrogation room with mirrored windows. The suit who'd spoken at the boat ramp sat across a heavy wooden table. The room felt hellish.

"Cigarette?" the suit offered as he took one for himself.

"No, thanks. What the hell's going on?"

The suit was extremely relaxed, almost nonchalant. "How about a soda or glass of water?"

He was pissed but still in control. "Why am I here?"

"Your infiltration into the Ultraist Group has bumped up against another high-level government operation."

"What the fuck are you talking about? I'm not involved in any operation with …"

"Look, asshole, we're just doing our job. Apparently, you're in danger out on the street, and you have a guardian angel. Some guy named Morgan wants you alive."

"How could volunteering at a free clinic put me in danger?"

"You figure it out; you're a cop."

The suit rose and knocked on the glass. The door opened, and he stepped out. He leaned back into the room and said, "In a few minutes someone will be in to brief you on what you can expect. After that, we'll move you right away."

The door closed, leaving him with his incredulous thoughts.

It was a short move from the warehouse to the safe house. Still, the agents hooded him so he couldn't disclose

the location. He guessed the movements just for sanity—
right turn back on to pavement, left, left, and right onto
another unpaved path that wound and bumped for fifteen
seconds.

As predicted by his captors, the house had two other
occupants who were also in protective custody. Also against
their will.

Like so many old Florida homes, this one had grown
up around its various occupants over the years, a bathroom
here, a new kitchen over there, a fourth bedroom in the
back. Jim looked out one of the windows. The house had a
dank wrap around veranda with a two-seater swing
suspended from the ceiling. Live oaks, bamboo, and
brambles blocked all views of the road and neighbors.

He tried to slip out the back door.

A huge African American suit blocked his advance.
"Hello, I've been instructed to keep the three of you in and
everyone else out." He smiled broadly, but there was no
mistaking that he meant business.

"Nice to meet you, and thanks for your help."

He knew the front door would have similar security.

Chapter 48

Sunday, December 1

Masters took the call on the veranda overlooking the Gulf. His eyes didn't take in the stunning beauty of the infinity pool as it flowed into the serene sea.

"What have you got for me, Bill?" He paced between the pool and the house listening. "Do you think Morgan suspects? . . . How sure are you that your identification is correct? . . . So DNA testing bears it out. Twins?" Masters shook his head. "Any idea why the government never caught this?" He walked down toward the beach. "No one can know about this. If McDonnell or her brother suspect, all bets are off. . . . "So, you're sure this information is accurate? . . . "But we have no idea whether Hafley or Morgan know? . . . Okay, Bill, thanks."

He sat on the sand and watched the trailing edge of the sun kiss the Gulf. He suppressed his fury and contemplated his next move in complete awareness that the entire call had been monitored.

Chapter 49

Markus plucked the hat from the pizza delivery boy's lifeless body. As he opened the car door, the sickening smell of stale fast food and melting cheese belched forth. He waved the hat in a vain attempt to clear the stench from the Dumpster on wheels.

"What a loser that kid was." He doubted anyone would even miss him.

He pulled out of the secluded parking lot in Mango and headed east toward Seffner. Sunday evening traffic was light. It would be days or weeks before anyone found the kid's body.

Jim Meyer looked out the peephole. The area was clear and well lit. A thirty-something pizza delivery guy waited on the porch. He pressed himself against the wall, wishing for a gun. Experience told him bullets or a battering ram would come through at any second. "I didn't order any pizza."

"All I know is it's paid for. Even the tip. Some guy named Morgan did it over the phone. Besides, I've already come through your guards."

Meyer let out a long sigh and reached for the lock.

Markus unzipped the pizza thermal bag. Meyer never saw the gun or the slug that ripped through his heart. He staggered back and fell to the floor.

Straddling Meyer's bloody chest, Markus put another 9 mm in his head. He chambered another round and stepped over the still form.

"God, I'm going to have to wash this fast food smell off."

He moved quickly through the house, catching the ATF agent on the toilet. He put one shot cleanly through his right eye and another through the heart as the half-naked body teetered against the wall.

The DEA agent was making popcorn in the back of the house. He was dead before he hit the floor, one shot to the back of the head.

Chapter 50

Monday, December 2

Morgan was unusually distracted as he moved from the elevator toward his office. His weekend had been busy and he hadn't been able to contact Thad. As he moved through the gray cube farm, he didn't notice the quick glances filled with primal fear.

He stopped at a cube. "Hi, Dick, how are you today?"

Dick's eyes went wide. "I, ah, I-I'm fine. How are you?"

"I'm okay, I guess. I had a tough weekend."

"Oh." Dick looked away, barely opening his mouth. The sound came out somewhat involuntarily, as if he wanted to avoid further conversation.

"Are there any messages for me?"

"Yes, Mr. Hafley requested a meeting with you at eight-thirty. He said to plan for it to take all morning." Dick sat vacantly, in a near catatonic state. "I blocked your calendar."

"Thanks. Are you sure you're feeling all right. You look pale."

Dick shook his head, as if waking up. "I'm fine. It's just Monday, I guess."

Morgan walked into his office and closed the door, thankful he didn't have to use a back-story to explain his weekend or listen to some long, dreadful gripe about someone else's problems. If it hadn't been Dick he'd been speaking with, he wouldn't have even made the second inquiry.

He plopped down in his chair and mulled over a feeling that something wasn't right. "Damn it, I don't like having Thad around this op. It's too dangerous."

As he looked at his watch, he realized his fists were clenched and he'd been motioning and speaking aloud.

He still had fifteen minutes until his meeting with Hafley. Maybe he could reach Thad before he had to leave.

Voicemail for the fifth time in ten minutes. "Goddamn it, Thad, pick up." He snapped the phone shut and headed out the door.

Karen waved him into the luxurious suite. No one had time for small talk this morning.

Hafley motioned toward an overstuffed leather sofa. "Welcome, Morgan, have a seat," he said in a no-nonsense manner, then smiled. "You've had a busy weekend."

Obviously, the news concerning the three threats had pleased him. Morgan gave a tired, wry smile as he sank into the comfortable seat. He took note that Markus, or Beelzebub, as he'd come to think of the man, was present for the meeting also.

"Why don't you fill us in on your activities?" Hafley said.

Markus gave a strange smile as Morgan began to speak.

Morgan couldn't help but feel as though Markus knew something he didn't, but he let it go. "Let's just say that I've fixed your leaks." He launched into the back-story he'd prepared in advance.

As he finished his narrative, Hafley rose and stared out the south-facing windows, toward MacDill Air Force Base. "It's time you joined us, Morgan. We need someone of your caliber in our inner circle. As I mentioned the other day, few people in the world understand the true capability and significance of what can't be seen from these windows—the city under the bay."

"What do you have in mind?"

"Let's drop the pretense. We both know what I want—Echelon. The heart of the most sophisticated surveillance complex on the planet is seven miles to the south, down about a mile.

"The NSA has designated TUG as a national security risk. They're idiots. They have no idea what we can accomplish. They can't even track our communications. We

189

can replace this government in a day. In less than eight hours, I can render them blind, deaf, and leaderless." Hafley seemed to gain a megalomaniacal high from his speech. "And I can repeat that all over the world, Asia, Australia, Africa, Europe, and South America.

"A four and a half square mile underground labyrinth spreads out to the southwest of MacDill, halfway across Tampa Bay. Through our intelligence, we know there are several entrances located on the base and in south Tampa. We know the northeast piling of the Skyway is an emergency exit. The Skyway is the world's largest satellite receiving antennae functioning as the eyes and ears of a corrupt system. Soon, I'll take control of Echelon and destroy that system."

Morgan felt as if he'd been water-boarded. Only a handful of high-ranking personnel could have given Hafley that kind of information. McDonnell, his boss, would be on that list.

"It's an awe-inspiring human achievement. Our shadow government has created a network capable of intercepting nearly all global electronic communication, examining, and codifying it into categories for further analysis. It's the quintessential supercomputer."

"If you know all that, then you know Echelon is worthless without the NSA computers in Washington," Morgan said. "Even with them, you still need an army of analysts to sift through the data."

"You misunderstand. I don't want to have Echelon; I want to destroy it, along with the corrupt global oligarchy it enables. But before I destroy it, I'll turn the beast against its masters."

"Did you know the accident that took out the original Skyway was staged in order to create the main antennae that drives Echelon? The builders hadn't intended for anyone to get hurt, but things went wrong. Thirty-five people plunged to their deaths when they wiped out that span to make way for the Echelon complex." Hafley smiled and shook his head. "Fucking morons didn't think there would be traffic at 6 a.m. Can you imagine?" He gave an involuntary chuckle.

"There are several other escape exits from the facility, and thanks to General Haddon, we know the precise location of each. Obviously, the main entrance is in the central command building on the base. That would be impossible for us to take out. But by a strange twist of fate, one of the auxiliary exits is right next door to your house on Treasure Circle."

That's how they'd accessed classified information. Haddon was a conspirator. He couldn't help but wonder what could have turned the general.

"Won't it be ironic when the same system they've used to monitor and manipulate is used to track them down and orchestrate their deaths? Have you met Dr Unger?" Hafley veered the discussion in a bizarre manner. The digression made him appear even more unstable. "Mike, please invite Doctor Unger in."

Markus rose and left through a door on the east side of the suite. He returned within seconds, leaving the door ajar. "He'll be right in."

Morgan was shocked when a gaunt man shuffled into the suite. With shoulders slumped, head bowed, and hair unkempt, Unger looked more like a soon departing resident of an elderly care facility than a distinguished scientist in the prime of his life. The contrast between the images he'd seen in the briefing and the man before him was so great it felt like there had been a mistake.

He rose to meet the new arrival, extending his hand in greeting. "Doctor Unger, it's a pleasure to meet you."

Unger just shook his head and mumbled as he moved to the other end of the sofa. He pushed himself into the corner and drew his arms into his chest, assuming a preying mantis position. His eyes averted from the others in the room as he rocked ever so slightly.

His behavior indicated that he'd either been tortured or was living in a delusional state, maybe a little of both. Gone was the beautiful tan of his publicity "headshot." Gone too was the salt-and-pepper styled hair. It was a greasy jumbled mess of salt now. If he'd aligned himself with the radical faction of TUG, it had been through madness alone.

Hafley stood behind the man, a hand on either of his shoulders. He massaged them gently as he spoke. "Doctor Unger is the architect of the space shuttle computerized flight systems. He personally led the teams that developed and perfected the automated re-entry, decent, and landing capabilities. Isn't that right, Stevie?" he said in a derisive snarl.

Unger just sat rocking and shaking his head, warding off invisible demons of the mind.

"Doctor Masters and I agree on things down the line, with one key exception. I don't believe the transition to his utopian society can happen peacefully or 'by the people'. He believes in evolution and God. That's insanity. I believe God gave us intellect and the power to create for a reason. We need to make this happen. The only way Masters's society will be ushered in is through a benevolent dictatorship acting as an interim government leading to Masters's ultimate goal. The only thing that will wake the American people and cause them to rise up against the growing tyranny is an opportune crisis. And that is exactly what I plan to give them. Thanks to the Internet and David Masters, TUG is nearly twenty million strong and growing. That's twenty million dedicated and highly motivated people. Soon we'll be ready to strike and create chaos. Out of the ensuing anarchy, we'll see the birth of a new and glorious nation."

Hafley was insane, but well informed, outfitted, and quite determined.

"Do you know what GCCS is?"

Unger flinched, as if a demon had broken through his defenses and stung him in the neck.

"Ground Control Computer System—it's Stevie's baby. It's the tool that gives us the ability to create chaos. After

9/11, the government rushed to increase airline security. They kept the public's eye focused on new TSA measures and Homeland Security, which was just a ruse to distract everyone from their real solution, installing GCCS. GCCS gives its masters the ability to control the skies. Every aircraft can be controlled remotely. It was a great idea. With GCCS in place, the public would be safe from hijacking and terror in the sky. There was just one thing the government didn't take into account: paranoia. Unbeknownst to them, Stevie built a back door into GCCS. He didn't trust them, so he wanted to be able to take control from them should he need to do it.

"In a few days, the Air Force will complete retrofitting military aircraft with its own version of GCCS. With a smart phone or other portable wireless device, we can take over any aircraft in North America—passenger, cargo, or military. As soon as I take control, I can shut down the onboard monitoring device. The pilot won't even know the communication is coming from onboard his plane. Or, if I'm not feeling suicidal, I can do it from the ground. I just need the right frequency and a thin client, both of which have been graciously provided by my pal here. Shit, once you have the information about Unger's hack of GCCS, any kid with a wireless software development kit can write a small footprint wireless application protocol program. It's a home automation program for airplanes."

Hafley flipped open his cell. "Think of it; a low power CPU, almost no memory, a weak battery, and a tiny little screen. Yet I hold in the palm of my hand the power to rule the world."

Clearly disturbed, Unger rocked more aggressively. He mumbled the same thing repeatedly but Morgan couldn't make it out. It sounded like a rhyme or limerick. He put the thumb and first two fingers of each hand together and alternately turned them, as though manipulating or twisting an object.

Hafley had been torturing the poor guy. Mixed in with the gibberish were several intelligible words, "Rose . . . key . . . tree . . . abbey." Nonsense dribbled from the once beautiful but now utterly destroyed mind.

Morgan reached out to comfort him, but Unger jerked away. He covered his ears and began to wail.

Hafley moved behind him, spoke soothingly into his ear, and massaged his shoulders. "It's okay, Stevie."

Unger quieted down. Morgan couldn't tell what the hell was happening.

"So, you want to take out Echelon and our corrupt government by accessing GCCS to control aircraft. But you're crazy if you think you can create a crisis big enough to cause the American people to rise up against its leaders. And why would they want to create anarchy. Why not just replace this government with one of their own choosing?"

"Did I say they would create anarchy? I'm sorry; I meant to say they'll be in anarchy, crying out for help. But there will be no help. That is, not until I think they're ready to receive help."

Morgan couldn't help but wonder at how ridiculous it all seemed.

Hafley moved his head up and down in a cocky, crazy way. "I'll create anarchy by striking every listening post attached to Echelon with flying bombs. All across the globe on one day, we'll strike them blind and deaf. France, the UK, Japan, Russia, China, Australia, and Germany, all hit at the same time. The most powerful governments in the world blinded; they won't be able to fly their military fleets. Strike the antennae, strike the escape routes, and destroy the facilities—one, two, three—it's all over. Since there will no longer be an effective means of tracking terrorist, those activities will shoot off the chart worldwide. Chaos will spread across the globe."

"Hafley, there's no way Masters will allow this. It's against everything he espouses."

"I don't give a shit what that fool wants. He thinks he can bring about change through pacifism. What an idiot." Hafley spat the words out like poison. He stood, pointing toward the Skyway. "While that base and bridge exist, Masters doesn't stand a chance of successfully overthrowing the current regime."

"Was Gandhi a fool?" Morgan posed. "How about Jesus? Was he a fool? Didn't they bring about real change without aggression?"

"So, you've really bought into his bullshit, haven't you?" Hafley sneered, "You're as stupid as he is, you dumb bastard. We'll take the city under the bay and use it against them. We'll create chaos. Once everyone is ready, we'll restore order."

The intercom buzzed. Hafley hit speaker. "Yes?"

Karen's voice was harsh as it filtered through the speaker. "The package you were expecting has arrived, sir."

"Thanks, bring it in."

"Of course, sir, right away."

Karen placed a large padded envelope on the corner of Hafley's desk. Without a word, she left the suite without making eye contact with anyone.

Hafley picked up the parcel and tossed it from one hand to the other, making his way around the massive desk. Gathering his thoughts, he opened a drawer, took a pair of scissors, and broke the seal. He sat down and pushed the envelope toward Morgan. "Let me be perfectly clear. I admire you and believe you have great potential within our organization. Hell, you could have a significant role in the New World Order."

"Why would I help you?" He half laughed but noticed an imperceptible moment of awareness flit across Unger's face.

Hafley ignored the question. "Did you do humanity a favor when you killed the bad in those three yesterday? You know you can be inextricably tied to those executions."

"I'm not worried about that."

"Maybe not, but you need to choose which side you're on: the winners or the losers."

"I've already decided."

"I thought you might say that, so I bought a little insurance." Hafley pointed toward the package. "Open it."

Morgan emptied its contents onto the table, then closed his eyes in an effort to erase what lay before him—a purple ear with a bloody earring in the shape of a winged circle with a heart in the center. Waves of nausea and despair came at him from every angle. He lost all orientation to time and space. He mouthed one word, "Thad," and began to cry.

Unger wailed, only this time, no one got up to comfort him.

"You fucking bastard. What do you want?"

"I want your full cooperation, which includes taking the rap for several nasty bits of espionage." Hafley turned to Unger. "Do you see, Steven? No one is immune, given the right leverage; not you; not Mr. Morgan."

"There's something else you should know and it seems like this is the time to make it clear."

Markus looked concerned as though some improvisation was happening.

Hafley turned back to Morgan, "You don't have a fucking clue who I am, do you? You're so stupid. Remember Skip Hutchins, the guy you left for dead?"

Morgan tried to put the facts together but nothing fit. "I didn't leave him for dead."

"You *did*. You left me for dead." Hafley gave an involuntary double blink. "I've known every move you were going to make from the beginning. You fucking puppet. Payback's a bitch, ain't it?"

"Did you say I left *you* for dead?" The reflex finally registered with Morgan. Skip had developed that blink in junior high school. In fact, he'd taken it on himself as a cool habit until his father had derided it out of him. He'd noticed it with Hafley before but couldn't placed it. *Hafley is Skip Hutchins.* "Skip?"

Markus expression soured. "Sir,"

"Shut up," Hafley, or Skip, turned on Markus. "Get him out of here, Mike. There's nothing worse than an imbecile."

Markus looked perplexed. "Which one?"

"Both of them, goddamn it. Get them both out of here."

Morgan staggered into his office and slouched into his chair. Things were out of control. He needed to get out of there and gain some perspective, find Thad.

The *St. Petersburg Times* sat on his desk. He stared at the newspaper in disbelief. The bodies of three men found . . . Seffner home . . . a gangland-style execution. The words swam off the page and fucked with his head. *Hafley, Skip, had found them and killed them. Skip was alive after all these years and he was Hafley.* It didn't make sense.

I'll be the only suspect. I set it up that way. All evidence points to me.

A mole at the highest levels of his organization had set him up to take the fall for all of this. Skip Hutchins was alive and looking for revenge.

He pulled the handset from its cradle. "Dick, notify everyone that we'll have a brief staff meeting at one-thirty."

He tossed the *Times* onto the conference table. "You can't seriously believe I had anything to do with this?"

No one spoke; no one dared to.

Dread and guilt had spread through the team. They all knew that the three men they'd identified had died over the weekend. No one knew why it had happened, but they knew how it happened. That answer stood in front of them.

Morgan left the room in disgust and panic. He had to get away and think. He needed help fast. Skip was alive and someone powerful was helping him.

Chapter 51

Fearful but needing answers, Gillian caught up to Morgan in the parking garage. Without a doubt, he was the most dangerous person she'd ever met. Even more terrifying, instinct told her that the killing was just getting started. She couldn't trust him anymore. *He's involved in all this.*

Shit, how can I approach him without getting myself killed? She couldn't just say, 'FBI, freeze.' She decided to play the relationship card.

He turned toward the clattering high heels of imminent confrontation, surprised to see Gillian charging up the ramp toward him. Her greeting surprised him even more.

"What the fuck did you do?" She slammed her fist into his chest. "You killed those three guys."

"I didn't kill anyone," he stammered. "I hid them. Don't you think it's time we were straight with each other? You know about the TUG private security force. Those three guys were the witnesses I needed to see Hafley prosecuted for his crimes."

While it was highly unlikely he'd been involved in the Benjamin Bradley incident, Gillian couldn't be sure. The TUG security team had conducted numerous questionable activities. "What are you talking about? You're so full of shit. Now you want me to believe you're an undercover cop?"

Her handler had told her that he belonged to a Special Access Program unit. Call it plausible deniability or discretion, either way, those units operated as black boxes. No one could see in and no information about personnel or operations ever came out. People lived and died within SAP groups as ghosts. As stereotypical as it sounded, people never left a group. They might become inactive for a short time, but if they tried to leave, they were dead.

Not even the FBI was privy to National Program Office information. SAP units operated without restraint, under cover of darkness. They were invisible.

Her thoughts berated her. *I've been falling for this guy. I can't believe I had feelings for someone who could kill at a moment's notice, without provocation.*

"Look, I'm part of an SAP operation to stop a global terrorist strike. Hafley did what I would have done in the same situation. He eliminated the hostile contacts and created a diversion."

"But why?" She was puzzled that he'd use the term *SAP*. Her cover was blown. It was the only explanation.

"Isn't it obvious? He did it to set me up. Now I'm completely under his control."

"You don't have to be." The words betrayed her desire to trust him.

"Unfortunately, I do. There're a couple of things you don't know."

His eyes pleaded and she caved. "Let's hear it." She still wasn't sure about trusting him, though. *Give me some insight into your plans.* She needed to drill down to his real reason for infiltrating the Ultraist Group.

"Come for a ride with me?" he said wearily. "It's not safe to talk here."

She nodded.

He reached in the glove box and pulled out a handheld RF detector capable of picking up high-end government-only frequencies. He scanned the cab, the fuselage of the truck, and the length of both their bodies.

Gillian was stunned when the scan revealed three LPD/LPI burst transmitters on her—a pen, a pendant, and one in the heel of her shoe. He held his finger over his lips and reached under the seat to pull out a large thermal grocery bag. He tossed the devices inside and rolled the bag up tightly. "Did you know those were on you? They're government-frequency, low-probability detection and interception devices."

The revelation was staggering. How the hell had that gotten into her shoe? *God, they've been in my house.* Anxiety dropped over her like a thick blanket. *Shit, I have to get Maddie and my mom somewhere safe.*

"They're the latest generation that utilizes ultra-high-frequency, direct-sequence-spread spectrum-signal technology. Only SAP groups can access those. We'd better throw our cell phones in here, too. Someone could track us through the chips."

He tucked the bag between the outer wall and a piling, where no one would find it.

Neither of them spoke as he drove out of the garage, into glaring sunlight.

***

"Should we keep line of sight on them, sir," the watch commander asked.

Hafley and Markus stood in the inner sanctum of the TUG security center. "No, let them have their private discussion," Hafley said. "We've got them exactly where we want them. When we're ready, they'll take the rap for everything."

"Pick them back up when they come in tomorrow morning," Markus said. "We'll just let paranoia do the work for now." Turning to Skip, he said, "It didn't take them long, did it?"

Skip's face twitched with delight. "Let them have this pleasant fantasy."

***

Morgan worked his way through several neighborhoods to ensure they didn't have a tail. Finally, he turned south on the interstate and pulled the truck off at the north end of the Skyway fishing pier, where he parked in a nearly deserted lot. He grabbed the RF detector off the seat and slipped it into his back pocket. "It has a line-of-sight range of five hundred yards."

They wandered silently along the little peninsula until they reached a sandy point looking across the bay, toward Fort Desoto. He wasted no time as he double-checked the RF detector and launched into his plea.

"A radical faction inside TUG is planning to use commercial and military aircraft as weapons to shutdown the country. Hafley laid the whole plan out to me earlier." He jerked his thumb over his shoulder. "That bridge is the main antennae for Echelon, the largest electronic communications gathering system in the world. Hafley wants to use it to take out our government and create anarchy." He paused to think.

"The NPO sent me here to identify and eliminate the radical faction of TUG. A mole inside the National Program Office set me up." He shrugged. "I don't have a credible alibi, nothing to back me up." He kicked at the sand. "In fact, all the evidence says I'm the lead conspirator."

"Why are you telling me all of this?"

"I know you're FBI. I need help. Someone inside my group has turned and thrown me under the bus."

"You think? I'm not stupid; you're the one who's turned."

"Why would I lie? If I'm the mole, why would I tell you any of this?" He sighed in exasperation. "Look, I'd have killed you already if I was what you suspect."

"Don't think I haven't thought of that." She pulled back her jacket to reveal a weapon. "I'll tell you why you're lying. You need me to get what you want."

"Hafley has Thad," he blurted out, then wept.

She touched his shoulder. "Are you sure?"

He nodded silently and pulled an envelope from his pocket. He choked out the words, "Hafley just gave me this."

She tilted it into the sun, looked away and looked again. She squinted and blinked, then retched all over Morgan's shoes.

"Oh, God." She threw her arms around him and held on.

Long minutes passed before she spoke. "What really happened to those three guys?"

"They were taken into custody by the FBI."

"The Bureau didn't participate in that op. I checked. We didn't have anything to do with it."

"Fuck . . . I told you there's a huge problem inside my unit. I arranged that op through the program. I have the confirmation numbers and everything." He stared at the sand and sea grass. Miniature waves lapped gently at their feet. "I'll admit I've struggled lately. For years, I believed in my work. I believed in our government and its work around the world. But over the past year, I've realized I can't keep doing this. They're wrong—plain and simple. But I'm no traitor.

"Last Friday night, everything started to come together. I realized it wasn't enough to think differently. I had to act different. I had to stop justifying my lifestyle and actions like some Nazi-prison-camp guard. The philosophy and actions of my organization are wrong. If I disagree with them, I need to act on that disagreement. So, I arranged to have those guys taken into protective custody."

She shook her head. "I'm sorry, but there's no record to corroborate your story."

He plopped to the ground and stared blankly at the RF detector. "I'm done. No more ops after this. I don't know what I'll do, but anything's better than *living* a lie."

"Unless something changes, you'll be living in jail."

"If that'll help me atone for what I've done to the people I care about, so be it." He sat, nodding his head. "I don't want to be an alarmist, but we have to get Maddie and your mother somewhere safe before they end up with Thad."

"What do you suggest? It's obvious Echelon is being used against us."

"Get a lot of cash. Take this scanner. Sweep your mom's car. Tell her not to use any credit cards or make any phone calls. She can't even have a cell phone with her. She can't call anyone that she knows. I have access to a cabin in North Carolina. As long as she doesn't speak to anyone and only uses cash, they should be safe there."

***

Morgan had to drive through two Mega-Mart parking lots before he found the right make, year, and color of car with a North Carolina plate. He swapped Mrs. Anu's plate with the unsuspecting tourist's.

He paid cash at the Kentucky Colonel, a sleazy by-the-hour motel on the strip. He secured the whole night even though he only needed a few hours. Then he slipped into a pharmacy and purchased black hair dye. Afterward, he crossed the north bridge over the river and stopped at a neighborhood basketball court. A lone teenager endured the steamy afternoon. Waves of heat radiated up from the asphalt as he approached the perspiration-soaked kid. "How would you like to make a hundred bucks?"

"Is it legal? I don't want any trouble."

"Yeah, it's legal. My mother-in-law has been laid up in the hospital. I need someone to help me get her car over there."

"You want me to help you get a car to the hospital for a hundred bucks? Where is it? Miami?"

"No, it's just across the bridge. I just want to pay enough so I can trust it to get there."

"No problem, man, I'll help you. When do you want to do it?"

"Right now, if you can."

"Sure, just let me call my mom."

***

The man who'd hired him to transport the car to the hospital pulled over at the corner of Second Street and Third Avenue East.

"Walk down Third to the traffic circle." He pointed down the block. Towering palms ringed the outer edge of the circle with their trunks the color of aged concrete. "There's a white two-story house on the southeast. It's the only two-story on the circle. You'll see a light blue Ford Crown Victoria in the driveway. Here's the key. Drive it over to the hospital and park it in the back of the lot." He gave him the key. "Here's your money and an extra ten for cab fare."

"Thanks, mister."

"Don't stop anywhere, don't talk to anyone, and don't brag about this. If you do, I'll kill you." The man didn't smile, nor did boy.

"Yes sir, I won't stop, won't talk, and won't brag. Got it." Obviously he was someone of above average intelligence.

Morgan watched as the boy got out of the car and walked up the street to the roundabout. Two houses were situated on the circle's island interior. One, a sprawling Florida ranch, had been converted into an odd duplex with a low, frowning roof. The other was abandoned, the grass high and the house neglected. Without a doubt, vermin of every type populated the place. The kid skirted the island wide and crossed the street.

Morgan inched the car forward to keep him in sight. His body language said he was spooked. Morgan recalled those deserted, eerie feelings that can descend on you at times like these. He hoped this wasn't a mistake. He could see the boy forcing his legs to overcome his paralyzing fear. Nothing stirred along the arc of the rotary, not traffic, not people, not the wind. *Come on kid you can do this.* Morgan felt his own heart fill with cold dread. The boy crossed Third

Street passing a single-story row of dilapidated green apartments resembling 1950's motel architecture. A screen door hung off-kilter on one hinge. A large Hispanic man leaned against the front wall, seemingly asleep on the two back legs of an old wooden chair.

The boy quickened his pace as the man looked up and brought the chair down on all fours. The kid rushed toward the two-story with the towering oak in the front yard. Morgan pulled forward and spoke to the Hispanic who had walked down the sidewalk to see what was happening. The light blue Crown Vic backed out of the drive and left the neighborhood. Morgan sped away.

***

Shortly after the car left the driveway, a taxi pulled up and honked the horn. Jean Anu came out with Maddie in her arms. The shaggy driver made her nervous as she got in. Filth covered every surface of the car. Mega-Mart bags covered half the back seat as though the driver lived in his cab. At the first traffic light, he turned and spoke through his scraggly beard. "Hi Jean, you and Maddie are safe now. We'll get you somewhere else until all this is over."

"Oh, my, Levi. Thank God, it's you. I'm so scared."

"There's a bag on the back seat for you. I've written out what you need to do. Do you see it?"

She turned to the mountain of Mega-Mart bags full of clothing, toiletries, and snacks. Gillian's loving touch was evident.

She searched through two or three bags before she found the yellow legal pad. "I found it."

"Good, can you read it to me?"

"Number one, dye our hair black. Number two, stay in the hotel until 9:30. It'll be dark by then. Call a cab, pay cash, have it drive us to the emergency entrance at the hospital on the west side of town. Number three, go inside, and sit for fifteen minutes. Once I'm sure the cab is gone, walk out to the back of the main parking lot. My car will be there with a North Carolina plate on it. Get in and follow your driving instructions."

"Do you understand the instructions?"

"They seem straightforward."

"Maddie, you and your grandma are going to play a game of dress up tonight, okay."

The little girl was thankfully clueless to any danger. "I like dress up."

"Jean, remember it's absolutely imperative that you don't call anyone on any type of phone. Don't use credit cards, bank cards, or checks of any kind. Only use the cash Gillian gave you. She and I are the only two who know where you'll be. We'll contact you when it's safe."

"Okay. She gave him a concerned look. "Please take care of her."

"You can count on it."

She smiled. This man loved her daughter.

Chapter 52

Tuesday, December 3

Morgan didn't sleep at all that night. He followed Jean and Maddie, using a broad-spectrum RF detector and fifth generation night-vision equipment. He'd directed Jean to use secondary roads rather than the highway and she'd done so without fail. The Florida landscape along these lonely stretches of road seemed impervious to light. He strained to see deeper into the blackness.

The night mirrored his predicament. He had to straighten this mess out for Maddie, Jean, and Thad.

The thought of Thad made him feel weak.

He pulled himself together and made a game out of the journey. He dropped back nearly a mile, watching the traffic and sky. Then he passed Jean, racing ahead to see if he could identify any predators waiting to intercept his charges. Most of the drive, he followed about four hundred yards back, close enough to monitor anyone trying to follow and listen.

He remembered a mouse he'd once seen when his family had lived in a dilapidated apartment, part of base housing at Norfolk. He'd ventured out one morning after a fresh snowfall and had discovered two sets of paw prints in the virgin snow, one small and one large. A field mouse had become a tabby's entertainment. In the tracks, he could see where the cat had repeatedly tossed the furry creature. As a boy, he'd been unable to empathize with the cycle of terror and hope that must have played out. The rodent seemed to have scampered off, only to have the tom pounce and fling it yet again into the air. Eventually, he'd come upon the creature lying lifeless in the bloody snow, a victim of destiny.

He empathized now. A silent opponent was manipulating him. He couldn't quite figure it out. Some clue was still missing. The memory made him think of Skip.

How did he survive? Where had he been? What was his real connection to Masters? Who was helping him? No answers just questions about his all-seeing assailant.

He'd never felt so off-balance, so disoriented. Of course, he'd never been on such a complicated mission. For years, he'd just collected the dossiers and dealt with identified problems. This assignment had sent him deep into something he couldn't comprehend—someone's sick game.

Convinced that Jean and Maddie weren't being pursued, he turned back at Lake City.

He thought about a traitor within the National Program Office. It had to be McDonnell. No one else could have accessed such a broad swath of information. Haddon could tell Skip about the city under the bay, but there was no way he was privy to SAP information. All clues pointed toward McDonnell. It had to be her. That was the only explanation for the intelligence Skip had accessed.

The possibility perplexed him. *What could have made McDonnell turn? Skip was using Thad to control me and he had something on Unger. Could he have something on her, too?*

As he approached home, he decided to pass by Gillian's place to give her an update. Even though it was three a.m., she opened the door as he came up the walk. Clearly, she hadn't slept. "Can we go somewhere and talk? I don't feel safe here anymore."

***

They drove in silence toward one of the barrier islands. Levi pulled off at a deserted fishing pier looking out over the Intracoastal, where the Gulf, bay, and river met.

"I think we're safe here. But just in case . . ." He pulled out the RF detector, performed a self-scan, and handed her the device. They were both clean.

The couple walked down the narrow strip of beach, away from lights. The cloudy moonless night created a treacherous pitch-black environment. Morgan used the gentle glow of the detector to light their way. A slight breeze produced a gentle clattering of palm branches. The salt air felt good after a sleepless night of worry.

Gillian was uncomfortable with the situation. "I had a face-to-face with my handler this afternoon and then again after Mom left with Maddie. "We know where Thad is, but he's so heavily guarded, we can't risk going in after him." She hoped Morgan wouldn't catch on and probe deeper.

"How the hell could you know where he is?" He was pissed. "Why didn't you tell me yesterday, at the bridge?"

"I didn't know then." *A little white lie won't hurt; I hope.* "My handler just told me."

"So, the Bureau witnessed his abduction and tracked him?"

As if on cue, the wind picked up, creating a clattering cacophony of branches. Even in the dim glow of the detector, she could see his ferocious expression. She prayed his anger was directed at the Bureau and not her. *Hell, I was furious when I found out they'd lost the boy.*

She took a deep breath and waited for the wind to die. "Apparently, we had you both under surveillance since you arrived. The Bureau didn't know what you were up to. We screwed up."

The wind dropped off completely and only the gentle lapping of the waves along the shore could be heard. "God, this is all so screwed up. Liz is dead, my son's been kidnapped, and God only knows who's tracking us right now." He shook his head in disgust. Sorrow crept into his tone. "I can't believe it. Just when I want to get my act together, everything goes to hell."

Gillian shrugged. "Maybe this is part of our path to awakening. As stupid as it sounds, try not to resist." She amazed herself. In the midst of all this, she was trying to fulfill her commitment to David. "Let what's happening be okay. You don't have to enjoy it. We just need to find a positive way to face it and then we'll understand what we're supposed to do."

"Great, we've become Zen fugitives. I've spent my whole life resisting and fighting. How the hell do I change now?"

They stopped and watched the sun peek over the horizon. It looked like a bright orange ball just below a vast band of storm clouds. The Skyway majestically spanned the mouth of the bay in the distance. Lamenting gulls pursued the fleet toward open water, their distant cries harmonized with the gently rustling palm branches. The village of Cortez sent her sons into the Gulf in hopes of a glorious catch. They would face a storm along the west coast of Florida today.

Gillian broke the spell. "Masters appears to be clean, just a man on a mission to save humanity from itself. Strangely enough, though, he openly claims to be the one who figured out how to beat Echelon. That claim opens him up to suspicion. I've been close with him for almost a year, but I don't see any indication of illegal activity."

"I agree. I've only known him a month, but if he's starting a revolution, it's of the heart not political. Echelon confuses me. How does he beat it?"

"Completely no-tech. It's genius, actually. He just doesn't use the systems monitored by Echelon. The amazing part is what he's been able to accomplish in creating a global communication network. It's required 'diplomatic' efforts on a Herculean scale. He devised a method of 'piggy backing' on the Hawala system to beat Echelon."

"But why?"

"Hawala is uniquely suited to this type of communication. As a relationship-based global money-transfer system, it doesn't have a logical infrastructure. The whole system leverages personal connections—trusted family ties and regional affiliations. As long as negotiable instruments are kept under ten thousand dollars, no one pays attention. In essence, it functions completely off the grid."

"That doesn't answer the why. If he's not a terrorist, why did he get involved with these people? I can tell he hates terrorists and spooks."

"He believes in personal privacy. He started using the network for communication only. People involved in Hawala were happy to make extra money with no financial exposure. Few carriers have been intercepted. Little to nothing is known about what's communicated. Masters took a page from DaVinci and developed an ingenious system for destroying documents before they fall into the wrong hands. With soluble paper and a special water pouch, they've prevented the capture of all messages. When a pouch is opened incorrectly, the lining breaks. The fluid releases and the message dissolves. We've caught several couriers and worked them over pretty good through the rendition process. They didn't know anything. They were pony express riders, plain and simple. Ignorant participants in black bag stuff."

"Don't you think you're being a little naïve? I don't think this is about personal privacy, more like a personal vendetta. I wonder if David could be using Hafley for something we can't understand."

"We know Hafley is leveraging the communication network to connect with the shadier organizations and individuals for his own purposes." Gillian appeared frustrated. "It's a shame Masters couldn't find other people to work with."

They turned back toward the parking lot. The beach remained empty. The salty gusts intensified as the storm approached from the west. Exhaustion and worry prevented either of them from appreciating the island community that had preserved its old Florida charm by banning high rises and franchised stores.

"The TUG security group is a different matter. Masters has nothing to do with it. In fact, he's unaware of its true nature. It's a small private army made of ex-special ops troops. At twenty-five hundred strong, it's a small brigade. They could repel quite an offensive if the need arose.

"Your information about Hafley's comments is the first specific evidence tying him to anything illegal. We've had lots of innuendo and speculation but nothing concrete." She contemplated her next words carefully. "I'm afraid without a wire, your information is worthless. You have every reason to lie.

"We've picked up bits and pieces of information through NSA analysis. It points to a plan to detonate a radioactive device near the capitol building. Whoever's orchestrating the TUG security group is staging an old Soviet suitcase bomb or some sort of dirty bomb. Apparently, they plan to take out as much of the elected government as possible. We suspect they're trying to invoke the Continuity of Government plan. If they can strike a fatal blow to the legislative, judicial, and executive branches, they could pull it off."

Levi seemed to come alive. "All right, let's make a plan. We need to get proof that Hafley gave the order to kill those men and that he's planning to attack U.S.-based targets. We have to get Thad out at the earliest possible opportunity, along with any other hostages they might have. Check out relationships for Steven Unger and Deb McDonnell, my boss. Hafley has something on them both.

"I'm sure he'll move soon. Otherwise, I don't think he would've let me in on his plans. He has to believe that it is too late for me to stop him. He waited for certain elements to come together, then selected me as the fall guy."

"My handler already has the information you shared with me," Gillian cut in. "He's working on ID'ing the mole in your organization."

"Fat lot a good that'll do." Morgan retorted. "We need to take Hafley down now. This is already out of control. We can't wait. We have to move on this by Sunday, at the latest. I may have to kill Hafley and take the rap for those three guys."

"Nonsense. If there's a mole in your organization, they're somehow involved in this. It won't end just because Hafley's dead. We need him to lead us to the others. No one's safe until we know who we're fighting."

Chapter 53

Morgan exited the elevator into what promised to be the longest five days of his life. His bloodshot eyes were the lone hint of the hell he'd endured over the last twenty-four hours. He ached to reach Thad and prevent further harm to him. The only thing that had staved off insanity was the activity he'd undertaken to protect Gillian's family.

An air of apprehension enveloped his staff. He marched straight into his office, called Karen, and arranged for a meeting with Skip.

***

Skip smiled effusively when Morgan entered the suite. "Welcome, Levi, I trust you've seen the light."

Markus stepped forward. He held the latest generation of RF detection equipment. "Give us the wire."

"I didn't know you could buy those at Sears, Mike. You guys must be accessing the SAP store."

"Just give me the fucking devices."

Morgan surrendered all but one inactive device.

Markus turned to Skip. "He's clean. I've switched the alarm to audio so you'll know if he activates anymore." He turned to leave.

"Please stay, Mike. I think you'll enjoy this conversation." Skip's lip twisted upward to give a devilish chuckle. When Markus pulled up a chair, Skip turned to Morgan. "Nothing you or the FBI do will free Thad. Once you've done everything I've planned, we can discuss arrangements for him."

"What the fuck are you doing Skip? Why would you want to hurt all of these innocent people?"

"Fuck you! It's none of your business. No one is innocent, not your ex, not Masters, not even your girlfriend.

I wouldn't tell you what or why for all the money in the world. You piece of shit!"

Morgan's face flushed and his stomach heaved. How much did Skip know about Gillian? He had to get her out of this. He could kill Skip before Markus could intervene. There was a pen on the desk. A quick jab through the temple.

He mastered his rage. He was just a tired middle-aged man who wanted his family back. He knew he had to stay alive for Thad's sake. "Tell me what you want. What do you need from me? You've got GCCS and Unger."

"I've waited so long for this. I'm not going to kill you. I'm going to make you suffer through the loss of all that you love. Then I'm going to hang all of this around your neck. You'll take the fall for everything. Originally, we were going to put it all on Unger and Masters. That fell apart early on.

Unger was much stronger than we'd anticipated. It wasn't enough that we had his wife and kids. He wouldn't tell us how to access the back door to the GCCS override system. We tried everything—drugs, torture, abusing his wife. You name it; he wouldn't crack. We brought his kids into a playroom with two-way mirrors. The sight of his children in the room with the men who'd brutalized him and his wife was all it took. He gave us everything we needed to take over GCCS. Sad really, the entire ordeal seems to have fried his brain. You saw him; he's an idiot. Once this thing is over, we'll put him out of his misery. For now, he's ours. We drive him between the office and home just so he won't bolt. Shit, he's so out of it, he sleeps on a couch in his office most nights. You can't be too careful, though."

Based on Unger's lucidity around GCCS, Morgan had a hunch there was more of him left than Skip suspected. "Can I see him?"

"Soon enough. This meeting is about making you miserable. There'll be no plausible deniability for you." Skip waved an unlit cigar in Morgan's face. "If they decide to take you alive, you'll pay and pay and pay."

The big man moved to the desk, flipped open a humidor. He placed his hand on a biometric scanner inside the box and keyed in a six-digit pin. The audio system sprang to life. "Please provide audio sample for final verification."

Skip spoke.

"Identity confirmed, engaging GCCS override system."

A panel on the west wall opened to reveal an electronic map and several large flat panel monitors.

"This is one of several panels which we currently have access to. Once we breach Echelon, we'll have even more access." Skip took a long pull as he lit his cigar exhaling smoke toward Morgan. "Two of us have full authorization, a silent partner and myself. I know you'd love to kill me right now, but that would be a huge mistake." He puffed his cigar before continuing. "Soon, you'll be set-up with full access. Of course, you'll never know your pin code. Then again, you won't need it." He took another drag on the stogie. "It's just another crumb on the evidence trail; another nail in your coffin."

"You know that's a phallic symbol, don't you?" Morgan tried to shock Skip back to reality.

Markus backhanded him.

He glared into Markus's eyes. "That's the last time you'll catch me off guard.

Skip laughed, "I've hated you ever since Junior High. You were always the golden good boy and I got the shit leftovers."

"That's not true Skip we shared everything equal up to that day in the jungle. You were my best friend, my only friend. I thought you were dead."

"You mean you left me for dead. You fucking coward."

"No Skip, they had to knock me out and drag me away. I would have gladly died to recover your body."

"Liar!"

Unger wandered into the suite, and Skip's demeanor changed like the channel on a television. "Morgan, I see you've already analyzed the situation. Each screen shows the view from the nosecone camera of an aircraft."

Unger appeared completely normal. "It's accessing the sense-and-avoid system, an on-board, wide-field of regard, multi-sensor visible imaging system operating in real time and capable of passively detecting approaching aircraft, declaring potential collision threats in a timely manner and alerting the pilot located in the remote ground control station. The GCCS technology allows us to see exactly what the pilot and ground traffic control see. Then it makes the programmatic transition to air traffic control."

It was amazing how lucid Unger sounded.

"Amazing, isn't it?" Skip said, tossing his head toward Unger. "Whenever he speaks about the GCCS, it's as though nothing's wrong with him. Watch this." He turned toward Unger, giving him his full attention, his voice soothing. "Stevie".

Unger fell into a trance-like state. Once again, he became the imbecile muttering nonsense. "Rose . . . key . . . tree . . . hook . . . how . . . abbey . . . aide . . . you and me."

"He's totally demented. His only touch with reality seems to be when he's describing the GCCS. Pathetic, really, isn't it?"

"The only pathetic thing I see is what you've done to him."

They listened in as air and ground traffic control managed the flow of aircraft in and around Mexico City.

"We conducted preliminary tests of the override months ago in Denver and just recently in New Jersey," Skip said. "Everything went as planned, without detection. Today, we do the final test of the GCCS override. We'll run Mexico City from here while we have personnel who'll use smart phones and wireless devices on other flights around the world." He smiled. "There shouldn't be any casualties yet, just some harmless accidents."

Morgan was riveted watching the screens. The upper right was captioned Lyon, France. It displayed the view from the approach of a landing aircraft. The jet should have been utilizing the computerized Instrument Landing System, or ILS, at this point. The audio and the visual both made it clear that something was wrong. The aircraft deviated to the left of the centerline and descended below the glide slope. It appeared that the onboard systems hadn't acquired the localizer signal correctly. The co-pilot called for a go-around and the engines began to spool up. The aircraft no longer responded to pilot input. The increased engine velocity caused the plane to hit the ground with incredible force. It bounced numerous times and struck several obstacles. It finally came to rest about a mile from the runway and caught fire. Though still upright and in one piece, it was highly unlikely that there'd be no casualties."

Skip had the elated look of a coach who'd just won a big game. "Bravo. Hopefully our Saudi friend survives that." He pointed to the far left screen. "Look at this, look at this."

A commuter jet turned onto the runway.

"What the hell are you doing, Ron?" The pilot spoke to the first officer. "We can't get off the ground on this runway. It's only thirty-five hundred feet. Call the tower. We're going back to the gate area."

Fear emanated from the first officer's voice. "I didn't turn the plane onto this runway. It came over here on its own."

"Have you been drinking? You're relieved of duty." The pilot didn't panic. "Tower, this is flight 125. Please be advised that we are on the wrong runway and will be returning to the gate."

"Roger 125. Please proceed to Northeast taxiway and return to the gate area."

The pilot seemed confused as the plane began to accelerate for takeoff. "Ron, what are you doing?"

"I'm not touching the controls."

"Tower, be notified that we're no longer in control of our aircraft. We're overweight for takeoff on this runway." The pilot's voice shook. "Rapidly approaching the point of no return. Applying full throttle."

"Negative 125, kill your engines and return to the gate area."

The jet continued to rumble down the tarmac, picking up speed at an inadequate rate.

"All controls are unresponsive at this time. Deploy emergency response teams."

The jet plowed through a fence and crashed into a line of trees. A ball of fire rolled above the tree line.

Skip gave a strange sigh, as though things hadn't gone exactly as planned. "Damn it, Mike, we don't want casualties yet. They'll ground all aircraft if they catch on."

Markus shrugged.

The screen with the caption Changi International Airport in Singapore displayed an image from a Boeing 737 on its final approach. As the plane continued its descent, the pilot reported that the landing gear had inexplicably retracted. The flight came in as normal, with the exception that a shower of sparks and howl of metal replaced the usual wisp of smoke from the tires at the point of contact with the tarmac. The aircraft came to a somewhat uneventful rest some fifteen hundred meters beyond the tarmac.

"All right, we're three for three. Now check this out as we control a plane in Mexico City from here."

Two of the other screens went dark, while the third displayed the GCCS override software. A brand new twin-engine Sabreliner airplane owned by a private cargo operator had been equipped with GCCS as part of their standard model. Manipulating the software, Markus requested a low approach landing. During the approach, he clipped several poles, causing the plane to cartwheel prior to impact in a residential area. A post-impact explosion and fire consumed the aircraft.

"Rose and Ricky fly around a tree; Look how happy they've made you and me."

Everyone turned to Unger. He'd finally recited his limerick and was pleased.

Morgan found his voice. "You're crazy. Not only will you never make this happen, you'll never get all these people to cooperate."

Skip beamed with pride. "Already done. You've just seen a proof of concept on the technology and the team. Come on Morgan, you know damn good and well that Islam has replaced Marxism as the political ideology of the angry and the violent. Marxists, Islamists, take your pick; they're blinded by their own anger and hate."

"So, you leverage their passions against them."

"God people are so gullible." Skip sneered. "These fuckers are so fanatical, its child's play to manipulate them. Do you know how easy it is to manipulate someone who believes 'the enemy of my enemy is my friend'? They're fucking morons. It's all one big crazy sermon. Destroy the Great Satan. Be rid of the oppressor; rule your country in peace and isolation. Goddamn, they're stupid. Just give them the hope of running their own fascist state and they'll sign on for almost anything. It's not even that hard to manipulate them toward a common goal as long as everything operates in silos. If they can't see each other's involvement, they're happy.

"Now, everything that flies is my personal weapon. With a dozen well-placed aircraft, I can cripple the US economy, along with the nationwide transportation network and food supply."

"Skip, release my son and I'll do anything you say."

"Fuck you," smoke furled about his head. "Get him out of here Mike."

Chapter 54

It was after six o'clock by the time Morgan left Skip's office and his world had spun out of control. Time had stood still in that house of horrors, while it had raced by in the sane world.

He had to call Gillian. "Can I come by and see you?"

She looked ashen when she greeted him from the porch. Her skin seemed waxy and appeared pasty white, as though all of the blood had drained from her body. She had all of the classic signs of shock.

He panicked. "Did something happen to Maddie or your mother?"

An eternity passed with no answer. He pulled her into his arms and held her tight. She began to sob. "Oh God, Levi, he's dead."

He reeled away and retched at the prospect of his ultimate failure. Thad, dead.

Gillian bent down beside him and pulled his head to her shoulder. "I'm not talking about Thad."

They stood and found one another's arms. Morgan shuttered with relief.

"My handler is dead. It was a professional hit made to look like a suicide."

After several moments, he found his voice. "This is crazy. They know our every move." He put both of his hands on his forehead, slowly pushing them through his hair. "I've got to get you out of here. Hafley is on to you."

"We've both been going thirty-six hours with no sleep. We've got to rest."

"Do you have any other contacts at the Bureau?"

"Just one in Washington. This is deep cover. I'm screwed if this goes any farther off the tracks."

"Can I stay a while? I need to talk to you about today."

"Sure, come on in."

They flopped onto the couch in the living room. Gillian leaned over, put her head on his shoulder, and sobbed. He put his arm around her, no words, just provided a comforting presence. Then the inevitable happened, and exhaustion pulled them into the deep recesses of sleep.

Morgan woke around three a.m., stiff and sore from the sofa. He carried Gillian to her room and placed her gently on the bed. He kissed her forehead and left the room, then lingered at the front door, ready to go home.

Rather than leaving, he turned toward the couch, grabbed an old afghan with the aroma of Gillian and lay back down.

At 6:45, he jolted awake and sat bolt upright. Gillian leaned forward in the recliner across from him. "Coffee?" She smiled and held out a cup.

Chapter 55

Wednesday, December 4

"Hello, Mr. Morgan. He's expecting you." The smartly dressed older woman rose and moved toward Masters's office. "Please follow me." She tapped on the door and gently pushed it open, "David, Professor Morgan is here."

"Show him in, Elaina."

Elaina was warm and charming, someone who could command respect from even the most illustrious business leaders. "Would either of you care for a beverage?"

"I'll have a coffee. How about you, Levi?"

"Black coffee would be great, thanks."

Affable as always, Masters moved forward with his hand extended, a genuine smile on his face. "Good morning, Levi. I'm so glad you asked for a meeting."

Morgan came right to the point. "How well do you really know Hafley?" He hesitated. "I mean, I know he saved your life, but how did he come to be second-in-command at the Ultraist Group?"

Masters gave him a broad smile. "I hate pretense, too. I understand your concern about Mr. Hafley." He paused. "Maybe even better than you do."

Elaina entered with the coffees. "Thank you, Elaina. That's all for now. Please hold all calls."

"Yes sir." She exited and pulled the door closed.

"Don't worry; I've known who Mr. Hafley is for quite some time. I'm not so sure you know who he is, though. He wants to take TUG in an aggressive direction." Masters stood and gazed out the window. His fingertips created a chapel setting, a temporary sanctuary for his thoughts. Slowly, he brought his index fingers to his lips. He dropped both hands and turned toward Morgan. "I'm concerned about your safety and continued growth."

Morgan exploded in frustrated confusion. "Goddamn it, David, I can take care of myself. I'm worried about you. People close to you don't share your aversion to violence."

"No one's going to do anything to me that I don't allow."

"You'll protect yourself?"

"We can't protect ourselves from everything, nor should we. The world isn't quite ready to evolve. Evil people want control. The signs of revolution are everywhere."

"Hafley," Morgan started but Masters simply raised his hand. The words died in his larynx. He needed to tell Masters to run from Hafley, to live to fight another day, but his throat was paralyzed.

"Arsenals won't provide security, governments will be impotent, and technology will become our greatest foe. The Furies will ravage the human race in one final cataclysmic cleansing. Without mercy, they'll persecute all that impede the natural order of evolution to the ends of the earth."

Morgan finally found his voice. "And you think this'll happen during your lifetime?" He dared not say what he was thinking, that this could all start today.

"No, but definitely during yours."

He was perplexed. "Are you giving up?"

"Like the phoenix, humanity will rise from the ashes and evolve." Masters shook himself, as though waking from a dream. "But we need to talk about you and complete your preparation."

"No, we need to talk about Hafley."

Masters shook his head.

"Hafley's going to kill a lot of people," he pushed.

"That'll keep."

A hysterical roll of laughter issued from him. "David, have you lost your mind? Hafley will kill you."

"Aggression and war reduce humanity to two classes: one non-functioning and the other dysfunctional. The dead and the survivors. No one goes unscathed, neither the aggressor nor the victim. All become disfigured, hollowed-out frames, the twisted wreckage of humanity on a collision course with itself, leaving bodies behind from which humanity has fled in varying degrees. You know what I'm talking about. You're trying to come back from that brokenness. I'm coming back from there myself. I only have one more task to complete."

Morgan sat in frustrated silence.

"To be truly whole, we must evolve. To evolve, we must embrace the divine within us, the One in All and the All in One."

Something triggered within Morgan. As a child, he'd been assailed by a nightmare. Ever fleeing in the dark, from streetlight to distant streetlight, his mysterious, terrifying pursuer drew closer until he forced himself awake to escape. How did that dream relate to what Masters had just said?

As if reading his mind, Masters continued. "We run from ourselves when we should embrace our true nature, admitting and accepting who we are."

His facial muscles twitched involuntarily at the thought. How could the dream be about avoiding his true destiny?

"Trust me," Masters said comfortingly. "Regret and avoidance can't heal. The samurai avoids the *suki* and so misses life. The Zen master embraces it, for therein lays the way. Time and honesty bring forth the consciousness necessary to evolve."

Out of nowhere, Morgan's thoughts shifted. Things began to resonate and fit together. "Thad. I've avoided Thad."

Masters put his hand on his shoulder. "Just do the next right thing. Everything will become clear in the moment."

Morgan trusted the divine within. His passions and base instincts lay quiet and subdued. For the first time, the fighter in him realized that time wasn't an enemy to be conquered. Time was irrelevant to his existence—to his essence.

His heart went out to his kidnapped son. He couldn't utter a syllable.

Masters changed the subject. "A few weeks ago, I undertook an investigation into Mr. Hafley." Agitated, he turned and looked out toward the Gulf. "About who he really is."

Concern for Thad continued to roil Morgan's thoughts.

"I've discovered things about him, things that involve your past—and mine."

The door opened slightly revealing Elaina's flustered face. "I'm sorry, David. He won't take no for an answer."

The door burst open as Hafley pushed past the oddly beleaguered assistant. "Don't let me interrupt."

Masters spun to face the intruder. "Don't be silly, Randall. We were just finishing up." He turned toward Morgan. "I want you and Gillian to join me for dinner tonight at Pedestals."

Morgan choked out the word, "Sure," then got up to leave.

Hafley just smiled.

Chapter 56

Muffled strains of laughter and clattering silver drifted into the booth occupied by the odd assembly. Flanked by Morgan and Hafley, David sat at a large table in Pedestals.

Gillian felt like shit. She still had the presence of mind to recognize the early stages of shock coming on but not enough to care about her makeup.

Hafley had invited two guests to join. Steven Unger sat to Gillian's left, across from Levi. Doctor Levine, a prominent Tampa Bay psychiatrist and a member of the TUG board of directors, was seated across from Hafley, to her right.

Soft murmurs, muted to perfection by the labyrinth of seven-foot vine encrusted trellises, echoed from the surrounding booths. Gillian felt claustrophobic, pinned in.

The waiters had just removed the soup course, providing everyone time to chitchat as they waited for the salad. She struggled to engage Unger. "Isn't this place amazing, Steven? Who would've thought you could turn an old warehouse into something this special."

Unger replied without hesitation. "It replaced the Basilica of St. Lawrence as the largest free-standing elliptical dome in North America. It's really cool."

Gillian couldn't believe it. He seemed perfectly lucid. *Maybe Levi is wrong.* "Sounds like you know a lot about buildings."

"Goddamn it." Hafley looked down at his trousers as if he'd spilled something. Most likely, he was making an excuse to swear at what he considered utter stupidity.

The aroma of roast duck wafted in from a passing tabletop, making Gillian feel faint with hunger and exhaustion.

She could see that Levi was spent. The events of the previous sixty hours had brought him to the brink of physical and emotional exhaustion. His head bobbed and he forced his eyes open just as the lids were about to fall shut.

David seemed unusually quiet. "How's Thad?"

Levi spoke as though he'd been punched in the chest. "I . . . ah . . . I . . . I'm not sure. I haven't seen him in a few days."

Hafley smiled. "Really, what's he up to?"

Levi glared. The snide remark seemed to give him energy.

The salad table arrived. Gillian noticed that one of the waiters was new; he hadn't served the other two courses.

An unfolded napkin lay on the end of the table. *Odd.* She thought. *Everything was usually meticulously in place.*

As the table was set in place, the waiter picked up the napkin. His right hand moved out of his pocket, while his left hand shielded it from view.

A shot rang out. David raised his hands in a blocking motion. Levi lunged toward him and threw both arms around him. Levi flinched in pain as the second shot grazed a forearm.

The first shot had pierced David's right ventricle, beginning his battle with death. The second shot passed through Levi's forearm, just missing an artery. The third shot disintegrated David's aorta, eliminating all hope for survival. He lay between his chair and the trellis, gasping for air. He had seconds of coherency before shock ushered him to the next phase of his spiritual journey. With every attempt at speech, a spray of blood appeared on his lips, accompanied by a hideous rattling sound. One of the bullets had ripped through his lung.

Instinctively, Morgan snatched a nearby napkin, wadded it up, searched for the exit wound, and pressed hard into David's back. He uttered the last words he would ever speak. They were simpler, more practical, than what would be expected coming from such a visionary.

"Take care of them." He gasped, his voice stilted. "Sist . . ." His hand was pointing toward Unger.

Morgan pulled his limp body close. "Stay calm David. We're getting assistance." Morgan looked up and saw Hafley smiling. *Could David have been pointing at him?* His tears fell on the now vacant face. He yelled to anyone calm enough to act. "Call 9-1-1."

Steven Unger clutched Gillian's shoulder and began a chant, timed perfectly to his rocking. "Rose . . . key . . . tree . . . abbey."

She looked over at Levine, who sat hugging himself in horror. "Holy fuck, holy fuck," was all he could find to say.

Gillian thought about pursuing the assassin but was trapped staring at David's body—powerless.

The assailant had disappeared into the labyrinth of Pedestals. Morgan had fled the booth in pursuit of the shooter.

She bit her lower lip, imploring anyone for help with tear-filled eyes. "Please, someone find a doctor." She reached for her spiritual father, tears streaming down her cheek. She didn't want to pursue anyone. She wanted more time with her friend, her master.

She reached over and placed her hand on Unger's. He squeezed back and wept.

She willed her weary legs into action.

Chapter 57

As eternity welcomed its child, Gillian exited the booth and followed a wake of frightened eyes.

She raised her badge for the first time in years. "FBI. Bring up the lights." Her cover was blown. It was futile to act as if it wasn't. "Everybody lie down. If you see anyone move next to you, call out."

People everywhere got on the floor. She listened carefully, hearing nothing but kitchen noises. Methodically, she advanced from booth to booth, moving toward the sound.

"Only talk if you see movement." Her appearance solicited fear from everyone. "Does anyone see movement?"

Silence was the only response. The shooter had most likely joined everyone else on the floor.

Gillian called out to anyone who would listen. "Seal all the exits. No one leaves until the police arrive." She bolted into the kitchen.

* * *

Her statement to the police completed, she slouched on the curb, head in her hands. She replayed the events of the past three days. Everything pointed back to Levi. *Could he be behind all this?*

Hafley had told the police that it appeared as if Levi was somehow involved in this shooting, as well as the deaths of the "Seffner Three", as they were now referred to. He claimed that Levi had held David so the assassin could get a clean shot.

Gillian couldn't believe it. *Could Levi be the lynchpin of this plot?* Could he have lied that convincingly? Her mind raced. He had her family.

She struggled with conflicting thoughts. Could Levi have orchestrated David's assassination? She was utterly confused, but one thing was clear. She no longer had anyone to trust.

According to the police, the paramedics had transported Levi to Tampa General for treatment. She called the hospital to check on him.

"I'm sorry, our records show he was treated and released."

Now he'd vanished. The shock of being alone crashed in on her. She sat and cried on the curb, just another heartbroken follower of David Masters.

Eventually, she got it together. Someone had to stop this and bring the conspirators to justice. She called a private number in Washington D.C.

Chapter 58

Morgan's truck headed south from the hospital parking lot as if it were on autopilot. Zombie-like, he unlocked the door to the house and headed straight to the master bath, where he showered, crawled into bed, and closed his eyes.

From every angle, thoughts came as though the darkened room produced them. They'd been waiting for him to stop moving. Now they clawed at every raw emotion, producing chagrin and shame. He looked at the clock. 11:45. Almost midnight. He'd struggled with thought-induced insomnia over the last year. This time, he couldn't afford the luxury of alcohol or sedatives to knock himself out.

He rolled over. Once again, he closed his eyes against the data assaulting his psyche. Three men under his protection, murdered; Thad kidnapped and brutalized; David Masters killed at his side.

His eyes sprang open as he contemplated Jean Anu and little Maddie.

He didn't dare contact anyone about them.

He lay for several minutes trying to divert his mind. His fatigue only fed the process. Finally, he rolled over and turned on the light.

As he reached in the bedside table to grab the TV remote, his eye caught a leather-bound notebook. Embossed on the cover was the image of a compass. A leather thong looped through a clasp held the book closed. He tilted it upward, noting the exquisite gold-leaf edges.

Of course, Liz would keep a diary.

He drew the latch from the clasp and opened the journal. In his wife's handwriting at the top of the first page was a date several years prior. He read her thoughts, feelings, and significant interactions for that day.

He read several others randomly.

She'd been seeing a psychologist, Doctor Levine. The guy had been at the dinner party tonight. *Odd*

Liz had felt comfortable with him. The visits and medication had helped. In fact, he could see that Levine had helped her view him differently.

Thank you.

Levine volunteered with the Ultraist Group.

Interesting.

Another entry intrigued him. Levine had told her that she suffered from empty-nest syndrome and needed a distraction. He tried to remember where he'd heard that.

He pulled on a silky brown ribbon bookmark, and the pages parted to reveal Liz's final entry. His world spun out of control as he began to read.

She hadn't been depressed at all. In fact, she'd seemed extremely excited. She'd been dating someone special—Mike Markus.

He closed his eyes in disbelief. Liz's sister hadn't been far off. She was dead because of him. How else could he explain Markus dating his ex-wife?

He flipped back several weeks and read feverishly through the entries.

November 1st

Dr. Levine suggested that I share a lot in common with a friend of his at TUG. Reluctantly, I agreed to meet him tomorrow night.

Things began to come clear. That's how Hafley had been a step ahead of him at every turn. They were using Liz and Levine to get information.

He knew I was coming. Hell, he was probably involved in getting me there. It's been a set-up from the beginning.

Deb McDonnell had to be involved. But why kill Liz? He read on.

November 3rd

The date with Mike was terrific. I can't believe how much we think alike. He's so gentle and understanding. Maybe I can trust again, maybe ...

November 8th

Had a wonderful evening with Mike tonight. I still miss having Thaddeus around every day, but Mike is helping put that into perspective. He even told me that Levi couldn't be all bad. You know, he's right; Levi did the best he could. I hope he and Thad can deal with their issues and have an adult relationship. Going out with Mike again tomorrow night. I can't wait!

He contemplated the calculated manipulation. *Fucking bastard.*

November 11th

The next time I see Dr. Levine I'm going to thank him for getting us together. For the first time in my life, I'm with a man I can trust. I'm with a man who makes me feel secure, wanted, and understood. He's coming over for dinner on the 15th, after that, who knows ... maybe he'll meet Thaddeus.

Gotcha motherfucker.

He could place Mike Markus in the house on the night Liz had died. The journal proved she wasn't suicidal and it established a link between the radical faction of TUG and his operation.

Why kill Liz?

Suddenly, things clicked into place—empty nest syndrome. McDonnell had said that to him. She knew Liz's death would destroy Thad. That thought led him back to what he really valued.

Screw all of this. If he could free Thad and wrap this up, they could start a new life. Hafley and Markus had destroyed his credibility. If he went public, no one would believe him. He was being framed as a murderer.

What could have provoked McDonnell to such a ruthless onslaught? He could see revenge coming from the families of his victims, but not from within his own organization, from his closest associate.

The only person who could have orchestrated this was Deb McDonnell.

He had to confront her. He was tired of being pushed around, tired of being a fool. She was the only one with the level of access required to manipulate all the pieces.

He grabbed the satellite phone and placed the call.

Chapter 59

The rich smell of freshly brewed coffee permeated the air of the SFO ATC complex. The evening shift had started and things seemed normal. Charles Brandon had been the Director of Air Traffic Control at San Francisco International Airport for the past ten years. This was his palace, his domain. He strode the perimeter observing his troops.

He stopped behind Drew Brailsford, one of his best. He seemed perturbed. "What's going on Drew?"

"I don't know. US Air Flight Eight to Charlotte has veered off course and banked toward Oakland."

"What do you make of it?"

"I'm concerned. It's strange, no word from the pilot, no apparent problems. The flight is deviating from plan and standard emergency protocols." The incident light began to flash yellow as he spoke to the pilot of the aberrant aircraft. "US Air Flight Eight, you have deviated from your filed flight plan. Are you requesting emergency status?"

"Affirmative SFO, we are experiencing helm and computer control problems. We're running diagnostics and will advise momentarily."

The director leaned over Brailsford's terminal. He had weathered the 9/11 attacks, and in their aftermath, had overseen the federal installation of the Ground Computer Control System at SFO.

Turning to his assistant, Brandon took control of the situation. "Get Oakland International's ATC director on the horn. Let him know we may have an emergency landing coming his way. Contact Alameda Nimitz NAS and let them know we're monitoring a developing situation." He turned back to the terminal. In this realm, his people would follow his orders to the letter. Without question, the jets from Nimitz could intercept and eliminate the threat if it turned out to be another terrorist incident.

The plane began to swing to the northwest, away from Oakland. Various relieved comments passed through the tower.

Brailsford spoke calmly. "Good job, Flight Eight. Bring that helm on around and we'll get you back on the ground here at SFO."

"Negative, SFO, that course correction wasn't a result of our efforts."

Brailsford went offline and spoke to the director. "Sir, current trajectory has them headed just off the northeast corner of San Francisco and then out over open water."

"Tell him to come about and prepare for emergency landing at SFO."

"Flight Eight, be advised that you have deviated from your filed flight plan. The director of ATC SFO requests that you come about and prepare for emergency landing at SFO. Please acknowledge."

"Affirmative, SFO tower. As soon as we've regained control of the helm, we'll come about and make an emergency landing at SFO."

Brandon couldn't help but think this was going to end poorly. Something didn't feel right; especially after all of the rumors he'd been hearing from New Jersey, Colorado, and around the world. Something was wrong with this new GCCS program. Since its inception, malfunctions and crashes had skyrocketed. "Jones, put the emergency landing contingency into effect. Notify all inbound and outbound aircraft as well as the FAA."

Brailsford called out the status. "Flight Eight, you are now at status yellow.

"This is Flight Eight, we have finished our diagnostics. All systems are functioning normally, but the helm is still not responding." The pilot sounded frustrated and confused. "Please advice."

The overhead monitor began flashing amber. The F-16's would start to scramble at Alameda Nimitz Naval Air Station.

Brandon needed information before he contacted the NAS commander. "Find out if there's been a cockpit takeover."

"Flight Eight, please advise, is the baby safe?"

"This is Flight Eight, affirmative, the baby is safe."

The director turned to his assistant, who'd just walked up. "Get the commander at Nimitz on the phone and let him know this is not a cockpit intrusion or a hostile takeover. It seems to be something mechanical or computer related."

"Pilot suicide?" Brandon wondered aloud without meaning to. "Brailsford, give them their status again."

"US Air Flight Eight, acknowledge that you have veered off your designated flight plan. Be advised that you are now in amber status."

"This is US Air Flight Eight. The helm is still not responding to my command. Repeat, the helm is not responding to my command."

Brandon was done playing around. "Prepare to override control of the flight with the GCCS program. Flight Eight, this is Director Brandon of the SFO ATC unit. I request permission to go to computer override to take ground control of your aircraft. Acknowledge."

"This is US Air Flight Eight granting permission for GCCS override of all onboard systems."

"Initiate ground computer override of US Air Flight Eight."

"Yes sir. The sequence is in and only requires your key and pass code to execute."

Brandon walked to the terminal, verifying that US Airways Flight Eight was the subject of the override. He inserted his key and gave it a turn. "Flight Eight, this is Director Brandon of the SFO ATC unit requesting reconfirmation. I request permission to go to computer override to take ground control of your aircraft. Acknowledge."

"This is US Air Flight Eight reconfirming permission for GCCS override of all onboard systems."

Brandon keyed in his code and executed the GCCS program. The terminal immediately displayed a flight simulator along with a coordinate input screen. The program was brilliant. It allowed an air traffic controller on the ground to take complete control of any aircraft in the commercial fleet.

He punched in the coordinates to bring the plane about and increase its altitude. He waited several agonizing seconds before he realized that the override wasn't working.

***

In fact, the override was working perfectly.

Hafley had entered the GCCS program via Steven Unger's back door. From his perspective, the plane performed marvelously. It had come about and locked on its target exactly as intended.

He could hardly contain his excitement. "Can you believe it? In a matter of minutes, we'll have taken out the west coast operations of one of the most secret and powerful organizations in human history. It's a simple calculation . . . a full load of fuel, the right velocity, and a direct hit on those external post tension cables. Bingo! The building will collapse."

True to his word, he would blind the government by taking out the large antennae that enabled the global monitoring network. Typically, those antennae doubled as bridges and other structures built with external post-tensioned steel cables. The cables provided a strong, easily maintained structure from an engineering perspective, while giving excellent reception capabilities from an antennae perspective.

The plane continued lumbering toward the Pier 39 parking structure at Fisherman's Wharf.

***

"Director Brandon, Flight Eight is just about to clear the city and pass over open water."

Brandon couldn't have felt more relieved had he been on the plane himself. "Okay, then, let's get the Feds on the phone to fix this glitch. If the plane doesn't start descending, we have plenty of time to solve this problem. Jones, cancel the emergency landing contingency and let's get traffic back to normal."

"Sir," Brailsford's voice quivered. "Flight Eight just dropped off radar. It's twenty-one thirty-eight, Pacific Standard Time."

"Oh shit! Is it in the bay? Activate emergency response procedures. Turn on the news." He couldn't believe it. "Check your equipment. Give me a status on our radar."

The mood in the tower instantly shifted from relief to dread and dismay. He knew the equipment was still working properly. It was Flight Eight that had malfunctioned.

Chapter 60

Morgan fidgeted with the remote as he waited for McDonnell to pick up. He pressed the power button and hit mute.

"McDonnell, go."

"Hey, Deb, have you seen the news?" He'd surfed to a cable news program airing footage of the exterior of Pedestals.

"Yeah, good job."

"I had nothing to do with it. I tried to save him."

"Hang on a second; you're breaking up. I'm just coming off the elevator into the parking garage. Okay." The connection sounded hollow and began to echo. "I'm running to catch the redeye. I'll see you in Tampa in the morning."

"We need to talk about a few things now, things that aren't easy."

"Masters is dead, assignment over. We'll pack it up in the morning, buddy."

"Just listen for a few minutes, will you?"

"Seriously, I'm getting in the car right now and I have a lot of work to do before I get on the plane. I'll see you in the morning."

"Deb, we need to talk about high-level leaks within our group."

"Not …"

The phone went dead. He looked at the clock. It was twenty-one thirty-eight in San Francisco. He hit redial, but the phone cut to voicemail. He'd never been able to talk with her about serious things.

Shit, she's ten times worse than me when it comes to avoiding conflict.

He brought the sound up on the TV. "Fuck it. She's trying to set me up."

Another sensationalized report on the death of David Masters flashed on the screen—TRAGEDY IN TAMPA— was the caption. A news anchor far from the scene droned insensitive babble designed to hold viewers through the next commercial break.

"We take you live to Tampa joining a police press-conference already in progress."

A well-dressed woman stood at a podium as cameras clicked and reporters jostled for recognition.

"Currently, we believe the assailant acted in congress with several radical evangelical groups and possibly with a rogue government worker. We are working every lead at this time. Thank you. We will not take any questions at this time."

The camera shifted immediately to the reporter on location. *"Again, we're broadcasting live, from Pedestals Restaurant in Tampa, Florida, where David Masters was shot and killed at approximately seven-thirty Eastern Standard Time. We just heard from Detective Sandy Resner, spokesperson for Tampa PD, make a plea for information regarding the assailant. To recap, police now believe that the lone gunman acted on behalf of numerous evangelical organizations."*

The government worker comment troubled him. He tried McDonnell again, muting the TV and flipping through Liz's journal as he waited for her to pickup. He tried for twenty minutes without success.

Out of the corner of his eye, he noticed a breaking news story. A US Airways flight had just slammed into a parking garage somewhere. He gave the TV his full attention.

He ground his teeth. "Fucking Skip. What have you done? Now, I'm going to have to kill you."

A newsperson interrupted the coverage of Masters's murder. *"Currently, it's believed there are no survivors on the plane or in the garage. We just spoke with an investigator minutes ago, who told us that in 1987, the garage had been rehabilitated utilizing post-tensioned tendons. The plane's impact and the ensuing explosion severed those tendons, allowing each level to collapse onto the lower ones.*

As of yet, no one has been able to explain why the crater is so deep. It looks more like a vertical impact, which wasn't the case here. All we know is that the plane crashed into the garage at nine thirty-eight this evening. All one hundred and eighty-seven people on board are feared dead. In addition, we expect numerous casualties on the ground. The initial fireball was so intense there's already speculation that many of the buildings in the adjacent area will need to be demolished. This is Lisa Arrington, reporting from Fisherman's Wharf in San Francisco. Back to you, Robin."

Morgan just stared at the TV. Each level of the parking garage had crashed down on the lower levels, leaving a massive tangle of rubble and wires. The crater belched smoke and ash, a pyroclastic nightmare. There was no way anyone could have survived that collapse. Much like the Twin Towers, it looked as though a demolition team had taken it down.

He noted the dateline on the screen—Pier 39 Parking Structure, Fisherman's Wharf, San Francisco, CA.

He sat on the edge of the bed, stunned. No wonder the phone had cut off. McDonnell was dead. The journal slipped from his hands and fell to the floor.

She'd been a long-time co-worker and his handler for the past five years. In theory, she'd been his closest associate. He dared to call her a friend. Only Skip had been a closer friend.

He felt strange. He would have expected pain, but all he experienced was emptiness and guilt. Had he loved McDonnell? He wasn't sure.

How could he have suspected her of treason—her of all people? The mole must have helped Hafley ferret her out. It couldn't be a coincidence. Hafley had taken her out along with the west coast operations center.

The doorbell cut through the fog of dismay. *Who the hell could that be?*

The bell rang irrationally, alternating with a pounding fist on the metal-clad core. He picked up the journal and tossed it on the dresser as he left the room.

Chapter 61

Still dressed in her skirt and heels from dinner, Gillian walked up the street. Under a streetlight, she noticed a trail of spots down her skirt, on to the shoes. Her pace quickened as heartache and rage swept over her; it was blood, David's blood. She ran across the yard, pounded on the door punching the doorbell without mercy.

She burst through the door as soon as the latch was drawn. Maybe it was his exhaustion, maybe it was her odd behavior, but she caught him completely off guard.

She pushed past him, into the formal living room. "What the fuck have you done?" She felt like two people: one in love and wanting to trust; the other, not so much.

Levi closed and latched the door. "Come on in."

He failed to muster the appropriate level of sarcasm. She paced erratically on the brink of insanity.

He looked exhausted, too. "Calm down; talk to me."

She pulled the standard FBI-issue Ruger P97 from the small of her back. "Shut the fuck up." She aimed at his midsection, giving him no time to assess the situation. "Where are Maddie and my mother?" Her voice cracked with exhaustion, but the steel barrel didn't waver. She rammed it forward, emphasizing the demand for an answer. In the dimly lit room, it would be impossible for him to see that the hammer wasn't cocked, the firing pin wasn't engaged.

He raised his hands in front of his stomach. The thirty inches between his fingertips and the barrel might as well have been a hundred yards. There was no way he could overpower her before she got off a shot. "They're in Bat Cave, North Carolina, at a house in the mountains." He slid one foot forward half a step. "I swear; they're okay. It's a small town. There's a stop sign, a mechanic shop, and a fire station."

She clicked the hammer into the locked position. Retreat was not on the agenda. "Call the police. You're under arrest."

"For what?"

"Three counts of murder, conspiracy to commit murder, accomplice to murder, five counts of kidnapping. Hell, you could've kidnapped your own son, for all I know. Espionage, treason, conspiracy to overthrow the US Government; take your pick." She shoved the gun toward his face. "Call the fucking police. Then call whoever it is you need to get my family back."

"Can I show you something first? After you've seen it, I'll do whatever you say."

She looked around. If they started moving, she would lose control of the situation. He was probably armed.

He held his hands closer together in mock restraint. "Do you have handcuffs?"

She shook her head. "You?"

He gave a weary chuckle. "Never had a use for them before tonight."

She sighed in exasperation. "What do you want to show me?"

"It's a diary, Liz's diary. I found it tonight."

"So?" The pistol shook as though it had asked the question.

"Just take a look at it. Please." He sounded submissive, almost childlike.

"I've had enough of your bullshit. You'd need more than a magic wand to get out of this."

"The diary proves that Markus and Hafley were using Liz to get to me."

"Where is it?" The gun demanded.

He lifted his head, indicating it was somewhere beyond her current position. "In the master bedroom."

Glancing over, she could see light streaming through an open door beyond the dining room.

"Sure, next to your gun, I assume." Cold and steely, her own voice sounded alien to her.

"Let's figure this out. You have the gun. The firing pin's engaged. If you keep me in line with that barrel, there's nothing I can do."

"Where exactly is *this* diary?"

"On the bed, no, on the floor. Shit, I don't know."

"Okay, we're going to move toward the bedroom. If I don't see a diary on the bed, you're dead. I'll say you rushed me."

"It's a deal."

"Stay in step with me. As I back up to the doorway, you maintain this distance. Got it?

"Got it."

"Put your hands behind your head and lock your fingers."

He obeyed. The bandage on his forearm had begun to ooze blood, a grisly reminder of the evening's events.

"Down on your knees."

"Hey."

"Just do it." The gun snapped toward his face.

He got down on one knee and then the other. With his hands behind his head, his upper torso became a massive target, impossible for an expert marksman to miss at such close range.

She stepped backward in the direction of the open doorway. He crawled submissively but teetered a couple of times on the thinly padded carpet. Seepage from the bandage dripped from his elbow into the beige pile.

"Stop. Don't move." She peered in the doorway. The covers were a mess. There was no sign of a book. She thought for a minute, moving her lips from side to side. "Don't move." She took another step through the doorway as she scanned the room.

She stepped out of the room, regaining command over her prisoner. "Describe this imaginary book." She towered over him, possessing the tactical advantage.

"It's brown leather, with a compass on the front and gold leaf pages."

She needed to get him into the room ahead of her, but the dining room table stood in the way. "Back up."

Dutifully, he began to inch backward.

"I want you to go around the table. You're going into the room in front of me."

As he approached the doorway, she moved to her right, giving her an optimal line of sight beyond him, into the room. "See that corner straight ahead." He nodded. "Get in the corner, face in, stay on your knees, keep your hands behind your head. If you move, I'll kill you."

She had seen the book on the corner of the dresser when she'd looked into the room. In fact, she could have grabbed it as she stood in the doorway, had it not left her completely vulnerable to attack.

She sat on the corner of the bed. Morgan knelt in the corner, about five feet away. She kept the gun trained on his upper back, her left hand pinning the book to the bed. Her fingers flipped the gold leaf pages. The gun never wavered. Without a doubt, someone had kept the journal over several years, a fact attested by the different types of ink used throughout.

A thousand feelings drained every ounce of logic from her mind. She snapped. Grabbing the diary, she rushed out of the room, slamming the door behind her. She slid across the dining room table. A heavy crystal vase smashed into the china cabinet, creating an explosion of wood, porcelain, and glass. She dropped off the tabletop and ran for the door. It felt like she was running through a vat of glue as she lumbered toward escape, not from the house, not from Levi, but from confusion and frustration.

She fumbled blindly with the latch, certain Levi was about to tackle her. She willed her shaking hands to turn the knob and free her from uncertainty. She needed space and time to think through everything.

She fled down the street to her car.

Chapter 62

Gillian drove blindly, heading wherever the car would take her, tears streaming down her face. She had to rescue Maddie and her mom. She had to stop this attack. *How could I be in love with this guy?*

The car stopped in a dimly lit parking space along the same fishing pier she and Levi had walked just twenty-four hours earlier. She sat there and cried, feeling small and frustrated.

Everything was a mess. *How had this changed from a simple operation to this fucked-up mess? Why had I gotten Maddie and my mother involved? How could I have allowed myself to become emotionally entangled with Levi?*

She looked toward the pier. That's when she noticed the journal laying in the passenger's seat. She picked it up and intuitively pulled on the ribbon to read the final entry. She was stunned. *Mike Markus killed Levi's wife. Why?*

She flipped back through the pages and read more.

Difficulty focusing at work today . . . Several entries later, Dr. Levine suggested that I share a lot in common . . .

Levine put Markus and Liz together? That doesn't make sense. Why?

She flipped through several more pages and it became clear. The sons of bitches *had been* using Liz to get information about Levi. With his ex-wife under their control, they knew exactly how to manipulate him.

She dug through her purse and found the phone. *There's no time like the present to apologize.* She dialed Levi.

"Hello."

She mustered her most humble tone. "I'm so sorry."

"Don't worry about it. You were right to suspect me. That's how they set it up."

"I should have trusted you."

"No, I'm glad you didn't. I take it you've read the diary."

"Yep, they've been manipulating you for a long time now. But why?"

"I don't know why they picked me, but they did. I'd like to say I'm getting too old for this shit, but they picked the wrong patsy."

"There's more about Levine. I'm surprised your intelligence didn't catch it."

"I'm not; my intelligence provided only what these bastards wanted me to know."

"The Bureau has tracked him for years. He's involved in performing mind-control experimentation. We've never been able to tie him to anything. This journal is the first proof of criminal activity and connections we've got. We knew Levine had tried to control Bradley. When it didn't work, they killed him and made it look like a suicide."

Levi cut in. "Hafley used Levine to break Unger's mind, accessing the GCCS system override keys. We need to get to Unger at TUG HQ."

Gillian choked up. "Thanks for getting my mom and Maddie to safety."

"I didn't kidnap Thad."

She sighed with relief. "I know."

"Seeing you work through this just makes me love you more," he said. The line was silent. Could a cell phone communicate embarrassment? "Are you still there?"

"Yeah." She whispered.

She ignored the declaration of love. "Okay, where do we go from here?"

"Meet me at TUG headquarters. I spoke with Unger; he's sleeping on the couch tonight. I have a sneaking suspicion he can help us. I tried not to give too much away. He's going to meet us at the elevators."

They stayed on the phone during the drive to Tampa.

"McDonnell, is dead," he said in anguish.

"Are you sure?"

"We were talking on the phone when she died. Hafley killed her with a plane crash that took out the NPO's west coast operations center."

"I'm so sorry."

"Me, too. I was just getting ready to confront her with the diary and accuse her of being the mole. It's bad enough I even thought it, I'm glad I didn't say it."

"That's a positive in this mess." She said.

Morgan continued. "The attacks have begun. Hafley isn't likely to start with a massive takeover. He'll begin small and build to a critical mass before he tries to take out the government."

Gillian agreed. "One thing is for sure; there's no one around here we can trust. That reminds me; I made a call to D.C."

Chapter 63

Thursday, December 5

Levi double-parked in front of the Plaza. Tires screeching, Gillian pulled up to the curb behind him.

The security guard abandoned his TV to confront Levi. "You can't park here."

Gillian flashed her shield. "FBI."

Levi flipped the guard his keys. "Park it wherever you want. There's an emergency up at the TUG headquarters."

They left the bewildered guard at the curb and bolted toward the elevators and the TUG security surveillance. If Hafley was running the attack out of this location, they would be under surveillance as soon as they entered the building. They were as good as dead.

They debated their exit strategy during the ride to the top floor. "Guns, no guns, what do you think?"

His shirt had a tear in it, and Gillian noticed his chest muscle beneath it. He followed her gaze. Instinctively, she pushed the flap of fabric into place.

What the hell am I doing? Self-consciously, she chambered a round into her Ruger and checked the spare clip. "God, I don't know. What do you think?"

He scratched his head with both hands. "Let's not scare the poor guy to death. No guns."

Gillian nodded, holstering her weapon and the clip.

As the doors slid open, they came face to face with the unexpected.

Barefoot and smiling, Unger stood facing them, a .38 caliber Smith and Wesson in his hand. The smell of gunpowder hung in the air. Beyond him, Larry Callahan lay on the floor, blood pooled beneath his head. He showed no sign of life.

"Poor kid," Levi muttered.

Unger displayed none of the erratic behavior of the past. He held the weapon steady and purposeful. "Please remove your weapons and throw them on the floor outside the elevator."

Astonishment gave way to obedience as they shed their weapons and stepped out of the elevator. Unger tossed Gillian a set of handcuffs. "Cuff his hands in front where I can see them." She obeyed, mouthing the word, 'Sorry', as she did.

Unger tossed her another set of cuffs. "Now yourself."

She winched in pain as Unger stepped forward to make sure the cuffs were tight and recovered their weapons.

They'd created this situation by calling ahead to let Unger know they were coming. He'd fooled everyone. Only time would tell if Unger was the ringleader or just cooperating with Hafley.

"Why did you shoot the kid?" Morgan said, thinking of Maddie or Thad. "He was harmless."

"He gave me no choice. He came up here to snoop around after he saw me on the video feeds." Unger thrust his gun into Levi's spine. "Move down the hall toward my office."

Sparsely furnished and sterile, Unger's office was tiny. The utilitarian furnishings included a plain Formica desk and a chrome-frame black couch. There were two doors. One led to Hafley's suite, while the other presumably led to a private bathroom.

As they entered the office, the already macabre scenario took on an air of hallucination.

"On the couch," Unger screamed. "Now!"

Levi and Gillian obeyed without resistance.

Strapped to a desk chair on one side of the room sat Levine. One of Unger's socks had been shoved into his mouth, which had then been taped over. Coagulating blood oozed from holes in the knees of his beautifully tailored pants. His eyes were filled with pain and terror.

"I believe you all met Doctor Levine at dinner last night." Unger chuckled. "We've been having a good session." He produced a digital recorder and pressed the PLAY button. His own voice came out clearly, *"Where are my wife and son?"*

Levine's words were measured and confident. *"You fucking idiot, I'm not going to tell you a damn thing. When Markus gets a hold of you, you're dead."*

"Oh, Markus," Unger said strangely dispassionately. *"He's out in the hall. Apparently, he couldn't withstand a bullet to the head. Do you want me to drag him in?"*

"You sad fuck, there's no way you took out Markus."

Muffled footsteps could be heard on the recording and then a sudden crack—a gunshot, followed by screaming. Gradually, the screaming died to an incessant cry.

"I'll blow your other knee off if you don't tell me where my wife and son are."

"Blow my fucking knee off. I'd rather face you than Hafley."

The sickening click of the .38's hammer could be heard, followed by Levine wailing for mercy, then another gunshot. *"Oh gawd, oh fuuuuuck, shit, goddamnit!"*

"You've been in on this from the beginning. You knew about their kidnapping. You helped Hafley get the GCCS code out of me." The firing pin locked into place once again. *"You were even in on Masters's murder, weren't you?"*

"Okay, I've been involved in the whole thing." Levine gasped. *"But you want Hafley, not me. He's the one behind it all."*

The recording ended. Unger turned toward Levine. Ripping the tape from his face, he removed the sock. The recorder beeped as Unger fumbled with the buttons. "Last chance. You're going to die right here in front of these two if you don't tell me where they are."

Levine sat whimpering.

Gillian cut in. "Steven, please don't kill him. We know where they are."

Unger turned to face them with a puzzled look. "What? How?"

"Stop the recorder."

***

If someone discovered Callahan's body they would never have enough time to stop Hafley. So they did what any sane person would do; they hid it.

Levi found a garbage bag in the utility closet and gingerly covered Larry's head, then they stashed the poor boy behind the couch in Unger's office.

Gillian heard Levi mutter under his breath, "Please don't let this happen to Thad."

She mopped up the blood, found an area rug and threw it over the bloodstained grout. "There, good as new."

Morgan chuckled, "That might fit a cereal spill clean-up but not a grisly soft-tissue mess."

"God, I've got to find a different line of work." She replied.

The three stood in the doorway of Unger's office.

"Now, what do we do with him? I think I've controlled the bleeding, but he'll need medical attention soon." Levi had wrapped the wounds on Levine's thighs. The makeshift bandages were already heavy with congealed blood.

"Let's lock him in my bathroom." Unger chimed in cheerfully.

Gillian looked at Levi. "I guess we could do that. As soon as we're out of the building, I'll call 9-1-1."

"It's a plan."

"Let's see if we can get some information from the television."

Chapter 64

Far from business as usual, a phalanx of cables and wires ran throughout the Plaza's lobby area. News crews staked out their territory and reporters wearing makeup bibs scurried about, radiating artificial importance. Fifteen to twenty news outlets, representing everything from the local to national media, had turned out to cover the death of David Masters.

TUG employees had the day off. The top floor remained completely deserted, which worked fine, considering the events that had recently occurred there. The unlikely trio sat in Unger's office discussing their next move.

***

"This is Valerie Malone, at the Plaza in downtown Tampa. Robin, we expect the interim director of the Ultraist Group, Randall Hafley, to arrive shortly. He'll be making a statement this morning about the brutal slaying of David Masters, the late head of TUG. As many of you may recall, we recently aired an interview with Masters, which revealed him as one of the foremost philosophers of our era. For a number of years he espoused a radical platform of change within the American political scene. His book, *The Ultraist Manifesto*, appeared on the New York Times bestseller list."

"Excuse me, Robin, Mr. Hafley has just arrived."

Randall Hafley appeared dapper in his fifteen hundred dollar suit as he stepped up to the podium. Surrounded by his entourage, he could have been the CEO of any Fortune 100 company.

"My remarks will be brief. As you know, at approximately seven o'clock last night, an assassin took the life of David Masters. Police have yet to apprehend the man who pulled the trigger. However, I am confident they'll catch him.

"As in ancient times, I believe a man David trusted turned on him. I suspect the U.S. government was involved in these dealings. In fact, several government agents were at the table with David Masters last night and did nothing to stop those horrific events.

"As he sought to bring about revolutionary change, David understood that he was putting his life on the line every day. He knew that standing tall and speaking out for human rights put us in harm's way. He knew that those who desire to maintain the status quo, those who want to oppress the masses, always seek to destroy the ones bent on liberation. He knew that pushing too hard was a dangerous game. We don't have to look far back in history to see that—John F. Kennedy, Doctor Martin Luther King Jr., and Bobby Kennedy—are but a few.

"There are things worth dying for. David believed that. Only through living our beliefs does death take on lasting meaning. Now is the time to get behind the movement that he started. Let us pay him homage by making his dreams a reality.

"To his followers, I say, don't lose hope. David Masters died because those with power—the economic, political, and religious powerbrokers—feared him. Ardent capitalists knew that David's teachings represent the end of their reign. Right-wing Christian power mongers—Fundamentalist, Evangelicals, Protestants, and Catholics—sensed that Ultraist Group as a direct threat to their established constituencies and dogma. Political bosses, both democrat and republican, understand intuitively that TUG represents the end of their oppressive system.

"He did not die in vain. His death serves to identify those who oppress us.

"I have lost a dear friend, but I will pursue his dream. I call on all of America to rise up against those who would manipulate and abuse us. Join with the Ultraist Group in the new revolution. That's all for now, no questions please."

Chapter 65

Levi flipped off the television and leapt from the sofa in Unger's office. "We're totally fucked. Hafley gave me access to GCCS, but I don't know the pin code. There isn't much hope of finding it." He shook his head. "We don't know enough to override the system."

"Wait a minute. What do we know?" Gillian asked.

"The attack started last night. So far, it's subtle, a few downed planes around the world. It'll probably pick up over the next several hours. They've already knocked out the Pacific rim intelligence gathering sites in San Francisco and Santiago."

"So the government has to know something concerted is happening."

"We've got Levine's confession on tape." Steven gave a sheepish shrug.

Gillian smiled. "I'm afraid that one won't hold up in court."

"We know they plan to render Echelon useless by taking out the Skyway."

"Don't you know someone in the military who would believe your story? Anyone?"

Levi covered his mouth with his hand, then scratched his stubble. He nodded. "That's a great idea. General Marsh owes me a favor or two. He could help. But how do I talk to him without tipping our hand to Haddon and Hafley?"

"At this point, I don't think it matters. I'll make a run for Sarasota. Hopefully, I can engage some help through the Bureau."

"Okay, that takes care of the city under the bay and hopefully captures Hafley. What about disabling GCCS?"

"I can stop GCCS," Steven said.

"I can't ask you to do that after all you've been through," Gillian said.

"Just get my wife and son to safety. I'll stop the GCCS."

"I didn't want to ask you, but I sure appreciate it."

Gillian feared for his safety given his fragile physical and mental condition. "You know how dangerous this is."

"Just help my family."

Levi held out his hand. "Let me see your weapon."

Steven dutifully handed over the revolver. Levi flipped the cylinder open. "You only have one round left," he said reaching into his pocket. He removed his own weapon and pressed it into Steven's hand. "Just in case."

"Where are you going?" He asked in a docile tone.

"I think I know where Hafley is running this op from." He gave Steven a wink as he walked through the door and headed to the lobby.

Chapter 66

Pleased with himself, Hafley strode through the reporters with a subtle smirk. He murmured to no one in particular, "Where the fuck is Markus? I can't believe he's missing a chance for glory."

With his retinue in tow, he plowed through the media hordes. Amidst their hollered questions and his people's cries of no further comment, they wound their way through the crowd to a curbside stretch limo with blacked-out windows. A large suit with sunglasses and an earpiece opened his door.

He'd begun to see himself as a world leader and felt he should assume the associated perks as well. "Take us to the rendezvous location."

"Yes sir."

With a black suburban in the lead and another on its tail, the limo was the center vehicle of a three-car convoy. The armada wound its way through downtown and into Ybor City, where it entered an abandoned cigar manufacturing facility. The procession passed through the open doors of the warehouse, and the doors closed behind them.

Five minutes passed and the doors reopened. Six black Suburbans with three limos exited the warehouse and left the facility, traveling in groups of three.

He wasn't taking any chances on his coronation day. Each set of vehicles headed in a different direction. In his mind, paranoia was essential to keeping one's throne. No one would have any idea which set of vehicles he traveled in. He was free to take care of business.

***

Unger stepped into Hafley's office and moved directly to the humidor. He flipped it open, confident no one had been smart enough to figure out his algorithms. He placed his hand on the scanner. The computer, recognizing the points on his palm and fingers, ran several secondary algorithms. No pin code was necessary. "Please provide audio sample for final verification."

"Rose and Ricky fly around a tree."

"Audio verified. Welcome, Doctor Unger." The panel on the west wall slid open.

Chapter 67

Treasure Circle was part of a newly gentrified neighborhood in south Tampa. A developer had come in and bought every house on the small circle just outside the main gate of MacDill AFB. He'd knocked all of the houses down, paired the lots, and built massive homes that appealed to the *nuevo riche* of Tampa.

Morgan had parked just up the street from the sublet house for about forty-five minutes when three vehicles arrived.

"Excellent. I knew this had to be the place." Morgan watched as Hafley went inside.

Markus had gone in just minutes before.

***

Gillian headed south toward the FBI offices in Sarasota. An old friend from her Academy days should be able to get word to the Director. Her phone rang; it was Levi.

"Gillian, time's up. They're moving." He wasn't panicked in the least.

"I got through to my DC contact. An FBI team is standing by."

"Have them show up at 4389 Treasure Circle; just outside the front gate at MacDill."

"They'll be there in half an hour."

"I can't wait that long. Tell them to come in and sort it out later. You've got to stop all traffic on the Skyway or every vehicle on the span will end up in the bay."

"Shit, I don't know how I can do that."

"You'll find a way. I'm going after Hafley. Take care."

***

Morgan sat in the truck prepared for battle. He set the rhythm of his breathing and visualized courage, honor, and integrity. Should it be necessary, he would arrive in Elysian with dignity. He entered his state of *mushin no shin*—mind of no mind—the samurai state of unguarded tension.

***

Gillian wrestled with guilt at having doubted Levi's motivation and loyalty. Swerving through traffic, she nearly crashed several times as she continuously dialed the Sarasota field office.

She stopped at the top of the Skyway. Traffic was at its peak. The bridge throbbed with life as Gillian hopped out and approached the median.

Scaling the median was more difficult than she'd expected. She leaned against the abutment and kicked off her heels. *Damn it, solid concrete, no way to threaten a jump from here.*

Hot air and exhaust made her queasy. Swirling wind turned her hair into stinging whips cracking against her face.

A highway patrolman stepped out of his car and looked her way. He tried not to scare her as he slid between the car and the concrete, preparing to talk her off the bridge.

She yelled above the din, "I'm FBI. I need you to clear this bridge. It's going to be hit by a commercial airliner any minute."

He hadn't expected to hear anything like that, but his facial expression didn't change.

The depressed and despondent who made up the true jumpers rarely stuck around to talk with anyone. They just did their business. Glory-seekers didn't find a lot of value in impersonating peace officers. He thought she was part of the lunatic fringe, one of the truly insane who dwell in the world of the mind. Those were the most unpredictable of the lot. You never knew what turn a situation with them might take.

"Ma'am, you're gonna hafta show me some identification. I cain't just take your word that you're FBI and stop all traffic on the bridge, now cain I?"

She started to freak out. Her shield was in the car. "Call the FBI; they can verify who I am."

Tires drummed steadily over the expansion joints, heightening her sense of vertigo. The wind swooshed erratically with each passing vehicle. She crouched instinctively to lower her center of gravity.

The officer inched forward at the opportunity.

She turned toward the northbound lanes. "Please sir."

He froze, apparently confused by her movement.

"I'm begging you; stop the traffic on this bridge."

She ran across the elevated concrete median, jumped to the shoulder, and darted across the northbound lanes, narrowly avoiding a tractor-trailer. The sound of breaks and horns was deafening. Trucks geared down, their engines making deep throaty complaints.

She gripped the railing. Far below, the wind whipped the water into frenzied swirling whitecaps. Her stomach lurched, her head spun. She instinctively drew back, but her hands wouldn't release the railing.

She was determined to survive this ordeal.

She looked back to see the trooper clambering over the abutment toward the northbound lanes. She floated upwards as another huge truck thundered past. Fear lifted her heart into her throat. She gripped the railing tighter.

"Ma'am, please come back over here where it's safe."

"Get these cars out of here or I'll jump. You already know I'm crazy. Do it!"

He had no choice but to inch his way through the steady stream of rubbernecking traffic. He stopped five or six feet away and started to direct traffic. "Please come down off that rail. Come over here where it's safe."

"Are you an idiot?" The entire bridge seemed to sway. "Get these cars off the bridge." She turned and faced east, coming face to face with her worst nightmare. A Boeing 747 lumbered across the bay at a much lower altitude than normal. The cop couldn't see it from his vantage point.

"Hurry up! Do it now!" She screamed.

All she could hope was that Levi could take control of GCCS before that plane killed everyone on this bridge. If he failed, Hafley would accomplish his main goal of sealing the western entrance to the city under the bay.

After several minutes of directing traffic and yelling over his shoulder, the officer turned toward her. His face contorted in confusion and terror as he saw the airliner about five-hundred yards out, coming straight at them. Encouraging words died on his lips, choked by primal fear into Neanderthal-like grunts.

"Stop gawking and get these cars off of the span."

The southbound lanes were nearly empty but the cop's presence actually slowed the traffic in the northbound lanes.

Looking over the edge was dizzying but she would jump if Levi failed. She wasn't about to leave Maddie motherless without a fight.

Chapter 68

"There you are. You missed the fun." Hafley was giddy with excitement.

"Check this out. I think you'll agree it was worth it." With the click of a mouse, Markus brought a digital video image onto one of the large monitors. The tape showed a scuffle and a shooting.

Hafley snorted, "Holy shit, I wish I could've been there for that. I bet that felt good."

Markus just grinned and nodded.

The TUG security watch commander reported. "We have men stationed throughout the area, ready to move on the emergency exit, sir."

"Perfect. Has Morgan taken the bait?"

"He's been watching the house for the past hour, sir."

"Let me know when he approaches. Gentlemen, are we ready to have some fun?"

A marine-like hoot went up around the room.

"Let's take over some aircraft."

Chapter 69

The B2 rumbled down the runway of Whiteman Air Force Base just west of Jefferson City, Missouri. The aircraft performed a flawless takeoff and climbed into the crisp blue skies. Several wisps of cirrus clouds hung in the western sky—a perfect morning for flying. Taking this bird up was a privilege beyond Bob McAlister's wildest childhood dream.

In addition to being the fastest vehicle known to man, the B2 Stealth Bomber was virtually invisible. Given its speed and maneuverability, it existed outside the seek-and-destroy capabilities of all earth- or space-based systems. Once airborne, it became a phantom even to its masters.

Bob opened the orders from USSTRATCOM out of Offutt Air Force Base in Nebraska. He spoke over the onboard intercom. "Holy Shit, Ace, we got a good one this time."

"What we got, Bobby?"

Ace Freeman had been Bob's mission commander since joining the Grim Reapers of the 13th Bomb Squadron. He'd run through three wives in rapid succession and had become a notorious womanizer in the process. He'd acquired his nickname several years back, the result of an unsuccessful bluff at the end of an all-night poker game. A mythological god to the immature, he was the stuff of underdeveloped legends—a walking cliché of Air Force flyers.

"COMPLAN 8022."

"Wahoo, this is gonna be fun. Let's make the 509th proud."

COMPLAN 8022 involved simulating a preemptive nuclear strike against a rogue state, presumably Iran or North Korea. The beginning of such an exercise opened a twenty-four-hour window within which strike decisions could be debated, changed, and finalized. The exercise would test the rapid course of action and execution capabilities of the Global Strike Integration Operations Command.

"Confirm air traffic transition to Offutt."

"Confirm that, Eagle One. Transferring to Offutt control for Global Strike Integration exercises."

"Offutt control, this is Global Lightening, do you copy?" McAlister said into the mike.

"Roger, Global Lightening, we have you. Confirm orders."

"Orders read 'Engage COMPLAN 8022.' Confirm."

"COMPLAN 8022 confirmed. Exercise is a go."

"GSI, confirm our position at lat 41.62806, lon 98.9525, climbing to 39/5, moving west-northwest at approximately 650 knots."

"Roger that, Global Lightening, our instruments confirm."

"You ready to rock-n-roll, Bobby?"

"This is going to be sweet."

"Global Lightening, this is GSI ground control, please confirm status of MHD systems."

Ace had been hyper-focused on system panels since hearing the words COMPLAN 8022. No one had come close to equaling his in-flight hours. His practical working knowledge of the system was unparalleled. In spite of his shortcomings, he'd mastered the magneto-hydrodynamic propulsion system that made this aircraft the pinnacle of human engineering and achievement. He referenced numerous digital displays, flipped covers off buttons, and pressed them to change settings. The antigravity system was charged, the cavitation projections read normal, and the ununpentium reactor was working normally. He loved this system the way most men loved a good woman, and it had become his mistress.

"All systems check out normal. MHD is ready to engage on captain's orders."

"Global Lightening, please confirm payload inventory and status prior to MHD engagement."

Ace checked several panels to his left. "GSI, this is Global Lightening, systems indicate five B61-11's at 300K per. Status of each is warm; repeat status is warm."

The B61-11 was the latest version of earth-penetrating nuclear weapons. A warm status meant the fuses had been loaded into each delivery device. Onboard and off-board codes were the only requirements to render the weapons capable of detonation. At 300 kilotons each, they were considered low-yield tactical weapons. Dropped from 40,000 feet, one could penetrate six meters of concrete or thirty meters of earth before detonating. The underground shockwave from the explosion would destroy everything in its path to approximately 200 feet. Detonation would create a massive crater and produce a narrow column of lethal gamma-radiation and a surge of air filled with radioactive dust flowing over a five to ten mile radius.

"Confirmed Global Lightening, payload is five B61-11's at 300K per with a status warm. Engage MHD on our mark, captain."

"Affirmative, GSI, awaiting your mark to engage MHD."

"Damn, I swear this is better than sex," Ace said.

"Global Lightening, engage MHD in five-four-three-two-one, mark."

"Moving to radio silence, MHD engaged."

As Bob spoke the words, Ace flipped the final switch. In a beam of light, the sleek aircraft burst forth from a yellowish plasma cloud of ionized air. By design, the shockwave and the sound dissipated into the high atmosphere. Within seconds, the jet hit mach eight and kept accelerating.

Bob flipped several other switches, killing the conventional engines and reducing the infrared footprint below detectable levels. Essentially, they'd become invisible. Twenty minutes later, they flew over the Pacific just off the coast of Alaska.

Chapter 70

The shrill whistle declared the morning break at the refinery in Chalmette, Louisiana. Marvin Breaux had lived his whole life on the river. In just a few weeks, he would retire and begin chasing his boyhood again.

He loved taking his break out at the picnic tables near the fence far from the hustle and bustle of the facility. As long as he didn't face the plant, it was easy to imagine himself on the bayou. He could stare out toward the delta and dream of a different time—a time that hadn't been ruined by big business and big storms. One could easily forget downtown New Orleans laying just eight short miles away.

He'd worked for most of his life at this refinery, producing high-octane gasoline. Even though he'd never smoked a cigarette, he'd lost one of his lungs to cancer about five years back. Hydrofluoric acid had caused it; he knew that with a certainty.

The company had patented a safer refining process already in production in California and Utah, but they chose to continue using hydrofluoric acid for the refining process here. It was cheaper and brought a significant improvement to their quarterly reports. What did it matter if a few people got sick? There was no apparent connection.

He was uneducated but he wasn't stupid. He understood that they'd made changes in California because they were more affluent and educated. The poor parishes of Louisiana would never benefit from the new process unless federal regulations mandated that big oil stop using hydrofluoric acid.

The wind blew gently from the east toward New Orleans.

***

Marvin knew something was wrong the minute he saw the commercial airliner come in low. Planes out of Louis Armstrong should have been miles high by this point—out of sight.

He stood in slack-jawed terror as the jet flew full-bore into the largest cache of hydrofluoric acid in the state.

The explosion roared and flames leapt hundreds of feet into the air as the jet fuel reacted with 694,000 pounds of acid. A toxic cloud began to drift westward on the gentle breeze.

He began to cry, not because his eyes suffered chemical burns, but because he couldn't understand the intolerable cruelty of fate. His skin began to blister and burn. His nose and throat swelled shut even as his lung began to hemorrhage. As his bones turned to gelatin, he lay down on the soil of his beloved Louisiana, letting the gentle breeze caress his weary brow.

Without hope of mercy, New Orleans lay in the path of its wind-borne killer.

Chapter 71

"GSI, this is Global Lightening, we are commencing targeting readiness, requesting permission to light the candles."

"Affirmative, Global Lightening enter your codes."

McAlister detached a key from his belt and inserted it into the safe. He removed a small canister. "Here you go, Ace. Key in the pin number."

Ace flipped the cylinder around and keyed in a six-digit code. He flipped it back around and twisted the cap off. Ceremoniously, he raised it and let the fob slide into his palm. It was the same shape and size as all remote ID devices on the open market.

Ace handed McAlister the fob. "Here you go, Bobby."

McAlister keyed in an eight-digit pin. The tiny screen displayed a twelve-digit number, which he wrote on a note pad. He returned the key to the canister and put both back in the safe and locked it.

He turned to one of the laptops they'd carried onboard and keyed in his user name and pass code. He launched several programs, each requiring a unique log-in and password. Finally, he reached the correct screen and spun the laptop around. "Your turn Ace, sign in to access the arming software."

Freeman entered the information and turned the laptop back to him. "It's all yours."

McAlister entered the twelve-digit code and hit the ENTER key.

"GSI, codes have been entered. I repeat, onboard codes have been entered."

"Roger that, Global Lightening, standby for communication of ground code."

"CENTCOM, upload code when ready."

At the heart of US Central Command at MacDill Air Force Base, in the city under the bay, General Haddon provided the final arming code.

"This is Global Lightening, on my mark, the candles are lit." McAlister keyed in Haddon's code.

"Candles are lit; I repeat candles are lit at eleven hundred hours CST."

"Well, Ace, only a Presidential order stands between us and history."

Chapter 72

"This is it people. This is why we've practiced thousands of hours." Hafley watched as his team seamlessly took control of the B2. "It's just a shame we couldn't do this on Pearl Harbor Day."

Instantly, the B2 began to alter its course.

Chapter 73

McAlister broke radio silence. "GSI, this is Global Lightening. Have you engaged the Global Hawk System?"

Global Hawk was the military's ground control system based on the NASA Remote Systems Architect's programming logic. It was the next generation in government efforts to create unmanned combat aircraft. Like its commercial counterpart, GCCS, it allowed full remote control of all military aircraft.

"Negative, Global Lightening, Global Hawk has not been engaged."

"GSI, the aircraft is no longer responding to pilot command, requesting permission for manual override of Global Hawk." Unlike other military aircraft, due to its astronomically high cost, the B2 was equipped with a mechanical means for disengaging from the Global Hawk control system.

"Roger that, Global Lightening. Override Global Hawk and return to base."

Ace cocked his service revolver. "Sorry, Bobby, I can't let you stop this flight. It's my ticket to the good life with a clean slate."

McAlister sat dumbfounded.

Ace had been bleeding money to loan sharks for years. Recently, an unknown benefactor had purchased his debt and promised to erase it, along with rewarding him handsomely for additional services. What did he care if a few bombs had to fall? He'd signed up to drop the damn things anyway.

McAlister started to protest. The projectile pierced his heart and came to rest near his left shoulder blade before he could utter a sound.

Ace began the process of re-targeting two of the warheads as someone on the ground maneuvered the plane east along the 38th parallel, toward its target.

***

"General, word has just come in that we're experiencing multiple hits on civilian targets. The President has issued orders to ground all commercial aircraft until further notice."

General James Barton had spent his life in the military. He'd been through Grenada, Libya, Panama, both Iraq offensives, and 9/11. He thought he had seen it all. "What the fuck is going on?"

"Sir, we have mass civilian casualties in Philadelphia and New Jersey. A toxic cloud of hydrofluoric acid has completely covered New Orleans. Reports are coming in from other major metropolitan areas, as well. It appears there's a concerted effort to use civilian aircraft as flying bombs targeting high-impact sites.

Barton let out a long sigh.

"It's worse, sir." The reporting officer shifted his weight. "These strikes seem to be happening on every continent."

"Contact General Marsh at CENTCOM and offer our assistance. Let's get this plane on the ground."

"Yes sir."

"What's the status on Global Lightening?"

"Global Lightening, this is GSI, we have readings from your targeting systems that must be corrected."

Silence.

"Global Lightening, this is GSI, do you copy?"

Dead air.

General Barton began barking orders. "Scramble fighters. Pick up their trajectory at the point of MHD engagement. Gentlemen, this is not a drill. We have a hostile aircraft over American soil with live nukes. I expect to take it down as soon as possible."

"General, two of the weapons have been programmed with new targets."

The Lieutenant surrendered a printout. Barton couldn't believe what he read.

```
Targeting    Schema    B61-11,    serial    number
00009950
Targeting    coordinates:    Lat    38.532401    Lon
77.003244
```

Handwritten next to the coordinates were the words 'US Capitol Building.'

```
Targeting    Schema    B61-11,    serial    number
00009951
Targeting    coordinates:    Lat    39.109608    Lon
76.774993
```

Handwritten next to the coordinates were the words 'NSA HQ, Fort Meade.'

He looked perplexed, then closed his eyes. "Are you sure?"

"Yes sir, we've triple checked."

"Get the President on the phone. Engage Continuity of Government plan. Scramble the Raptors out of Langley. This thing cannot get through. This is not a drill, people. Find that plane and destroy it. We have less than thirty minutes."

At his creative worst, Barton could never have imagined the 509th would be the source of a decapitation strike on Washington DC. "What American could put eight million people within the fatality plume of a nuclear warhead?" he muttered.

"General, we have F-22's airborne out of Eglin, approaching last known location of Global Lightening."

"Put them on screen and open audio."

Nosecone camera shots appeared on the screens but audio failed.

"Sir, apparently, the Global Hawk system is malfunctioning. All fighters report a loss of aircraft control. Two Raptors crashed on takeoff from Langley."

"Fuck!" Barton slammed a fist onto the console. "Ground all aircraft. What the hell is going on here?"

Chapter 74

Morgan dialed the personal cell number of General Marsh, an old friend at MacDill. "General, this is Levi Morgan."

"God, Morgan, what's going on? I've got a B2 with live nukes headed toward D.C. What can you tell me?"

"There's an assault team getting ready to storm the Echelon complex. They've taken control of the Global Hawk system and the civilian GCCS. They're using planes as weapons to stage a coup. I'm trying to restore Global Hawk control to you." He hesitated, knowing it would be hard for Marsh to accept what he was about to say. "General Haddon is a conspirator in the coup attempt."

"Goddamn it. Leave this line open so I can hear your progress. Notify me as soon as you've regained control. Good luck."

"Thanks."

He drove the truck up to the house and walked to the front door. He didn't bother to knock, just opened the door and walked in.

Skip seemed relaxed "'Bout damn time you showed up. I was beginning to wonder if you were going to sit out there at the curb all day and miss the fun."

"Fuck you, you're under arrest."

A strange, almost girlish laugh slipped from Skip's lips. "Goddamn, I can't believe it. You walk in here totally unarmed and outmanned, yet you still have the balls to spew bullshit. Amazing. I brought you here, arranged this house for you, killed your ex-wife, kidnapped your son, and framed you for murder. Everything that's happened in your life over the past month has been my doing. It all coincided with the government's test of their most sophisticated nuclear delivery device."

"Give it up, Skip, you're fucked. Unger isn't crazy. He's going to disassemble your little science project."

Skip's laugh turned devilish and throaty. "You mean this guy?"

A digital image flashed on a large video screen across the room. Morgan watched as Unger entered Skip's office and moved to the humidor. He opened the lid and scanned his palm.

"Rose and Ricky fly around a tree." Suddenly a panel opened before him.

Morgan looked on in horror as Markus slipped into the room. He circled Unger like a wolf cornering its prey. Unger pulled his gun and shouted obscenities. Markus just kept circling in an ever-decreasing concentric direction, frustrating Unger. At the last second, Markus looked to his left; Unger followed his glance, realizing too late that it was a ploy. Markus sprang on him, relieved him of the weapon with little struggle, and pushed him to the ground, where the desk obscured the camera angle. Markus fired twice.

Markus turned, holding Morgan's weapon, and walked to the humidor, which he flipped shut. The screen went blank. The panel closed.

"Man, I wish I had a close up of that. He was so fucking annoying. Good work, Mike." Skip turned back to Morgan. "He was killed with your gun and we have video of you leaving the complex. Oh well, I guess you're screwed . . . *again.*"

Morgan scanned the room for weapons, real or improvised. Nothing was available, not even a pen. The .38 in his pocket only had one bullet. He preferred to get out of this alive. "The FBI is outside right now."

Skip's eyes twitched in rapid succession. "Do you think I give a shit about the FBI? By tomorrow morning, I'll own this country and you'll be dead." He gave a triumphant sneer and then his face contorted. He began to cry. "You *did.* You left me for dead." Skip gave an involuntary double blink.

"Skip, don't believe it for a minute. They've used you for all these years. You don't have to be their pawn anymore."

Skip laughed but his words became increasingly incoherent. "I've known every move you were going to make from the beginning. You fucking puppet. Payback's a bitch, ain't it?"

"Skip."

"It's a bitch."

"Skip you don't have to live like this."

As if cued by some mysterious force, Markus stepped from behind Skip. He leveled a gun—Morgan's gun—at Skip's head and pulled the trigger. Blood and brains burst from the opposite side of his skull, splattering a rather large part of the wall. His body flopped uselessly to the ground, expelling the contents of his bladder and bowels.

Morgan stared in disbelief, then looked at Markus. "Whose side are you on?"

Markus just stood next to his kill, smiling.

McDonnell stepped through an adjacent doorway. ""Hello, Levi. I told you I'd be here in the morning to wrap this up."

"Deb?" He began to feel light-headed, disoriented. He turned to Markus, wondering if he were seeing and hearing her, as well. Markus seemed happy to see her.

"You're so gullible. You thought I was dead. I couldn't believe you called me at the exact moment I was going to call you. Hell, you thought Anu was my inside man. I've been leading you around by the nose for weeks."

"Why?"

Her face transformed in an unholy crimson rage. The words came forth as though spoken by some mythic creature filled with hate and fury and fear. "Because your father chose you over me."

The thought caused Morgan to breathe out an involuntary half-laugh. "What the fuck are you talking about? I hated my father, and he hated me."

280

"Bullshit! You're still trying to gain his love and acceptance, and he's been dead for nearly twenty years. You loved him and he loved you. He was so fucking proud of you. It makes me sick. He rejected me to stay and serve in Grenada with you. Then the fucking bastard got himself killed, and it was your fault." White, foamy spittle hung from the edge of her mouth.

"Deb, I don't know what you're talking about. Until last week, I had no idea you even knew my dad."

"Knew him!" Flecks of spit flew as she spoke. "You fucking idiot, I loved him more than you can imagine. We'd been lovers for years, and then you had to come along and steal his fucking attention." Her face contorted into a hideous inhuman shape. "God, I hate you. After you made the SEALs, he was on cloud nine. He wanted nothing more than to serve with you, even if it cost him his life. I've wanted to kill you for so long; I can't remember not wanting to kill you."

She shifted the subject, jerking her thumb toward Hafley's carcass. "I stumbled onto Hutchins in a pigsty in the mountains of Columbia. He was really just an empty shell, a modern Ben Gunn. I rescued him. It wasn't until the trip home, when I found out who he was, that I realized his bitter madness might come in handy. It was surprisingly easy to take that blank slate and create Randall Hafley. The plastic surgery was the hardest part." A look of regret came over her face. "Hutchins was more than happy to set you up, but he let the whole thing go to his head over the last few weeks. Unavoidable, I guess." She became calm. "We planned everything out to the smallest detail. We fucked with your head by fucking with your family. We used Levine to set Liz up with Markus, who wined her, dined her, and killed her. Fun wasn't it, Mike?"

Markus just grinned.

"I took everything precious from you, everything that you ever loved. The same way you took it from me."

He felt the weight of the .38 in his pocket. McDonnell would be unarmed. One shot was all he'd need to take Markus out of play. The son of a bitch had killed his ex and brutalized his son. His soul began to rage. His spiritual equilibrium destroyed, he plummeted from the mushin state, knocked out by his emotions. For the first time since Columbia, the urge to kill was personal.

He hated these two with a crushing, passionate hatred. He would enjoy killing Markus and giving McDonnell a painful, lingering death. There would be no mercy, no opportunity for them to slip the bonds of justice.

He flipped the safety off. "I'll see you in hell."

Guns appeared everywhere. In his rush to stop Skip, Morgan hadn't noticed that the technicians manning the computer terminals around the room were a bit too disciplined. His threat caused McDonnell's handpicked mercenaries to snap to attention, weapons trained on him.

"What are you, some fucking idiot? You might kill Markus, but you'll never kill me."

A perplexed look crossed Markus' face but he didn't divert his attention from Morgan.

A quiet inner voice challenged Morgan's explosive anger and hate. *You don't have to feel this way. You're free not to feel this way. The choice is yours.*

Like Christ in Gethsemane, he battled his impulses, the temptation before him overwhelming.

As he drew in a deep sobering breath, he recognized the distinct metallic taste of intimidation-induced adrenaline. Flashing before him was the dream of his youth, fleeing from streetlight to streetlight, his pulse thundering in his ears. It was time to stop and face his terrifying pursuer who he now knew was himself.

Massive, dormant gears within his psyche lumbered into action, opening the floodgates of his soul. The river of life flowed beyond the Mushin boundaries of battle and filled the boundless *now*. Here there was no honor or dishonor, no past or future. There was only the *oneness* as it washed away the illusion of separateness. In this place, logic, reason, and self-consciousness were pollutants.

This abrupt awakening accompanied the realization that he no longer needed to endure his waking or sleeping nightmares. Long-standing contradictions harmonized and reverberated within his essence. Suddenly, he felt comfortable resting in life's paradoxes, the need for vain analysis dropping away. He recognized the *One in All and the All in One* within himself.

This sacred event gave him peace. Separateness washed away. He didn't need to look back with regret nor fear the future. The *eternal now*, the Tao, had revealed itself.

Without warning the front and rear doors burst open.

"FBI, drop your weapons."

He pulled his hands from his pockets, letting the .38 fall to the floor. He lifted both hands over his head. In his left hand, he held the satellite phone.

McDonnell spoke first. "Thank God you're here. Arrest this bastard for treason."

Every agent in the house trained their gun on Markus and McDonnell.

Morgan pressed the speakerphone button. "General, we've taken control of the command center. You should have control of your equipment now."

"Negative, Morgan, our birds are still unavailable. You need to do something else or Washington is history. ETA to launch point is less than two minutes."

"General, you need to speak to the FBI Special Agent in charge."

The agent in charge of the strike force spoke up, "That won't be necessary. Are you Morgan?"

"Yeah."

"Anu's vouched for you. Do what you need to do."

Deb McDonnell screamed obscenities as the agents cuffed her. "You're dead, Morgan. My brother will make sure that you're fucking dead."

Morgan checked his watch and sat down at a terminal. *What had Unger been ranting all along? Could it have been a code?* He began to type.

```
Rose and Rickie fly around a tree.  Look how
happy they have made you and me.
```

He hit the ENTER key. Nothing happened. He looked at his watch. "How much time, General?"

You've got forty-five seconds before they enter the launch window."

"Damn, damn, damn! What am I missing?" He rubbed the stubble on his chin.

Each second resounded gong-like in his mind as the blood rushed to his brain; time stood still. The General counted down. Thirty seconds. Twenty seconds. Time continued to contract.

That's when he realized his mistake.

"God, I hope this works." He began to type again.

```
Rose and Rickie fly around a tree.  Look how
happy they've made you and me.
```

He said a prayer as he pressed the ENTER key.

The terminal flashed. The prompt read, *Welcome Dr. Unger.* The cursor kept winking at him. He glanced at his watch, fifteen seconds left. He typed, disassemble.

The terminal prompted, *Disassemble GCCS and Global Hawk code? (Y/N)*

Morgan entered Y and pressed the key once more. Ten seconds remained before the nukes could launch. The neighboring screen locked up. A warning dialogue box opened, "Connection to Global Hawk server has been lost."

He grabbed the satellite phone, "General Marsh, your birds are free to fly."

Marsh wasted no time. "Langley, send in the raptors and deactivate Global Lightening."

Chapter 75

On board the B2, Ace Freeman felt a jolt as the Global Hawk system went off-line.

"What the fuck?"

He looked at the controls and realized the plan had failed. "GSI, this is Global Lightening, do you copy?"

"Go ahead, Global Lightening."

Ace's voice quivered. "Someone overrode our communication equipment."

"Calm down, solider. What's your name?"

"Apparently, they were using Global Hawk to re-route us. Colonel McAlister was in on it. I overpowered him and shot him. But I couldn't take control of the plane until just a minute ago."

"Affirmative, Global Lightening. Someone has been using Global Hawk to redirect your aircraft. Identify yourself."

"Captain Charles Freeman, sir."

"Captain Freeman, this is General Barton. You've done a great service to your country. Now let's disarm those nukes and get you back home."

"Roger that, GSI."

Chapter 76

Gillian stepped onto the bottom rung of the rail, ready to plunge toward safety. The early morning sun brought clarity. A salty gust brushed the hair off her face, giving an unobstructed view of the 747 as it continued to bear down on the bridge. On her. There was no point in running. If the plane hit, the span—everything—would collapse, and her with it.

She wouldn't be around for Maddie's first day of school, for her graduation, her marriage, her first baby . . .

God, get me through this and I'll always put her first.

She would have to time this just right, jumping at the last possible second, just in case.

The bay looked like a steady progression of snow-capped peaks. The wind and waves reduced the likelihood of her surviving the fall.

It had become eerily quiet. The traffic was gone. A high-flying pelican glided nearby, scouting for fish. Wind whistled through the spans and girders blowing the last traces of exhaust out to sea. It almost felt serene. Almost.

One glance at the massive 747 banished serenity. She thrust her body upward on the rail and looked at the plane. Was it her imagination? Was she seeing the faces of horrified passengers as the aircraft strained against every joint in its effort to survive?

She leaned forward, hesitating one final moment.

Then . . .

Levi must have succeeded. The plane would miss the supporting towers of the bridge. Yet she clutched the railing, every muscle taut, ready to throw herself over in a final attempt to live. Could the pilot still get enough thrust to lift clear of the roadway?

The jets engines roared as it flashed past.

She eased herself down and dropped to the pavement, rushing to the patrolman. She gave him a hug. Heat shimmered above the concrete as she ran toward the nearest northbound car. She pulled open the door; the driver thought he was getting a hug too. She left him dumbfounded on the empty deck of the Skyway as she drove back toward Tampa.

Chapter 77

Ace landed the B2 with flawless accuracy. As he taxied up to the hanger, he saw General Barton. "Holy shit, I'm going to get a medal for this."

He shut the engines down and descended the gangway. Barton stood there, flanked by his entourage. Ace just smiled. He moved directly toward Barton and reached out a hand.

Security police slapped cuffs on his extended wrist.

Stunned, he exclaimed, "What are you doing? I just saved all three branches of the government and the fucking NSA. I'm a goddamn hero. Get your fucking hands off me."

"What? Do you think I'm stupid? You're under arrest for treason," Barton said. "You just sealed your own fate. Not only did you know exactly where those nukes were targeted, you also knew the mission objective. You better have a damn good lawyer." The general pivoted and walked away.

"You can't do this to me. I'm somebody."

"Sergeant, don't forget the flight recorder. It's evidence," Barton said as he kept walking.

Chapter 78

Gillian drove like a mad woman to Port Tampa to meet an FBI team less than two miles from MacDill. The early December sun was surprisingly fierce. Beneath a ballistic vest, sweat trickled down her torso.

Thunk-ca-thunk ca-thunk. Thunk-ca-thunk ca-thunk.

Gravel poured from a large ship onto a conveyor bound for a nearby concrete plant. Gulls swooped toward the cars screaming for food.

"Fan out and establish a perimeter. Alpha team comes with me; we'll board the tug."

The vessel appeared deserted, no movement of any kind. The team ascended the gangway, guns drawn. The deck was larger than Gillian would have suspected. The boat sat low in the water gently swaying. Massive coils of line, thicker than a man's arm lay along the gunwales. The superstructure was forward with a large open space in the back for tow activities and lines. It seemed clean and well kept but there was no crew. "Search everywhere, including the bilge. You two take the forward deck. You two take the pilothouse. I'll cover the left hatch of the deckhouse and you cover the right."

She stepped around the winch, released the dogs and opened the hatch. The pungent smell of diesel mingled with salty bilge water belched past her.

"Forward deck clear," the call came in.

She searched the galley—nothing. "Galley clear."

"Pilothouse clear."

She moved on toward one of the crew quarters. *Hopefully the hostages are alive and well.* She pushed the hatch open.

"Captain's quarters clear."

The call startled her. *What was that? Fuck is someone in here.* She flipped on the shoulder light on her vest. "Don't move, FBI." Nothing, no sound at all. Then she saw it. A rat had made a nest in one of the drawers. Thad was nowhere to be found.

"Left crew quarter clear," she called in.

Gillian arrived at the final hatch with a horrible feeling. She pulled it open, a black hole. The light revealed a steel ladder that led down to the engine room. A large diesel motor dominated the space. Pipes, gauges, tools and spare parts were everywhere. She pushed past the generator. A dark shadowy spot on the floor caught her eye. The decking had been pulled back exposing the drive shaft. She stared into the ugly dark space filled with brackish water. "Fuck, I bet there are rats down there too."

"Right crew quarter clear."

She shrugged off her vest and crawled between the generators. As she reached the hole, covered in grease and diesel, she realized … she could have simply walked around the other end of the generator.

She lifted the vest to shine the shoulder light through the opening. That's when she heard it.

"Help," a whisper roared. "Help me."

She thrust her head into the darkness. There lying on a pile of wet blankets near the shaft was a young man that she recognized. She had found Thad.

"Thad," she dropped through the hole into the darkness. "Thad it's Gillian. I've got you now. You're going to be all right."

"Located one victim in the engine room. Bring in the EMS crew."

She pulled Thad close and held him. He was burning with fever and delirious. "Thad your dad saved us." *God I hope he's alive.* "Your dad saved us all."

The boy smiled and passed out.

"Get a medivac chopper in here right away."

"Yes, ma'am."

"We've searched the entire vessel. There's no sign of the others."

Gillian watched as the helicopter lifted off, bound for Tampa General. Across the shipyard, she saw Unger standing by a black SUV. It looked as though he had been waiting to make eye contact with her. He waved, got in the vehicle and drove away.

"What's he doing now?" A nervous laugh escaped her throat. She had a sick feeling.

Gillian dialed Levi's cell, praying he was alive.

"I've got Thad; he's safe. Meet me at the hospital."

"I'll be there as quick as I can. Gillian," the line sounded dead. "Tell him I love him."

Chapter 79

Levi winced as they entered the room. Sterile, white gauze covered most of Thad's head; he had an odd shell-shocked look as he opened his eyes. Levi reached toward his own ear in empathy.

This young man, even though she only knew him through his father's words, somehow brought out the mother in her. Seeing him connected to monitors and machines made her realize the frailty of life.

The doctor had told them the first surgery was scheduled for tomorrow. It would take months, but they were confident they could fit him with a prosthetic ear. The ear would be the least of his worries.

"Hey, buddy, how you feeling?"

Levi bent over the bed and embraced him. Nothing could pry them apart. After a minute, he straightened and stepped back. He rubbed his eyes with the back of his hand, then stumbled into a serving cart.

Thad laughed groggily. "Careful there or you'll need a bed, too."

"God, I'm glad you're alive."

Gillian flinched at the wires and tubes tugging against Thad's veins as he pushed and twisted in an effort to find comfort with a view.

Then he spoke, the dehydrated words croaking out of his throat. "I did a lot of thinking in that hole." He took the cup of ice his father extended. "I'm sorry for the way I acted."

"Don't. You've got nothing to apologize for. I'm the one who needs to confess."

Gillian put her hand on Levi's strong shoulder.

"Dad . . ."

"Let me finish, please." Levi paused and leaned onto the bed rail. "It's going to take a long time to sort through all this. I'll be here no matter how long it takes. I love you, and I'm proud of you."

Fatigue might have facilitated a forgiving spirit. Thad looked up at his father and said, "I love you." His eyes grew heavier.

Levi gave his shoulder a reassuring squeeze. "Get some rest. We'll be outside if you need anything."

Gillian bent down and kissed Thad's scruffy cheek.

"Hmm, I love you, Mom." He slurred.

She felt embarrassed and didn't know what to say. "Your mom loves you, too."

The boy drifted toward sleep with a smile on his face. Levi looked at her across the bed. "Can we go for a walk?"

"Sure. But I need to speak to Maddie and my mom soon." The words came out snippier than she'd intended.

He knew she had to be yearning for her daughter. "They should be calling any minute now."

She checked her phone to make sure it had a signal. They left the building and followed a sidewalk along the river.

"I can't believe McDonnell duped me," he started. "I hated her in that house, and then something happened, changing that. Now I don't think I can bring myself to hate anyone, even her. I won't even try to explain it, but I feel full, not empty. I feel everything and nothing." He stopped and looked into her eyes. "I know it sounds crazy, but I feel peaceful for the first time in my life."

"It doesn't sound crazy. Hate, bitterness, and resentment twist us and destroy our humanity. That's what happened to Deb. I'm glad you didn't become like her." They continued down the promenade. "By the way, what's Unger up to?"

"Shit, I forgot to tell you. He's dead." He shook his head. "Poor bastard."

She frowned. "When was the last time you saw him?"

"Markus killed him right after we left the office."

293

Gillian stared at the river and thought. Music drifted in from an angler's radio. A thin figure approached, the orange glow of a cigarette punctuating its silhouette.

"Mr. Morgan?"

Levi stopped dead, positioning himself in front of Gillian. He didn't shake the man's extended hand. "Do I know you?"

"No, but I've been an admirer of your work for quite some time."

The stranger's effeminate voice sent a shiver up Gillian's spine.

"Good work out there today."

Like a hackled old guard dog, Levi crouched slightly. Every muscle tightened as he demanded, "Do I know you?"

The man waved dismissively. "A Federal grand jury will convene on Monday. Markus and your boss will face a capital murder indictment, as well as domestic terrorism charges."

"Who do you work for?"

"We've got McDonnell and Markus in custody, but watch your back. Unger's still running around out here somewhere."

Gillian threw up her hands in frustration. "Who the hell is Unger anyway?"

"McDonnell's brother." The man spat an imperceptible piece of tobacco. "He's a crazy fuck. They faked his death to fool Hafley. He was McDonnell's inside man."

"That makes sense," Levi said. "She yelled something crazy about getting even." He held out his hand.

The man ignored the gesture, took out a fresh cigarette, and lit it from the smoldering butt, which he dropped. He skidded his foot over the glowing embers to put them out. Only then did he reach out and shake Levi's hand. "I'd known she was a traitor for a while, but I needed you to prove it. They were trying to sell GCCS and Echelon to the highest bidder. They would have succeeded if it hadn't been for you two." He took a long drag and exhaled. "I've got an opening in the NPO now. Why don't you work this professor gig and think about running a SAP group for me?"

"I'm done."

"Take your time." The man turned to walk away. "Don't forget to keep an eye out for Unger."

The couple drifted past the hospital's helipad and stood on a patch of grass at the river's edge. A breeze danced across the river, rippling the turbid water here and there. To Gillian it felt like David's chi moving through the world, assuring her that things would work out.

"How do I keep you in my life?" Levi asked.

"What about your work?" Fear gripped her heart. Not fear of Levi, but fear of the unknown.

"I'm done with SAP. I've hidden under the leaves for too long. Thad needs me, and I'm going to do everything I can to support him. I'm scheduled to start teaching in January. I have two houses here, so I'm staying for awhile."

"Well, my work here with the Bureau is finished." She scuffed at the concrete. She desperately wanted to stay; to start a new life, a life free of confusion and deception. "I've got to support Maddie."

"Will you stay and see if we have a shot at a relationship?"

"To be honest, I've been looking for a change. But my resume sucks; undercover work doesn't exactly help your career in the real world."

"What about staying on with TUG?"

"That's what I'd love to do. It's the one thing I've really enjoyed."

"Give it a shot. There's no way they can refuse you. You're intelligent, funny, kind, and compassionate. Oh, and you're beautiful." He turned red. "Give *us* a shot. I've fallen for you."

Her past welled up and told her to run. She was happy and content without men, just her and Maddie and Mom.

The full moon shone through a separation in the racing clouds. The river had no choice; the moon was there, it reflected it.

Her hesitancy fled with the clouds. She turned and faced him fully. "I've been feeling the same way."

They fell into a weary yet comfortable embrace. She welcomed the attention. This man felt like home. Her skin blushed and rippled as he touched her cheek, his eyes never moving from hers. Gently, he moved his mouth towards hers.

Their lips caressed, and she relaxed in his embrace. They continued that one long kiss, ignorant of the intermittent irrelevant passers-by. Electricity coursed through her body and she pulled him closer. "I love you."

"Thank God."

She rested her head on his shoulder. "I couldn't agree more."

They stayed that way for a long time.

Morgan's satellite phone rang.

"Hi, Levi."

"Unger?"

"Do me a favor. Tell Deb I'm coming to pick her up." The line went dead.

As darkness approached, a stranger came to the door of the cabin. The moment that Jean Anu had been dreading had just arrived.

"Hello Mrs. Anu, my name's Tom." The man was medium height and build, sporting a short goatee. His blonde hair had long given way to a bronze tan patch on the top of his head. "This is my cabin; Mr. Morgan called me and asked me to bring you this cell phone. He said you could call Gillian now."

End

ABOUT THE AUTHOR

David "Hap" Hapner lives in the Philadelphia area with his wife Camilla. They have three children, two grandchildren, and a dog named Boone.

The idea for the character Levi Morgan came to Hap at the age of nineteen while he was serving in the U.S. Navy. It took more than twenty-five years to put those ideas on paper. Years of living abroad and traveling in the Balkans, Eastern Europe, Scandinavia, South America, and Southeast Asia have provided an ample foundation for the action in his writing.

Wireless has been a labor of love accomplished through the encouragement of Hap's wife, Camilla. He is currently working on a second novel entitled, Revelation J.

DON'T MISS IT

Visit www. ultraistgroup.com to explore Hap's other short
stories and projects.